CW00750035

THE WORCESTER
WHISPERERS

THE WORCESTER WHISPERERS

a Victorian Crime Story

Kerry Tombs

ROBERT HALE · LONDON

© Kerry Tombs 2008
First published in Great Britain 2008

ISBN 978-0-7090-8688-8

Robert Hale Limited
Clerkenwell House
Clerkenwell Green
London EC1R 0HT

www.halebooks.com

2 4 6 8 10 9 7 5 3

To Jess and Ted, my parents –
who gave so much to me and to Worcestershire

Typeset in 10/14pt Plantin
by Derek Doyle & Associates, Shaw Heath
Printed and bound in Great Britain
by MPG Biddles Limited, King's Lynn, Norfolk

PROLOGUE

WHITECHAPEL, LONDON. AUGUST 1888

She paused beneath the archway of the old building, drawing the veil slowly down across her face, seeking to distance herself from the world into which she now entered.

This was not her first visit. During the past year she had ventured into the labyrinth of streets and alleyways on numerous occasions, seeking out the information she had required, fitting the fragments of the past together, ever discarding the lies and the deceitful, and always seeking to understand why it had come to this.

She remembered the first time she had entered this other, strange place, with its loud noises and never-ending activities, its overcrowded hovels, its lingering smells of decay and death; places where the thick sickly air had sought to encompass her within its darkness and choking vapour. On that first visit she had been easily repelled and had fled quickly from its streets, gaining the sanctuary and relief of the country-side, vowing never to return, and deciding to relinquish her quest before it had begun.

But then as the months had passed, she found herself unable to rest, and the old desires had come once more to play upon her mind, eating into her very soul, until she had felt compelled to accept the inevitable – and knew that she would have to renew her journey, before she could ever hope to be at peace with herself.

At first she had only dared to return to the area during the day, attemp-ing to gradually familiarize herself with the streets and buildings, the shops and drinking places, the markets and cheap lodging houses – and

5

always changing her appearance so that she would not become noticeable, or thought different from those around her. Then as she had become familiar with her new surroundings, she had returned during the hours of darkness, walking the narrow alleyways, always seeking to converse with those who lingered beneath the shadows of the crippled buildings to slowly gain their confidence. When she had learnt all that she had sought, she had withdrawn into the dimly lit corners and doorways, where unnoticed by all those around her, she had begun to watch those who now interested her.

Now she knew that the time had come.

She waited anxiously. Somewhere in the distance she heard a clock chime the hour. Perhaps the boy would not come after all? He had taken her money – perhaps he would have decided that the prospect of further recompense was not worth the effort. She would have to find someone else who could lead her to the man whom she now sought above all others.

She paced back and forth, straining to peer through the lingering fog at any noise she could hear, waiting to commence the sequence of events for which she had planned for so long. The idea that she had come so far, and that she might yet be turned away from her purpose, was a thought she could not bare to countenance.

'Miss!'

It was the voice of the child. So he had come after all. Money was always the persuader.

'Miss!'

The speaker emerged before her; a ragged child not above ten years of age, but no doubt far more knowledgeable, above his years, in the ways of the street.

She felt in her purse and took out the shilling.

'Take me to him – and there will be more,' she said holding out her hand.

The child seized the coin from her outstretched palm, and looked up at the strange woman who was dressed entirely in black from head to foot, and whose face he could barely see from beneath her veil.

'Follow us, lady,' he said, turning away.

She nodded and followed the boy down the dark alleyway.

They made their way down a succession of streets and narrow twisting walkways, the boy pausing momentarily now and then to glance behind him, to see that he had not lost his companion in the darkness of the night.

Their journey took them past a number of drinking dens where the noises of the revellers and the songs of the piano escaped through the open windows before drifting upwards into the enveloping fog. Then onwards past the rows of squalid houses with their ever changing smells and decaying fabrics – until she began to realize that they were gradually making their way out of the streets with which she had become so familiar during the previous months.

Now they appeared to be walking into an even darker unknown world, where the sounds of the night seemed to fade away into nothingness, until all she could hear was the noise of her own boots on the cobbled pavements. She began to feel afraid that perhaps the child was taking her to a place from where his accomplices might be lying in wait for her, and from whence she might never return. Her own life was of little consequence to her, but it was the sudden realization that her mission might then come to nought that now increased her anxiety.

'How much further?' she asked, seeking to regain her breath.

The child said nothing – and continued on his way.

She paused for a moment. She told herself that there was still time to put an end to it all, to abandon this mad desire, that she should retreat from the darkness, and return once more to the world of purity, light and sunshine, and to the hills which she had known for nearly all of her life.

'Down 'ere!' said the boy, breaking into her thoughts, and suddenly turning off the alleyway. 'Mind the water miss.'

She realized that they were now walking by the side of a canal. She could hear the gentle lapping of the waters as she pressed her handkerchief close to her nose in a vain attempt to extinguish the smells that rose from the decaying waterway. Occasional glimmers of light from the hanging lanterns of the barge boats lit the cobbled towpath before them, making their way easier.

Suddenly the child led her away from the canal and down a narrow passageway where the darkness seemed to close in around them once more.

'Monk, up there!' The boy pointed upwards towards a light that flickered at the top of a flight of steps, which led from out of the yard in which they now found themselves. 'He be expecting you, miss.'

So this was where he had brought her, to a lonely warehouse in this dark forgotten corner of London. She felt inside her purse and took out the crown. As she placed the coin in the child's hand she could see the light reflected in his eyes as his fist closed greedily around the coin.

'You must wait for me here,' she began, but the child turned on his heels and ran quickly down the alley, leaving her alone at the foot of the steps. Had he taken her to this lonely place merely to abandon her? Clearly he had been only interested in her money. She could have expected little else. Perhaps the man she sought was nothing more than a figment of the child's imagination, but then she remembered it had been she who had learnt of his arrival in the city and who had instructed the boy to find him.

Slowly, knowing not what she might find, she made her way up the narrow steps on the outside of the old warehouse, until she reached the door at their head. Realizing that it was slightly ajar, and that she would be expected, she pushed open the door and entered.

At first she could see nothing in the room, except the flickering flame from a solitary candle that burned somewhere in the distance. Cautiously she drew near, saying nothing, but aware that there was another there who had awaited her arrival, and who was now observing her every move.

'You are the man they call Monk?' she enquired, in a voice that seemed unlike her own.

'The child said you would come,' said a voice from somewhere in the darkness beyond the candle. 'Take a seat, my good lady.'

She almost stumbled into the wooden chair that had been placed before the table, but quickly recovered her composure and seated herself.

She waited for the other to speak, and began to wish that she had never come. Even now there would be time to draw back, to make her way out of that room, and to escape once more into the outside world.

'I would prefer to see your face,' said the disembodied voice suddenly. 'Why have you sought me out?'

'I believe that you are the only man who can undertake that which I most desire,' she replied, ignoring his request to lift her veil.

'And what is that?' he enquired, in a voice which she thought sounded both harsh and distracted.

'To gain my revenge on those who have caused hurt to my family.'

'A noble sentiment, my dear lady – and why do you think that it is only

I who can assist you?'

'I have learnt much about your activities since your arrival in the city.' She paused, not knowing whether she had been foolish to disclose so much.

'Then you must know that I could kill you right now, in this room tonight, and that your body would never be found in the lower depths of the river that runs through this festering city!'

She sensed the anger in his voice, but feeling her own inner pain, quickly replied, 'But you would be foolish to do so, when you could gain so much.'

He said nothing and she grew anxious. All she could do was to wait, watching the candle flickering in the cold air, casting fleeting shadows on the walls of the room.

'I have money,' she said, breaking the unbearable silence.

'It always comes down to money,' he sneered.

Quickly reaching into her purse, she took out the small pouch and placed it carefully down upon the table. 'Ten sovereigns' she said. 'And there will be a further twenty when you have carried out what I desire of you.'

'And what is it exactly that you so desire so much?'

She hesitated for a moment, affronted by the contempt in his voice, but then, leaning forward in her chair, she removed a small piece of folded paper from her purse, which she then placed upon the table. 'This paper contains the name and address of a certain person' – she hesitated for a moment – 'whom I would desire you to kill.'

'You think I am a common murderer!' he shouted suddenly.

'I am sorry. I have made a mistake. I should not have come,' she said quickly rising from her seat. 'Please forgive me. It is foolish to proceed.'

'I have not declined your request,' said the other reassuringly, and with firmness.

'But—' she protested, unsure of whether her mission had succeeded.

'Twenty sovereigns you said?'

'Yes' she replied, regaining her seat.

'Very well.'

A hand appeared from out of the darkness and took the paper from off the table. He unfolded the sheet and, as he leaned towards the flame to read its words, she thought she caught a brief reflection of the light across his eyes. He gave a grunt of recognition, before tossing the paper down upon the table.

'You know of her?' she asked, recovering her composure.

'I have heard stories, gossip no more. They say she is a common whore. Why would you seek to rid yourself of this person?'

'There are to be no questions asked,' she replied, gaining in confidence. 'You are to be given no further information, you must make no enquiries regarding myself and you must forget that I ever came here tonight. I will return here at the same time next week. If I have read in the newspapers that you have carried out the deed, then you will receive your payment. If I learn that you have failed me, you will see no more of me,' she said, standing up, indicating that their meeting was at an end.

'Wait. How do I know that you will not betray me to the authorities?'

'Because we have need of each other – and because, there will be further work to be undertaken, for which you will be more than amply rewarded.'

'There will be others?' he enquired.

'Yes. There will be others.'

She walked quickly across the room, anxious to quit the darkened space as soon as possible, now that he had accepted her payment.

He watched her close the door behind her and listened to the sound of her boots on the steps as she made her way down the flight. Then he opened the paper once more and looked down at the name he saw there—

MARY ANN NICHOLS. WHITE HOUSE. FLOWER AND
DEAN STREET.

—then, bringing it towards the candle, he allowed himself a brief smile as the flame quickly consumed the words.

CHAPTER ONE

WORCESTER – SEPTEMBER 1888

The church clock struck the hour of eleven as Nicholas Evelyn made his way between the rows of old houses that formed the area known as the Shambles in the city of Worcester, drawing his long coat closer around himself despite the late warmth of the summer evening.

He had known this street all his life, and in those sixty-two years it had seemed to change very little. By day the traders spread out their wares before their premises and the place was alive with the sounds of argument, transaction and vulgarity. In the evenings there seemed little alteration, for although the shopkeepers closed up their places of work and retired to their living quarters on the floors above, the area took on a more aggressive, unsure aspect with its late night revellers, and women of dubious certainty who called out to their prospective clients from dimmed doorways. Nicholas had long learnt to avoid the former, whilst the latter had long since learnt to ignore him.

Nicholas continued on his way, down the narrow passageway that opened up into a wider road, passing the music shop on his left and the old inn on his right, before the cathedral came into view. He paused momentarily to look upwards at the great building, as he had done so in the same place for the past forty-five years, and felt humbled once more by its magnificence and its mystery. A few minutes ago he had sat writing in his rooms near the old Cornmarket, straining to see the letters in the dim light, and taking sips from his tankard of ale as if trying to give himself the courage that he knew would shortly be required of him.

He made his way across the grass towards the building, but instead of entering by the door immediately in front of him, he slipped quietly to the side, letting the darkness conceal his presence. It was important that tonight – above all others – that he should not be seen by anyone either entering or leaving such a place.

Eventually he reached the side door of the cathedral and, after glancing over his shoulder to see that he had not been followed, he pushed gently on the wooden panels. For a moment the door failed to yield, and the sudden realization that he would perhaps be unable to carry out his mission made his heart beat faster – but then he applied more pressure and was relieved to see that the ancient woodwork move slowly inwards, creaking as it did so.

He stepped inside, and stood silent for a moment, listening for any sound that might indicate that his arrival had been observed, and so that his eyes could adjust to the dim lights on the wall in the distance. Reassured that all was well, he turned around and closed the door behind him.

Keeping to the areas of darkness at the side of the building, he made his way step by step towards the small side chapel, his ears straining to hear the words of prayer. He knew that Brother Jonus would be offering up his words of penitence, as he did every night at this same hour and, as he came nearer he was almost relieved to learn that the familiar ritual had not been broken. There was the solitary monk kneeling before the altar, his hands clasped before him, a single candle casting light on the gold cross that stood on the table.

Nicholas pulled his hat closer over his forehead and slipped past the chapel, keeping his eyes in the other's direction, listening for any indication that he had been detected, but the monk continued with his prayers, and he knew that all was well and he could proceed with his undertaking.

Reaching the end of the building, he paused beneath the hissing gas lamp on the wall. Knowing that he would need light to make his way upwards, he took one of the candles from the offertory table and lit it from another that had almost burnt its course. Then, turning the corner, he found the door to the staircase he was looking for and began to make his way up the stone steps, holding the candle before him to light his way lest he stumble in the darkness. Although he knew that he would have almost another hour before the monks would enter the cathedral to conduct the midnight mass, he was anxious to proceed as quickly as possible.

At the top of the flight of steps he found a door before him and, finding it locked, reached into the pocket of his coat and took out the ring of keys he had brought with him. He placed one of them in the lock, turned the key and entered the vestry, and walked across to the large oak table where the guardians of the cathedral had conducted their affairs for centuries, seeking the candlestick which he knew he would find on its centre. Not disappointed, he fixed the dripping candle into its stem and taking his handkerchief from his coat pocket removed the hot wax which had trickled down on to his thin fingers.

Before continuing he listened to see whether anyone had followed him, and hearing nothing save the sound of the ticking grandfather clock in the corner of the room, decided that it would be safe to proceed with the next part of his journey. He crossed over to the corner of the vestry to the old winding wooden staircase and began to climb the well worn steps towards the library – the same fifty-eight steps which he had climbed twice a day, every day of his working life, for the past forty-five years.

As he went, he recalled the first time he had climbed those same stairs. He had been apprenticed then to Ganderton, the librarian, who had showed him how to care for all the ancient books and manuscripts in his charge. The old man had taken a fancy to his young charge and had even taught him how to read some of the fine words. In those early days Nicholas had been so eager to begin his duties each morning, he would run across the cathedral lawns and bound up the steps two at a time, and had suffered the elder man's reprimands for his youthful exuberance. Then as he had grown into middle age, his friend and mentor had died, and he had succeeded to the position of librarian. He began to extend his knowledge by reading those works that the older man had forbidden him to take down from the shelves lest his youthful clumsiness should damage their fragility, and in those many hours when there had been no visitors to the library he had sat at his desk turning the pages of the handwritten books, and running his fingers around the brightly coloured letters, as if seeking to encompass the past and to bridge the knowledge of centuries. To him, the books had gradually become his friends and he had been content that it had been so.

As his role had grown in importance, so his daily progress up the staircase had gradually become more sedate and dignified, – as befitted his austere position as the custodian of the cathedral's legacy. But as the years passed and his thinning hair became greyer and his eyes dimmer, he began to find the climb almost an unwelcome start to the morning, and lately there had even been days when the prospect of turning yet another page in the ancient volumes had begun to lose its appeal. There had been whispers between the monks that he should take on another, or even retire from his position, but he had known no other world and was not yet willing to pass on the mantle to a younger man.

All these thoughts, these fragments of his past life, seemed to crowd in upon his mind as he made his way up the staircase, holding the candle before him and sheltering its meagre flame with his other hand, lest a sudden draught should plunge him into darkness.

He pushed open the door at the head of the stairs and entered the room. There were the three candles on the table before him, just as he had left them five hours previously, and he leaned forward and lit their wicks. Soon the room was bathed in a golden flickering light, which shone forth, illuminating the rows of ancient books and glass cases that were situated there.

He stood gazing around the room for a moment or two, then made his way across to his desk and seated himself. Reaching to replenish the empty glass that lay before him from the jug of water there, he was surprised to find that his hands were shaking so much that some of the liquid spilled over on to the woodwork. Quickly he applied a cloth to soak up the water, before bringing the quivering glass to his dry lips and letting the water ease his throat. Placing the glass back down upon the desk, he cast his eyes around the room at the rows of books, drew his coat closer and, as the tears began to flow he covered his face with his hands.

For some minutes he cried uncontrollably, occasionally banging the table with his fist in his frustration, and cursing his fate that his life had now come to this.

Eventually the tears subsided and after glancing across at the old clock in the corner, he quickly dried his eyes and blew his nose before replacing the handkerchief. The hands of the clock had pointed to 11.30, and he realized now that time was short, and that he must complete his mission before the cathedral became busier again at the midnight hour.

He crossed over to the glass case in the corner of the room. There was the book, lying in its usual place on the crimson cushion, its brightly illuminated pages shining forth as they had done for centuries. Briefly he allowed himself the indulgence of viewing the open pages for the final time, before taking his ring of keys from his coat pocket and slowly turning the lock of the cabinet. He reached out for the work. His hands began to shake violently as he closed the volume shut and lifted it from its place. Quickly he crossed over to his desk and wrapped the precious volume in the piece of cloth that lay waiting there, and thrust the package deep into the inside pocket of his coat before returning to lock the cabinet.

Taking hold of one of the candlesticks, he snuffed out the candle, and bringing the stick above his shoulder he thrust it down suddenly on to the front of the cabinet. Startled by the flying glass, he backed away quickly, alarmed by the damage he had just caused.

He had not thought it would be like this, and the sudden realization of what he had done seemed to sweep over him, and he grew afraid.

Then a new desire took hold in his mind – now that the deed had been done, all he wanted to do was to leave as quickly as possible, to escape from the room, to seek the midnight air, and to ask God's forgiveness for the violation he had just committed.

Quickly he blew out the remaining candles, save one which he held before him to light his way. He closed the door of the library behind him, and made his way down the wooden steps towards the vestry, before beginning his descent towards the main body of the cathedral.

Suddenly his foot missed one of the steps and he felt himself falling. In blind panic he thrust out a hand and steadied himself against the side of the wall, dropping the candle as he did so. He almost cried out in the darkness and cursed his carelessness.

Nicholas felt the cold sweat on his forehead. He heard his breathing coming in short gasps, and it seemed as though the noise from his beating heart would split open his head at any moment.

Then he told himself he was nearly at the bottom of the staircase, and that if he kept his composure, he would be able to feel his way down the remaining steps.

After what seemed like an eternity, his hand felt the contours of the wooden door and he knew that he would be safe. Gently he pushed it open and stepped once more into the main building.

He stood still for a moment, listening and looking for any indication that others may have noticed his presence. Growing in confidence, he began to retrace his steps along the dark side of the building, passed the small chapel where old Jonus was still continuing with his prayers, until he reached the outer door and stepped out into the night air.

A welcoming cool breeze blew across his face, and he briefly removed his hat to wipe away the beads of perspiration which had collected upon his forehead. Now all he desired was to walk away from the building, and to complete his final task, so that he could begin to rid himself of the terrible act he had just perpetrated.

Crossing the Green, he found the steps that took him down towards the river. His pace quickened now as he realized the lateness of the hour. As he turned the corner at the end of the flight he collided with another who suddenly emerged from the darkness. Not wishing to be detained in conversation, he kept his head down, muttered some brief words of apology and continued on his way.

As he proceeded along the footpath at the side of the river, he could see the lights of far off dwellings on the other side of the water. He kept the old walls of the city on his left side, and soon distanced himself from the ancient cathedral. The sounds of singing and shouting drifted down from the Diglis Inn to the water's edge as he passed by. Soon he was leaving the distant lights of the city behind him.

Suddenly turning away from the river, he pushed open a wooden door in the wall at his side. He found himself in an enclosed garden and made his way through the undergrowth until he reached the remains of the ruined building. He had been here before, so despite the darkness of the night, he soon found that which he sought.

Sliding the stone to one side, he revealed the cavity. He reached into his pocket, withdrew the packet and laid it within the space, before replacing the cover.

Quickly regaining the river-bank, he began to retrace his steps towards the city. A feeling of immense relief began to overwhelm him as he realized that he had completed his mission, and tears again began to form in his eyes. He had kept his side of the agreement. Now perhaps his life would be given back to him – he could begin again. God had given him a second chance. He would be redeemed.

'Nicholas!'

The voice startled him, but before he could turn around, he felt a sudden pain on the back of his head. He cried out as he fell towards the ground.

He tried to look up at his attacker, to see who had carried out this act of brutality, to learn who had violated his person, but before he could do so, he became aware that someone had taken hold of his legs and was dragging his body along the ground.

He knew then what was about to happen: that he would be unable to prevent it. Nevertheless as he neared the edge of the tow path, he made a frantic effort to cry out, in the hope that someone might yet come to his rescue and that his life would be spared.

But then the icy waters of the river seemed to open up to receive his body, and he felt himself falling into a quieter, darker world, from which he knew there would be no return.

At first he struggled, but as the waters closed over him, and as the blackness took him down into the bitter, unknown depths, Nicholas Evelyn became resigned to his fate, and uttered a last prayer to his Maker begging forgiveness for all his past sins – and asking that his life might be better in the next world.

CHAPTER TWO

LONDON – SEPTEMBER 1888

'Call Samuel Ravenscroft!'

'Call Samuel Ravenscroft!'

Ravenscroft made his way into the number two court of the Old Bailey, and took his place on the witness stand.

'Please take the Bible and repeat the words on the card,' instructed the usher.

Ravenscroft cleared his throat and uttered the familiar words.

'You are Samuel Ravenscroft?' asked the prosecuting counsel. 'I believe you are an inspector in the Whitechapel Division of the London Constabulary?'

'I am.'

'Speak up! The court cannot hear you,' said the judge, leaning forward and peering over his glasses at the middle-aged, untidily dressed figure who stood before him.

Ravenscroft cursed his bad luck to be giving evidence before old Winslow yet again – deaf as a post, and irritable and sour to boot. He had a bad feeling about the outcome of this case. 'I am sorry, your honour. I will endeavour to speak louder for your honour,' he replied, as laughter broke out from the gallery.

'Silence!' shouted the judge. 'May I remind those present that this is a court of law, not a place of music hall entertainment. Proceed.'

'Thank you, your honour. Now Inspector Ravenscroft, would you care to tell us what happened on the night of 23 July last?' enquired the prosecutor.

Ravenscroft took out his notebook, and after adjusting his spectacles, addressed the court.

'Following information I had received earlier in the day, I took up my position that evening outside the house of Mr Charles Roberts in Shoreditch. At ten thirty precisely I observed the accused, Nigel Makepeace climbing into one of the downstairs windows of the property. Approximately ten minutes later I saw him making his way out of the window and I immediately raised the alarm.'

'What did he say?' asked the judge holding his ear.

'I think the inspector said that he raised the alarm when he saw the accused leaving the property, your honour.'

Winslow nodded. 'Well, go on then!' he demanded, a look of annoyance creeping over his face.

'The accused ran off and myself and two of my officers set off in pursuit. We shortly apprehended Makepeace and conveyed him to the local police station.'

'Did you make a search of his person?' enquired counsel.

'I did indeed, sir, and found two watches in his inside pocket. The same two watches which you have in court today,' replied Ravenscroft looking up from his book, and realizing that his left hand was shaking.

'Did Mr Makepeace then confess his guilt, Inspector?'

'He did not, sir.'

'But you were confident that you had arrested the right man?'

'There was no doubt about it, sir. We had caught him red handed with the goods upon his person.' Ravenscroft tried to sound as confident as possible, for he knew what to expect next. Opposite him the accused was looking up casually at the ceiling.

'Thank you, Inspector, you have been most helpful.'

The prosecuting barrister resumed his seat and as the counsel for the defence, Mr Sefton Rawlinson, rose to his feet. Ravenscroft's heart sank.

'Inspector, how long have you been a member of the London Constabulary?'

Ravenscroft knew that Rawlinson always began with the same question, smiling as he did so, ever seeking to ingratiate himself with the court. It was just unfortunate that the slippery old brief was on the defending side yet again.

'Fifteen years, sir.'

'Fifteen years, Inspector. Well, well.'

Always the same response, Rawlinson seeking to belittle his age and experience as usual. He would need to be on his guard. It would not look good at the Yard if he were to lose this one.

'You say you took up your position outside Mr Roberts's house. Remind the court as to the time, Inspector?'

'Ten thirty in the evening.'

'What time did he say?' asked the judge, to yet more laughter from the spectators.

'I think Inspector Ravenscroft said ten thirty in the evening, your honour.'

'Thank you, Mr Rawlinson.'

'A pleasure, your honour. Now, Inspector, you say you took up your station at ten thirty. When did you see someone climbing in through the downstairs window?'

'Eleven-ten precisely,' replied Ravenscroft, trying to sound as convincing as possible.

'Eleven-ten precisely, you say,' repeated the barrister brandishing a sheet of paper. 'How can you have been so sure of the time? Was it not dark then?'

'There was some light from the lamp behind us, which enabled me to read my pocket watch.'

'You say there was some light behind you. So there was no light on the front of the house?'

'No—' began Ravenscroft.

'Quite! So the front of the house was in complete darkness. Tell me Inspector, how was it that you could possibly identify my client either climbing in or out of the property when it was so dark?' asked Rawlinson leaning forward eagerly.

'There was some light,' protested Ravenscroft, feeling his neck becoming hot under his collar, and beginning to wish he was elsewhere.

'Ah, but according to you, Inspector, you stated that only light visible that night was from the lamp behind you. I put it to you that it was so dark, you could not make a positive identification that the man climbing into the property was my client. It could, in fact, have been anyone!'

'I am sure it was the accused.'

'Really, did you see his face?' asked Rawlinson, a note of sarcasm in his voice.

'No, but I knew it to be him.'

'How can you have been so sure?'

'I have known the accused for the past ten years and have arrested him on a number of occasions during that—'

'Ah, now we have it. Because you had arrested my client in the past, you assumed that it was him whom you saw on that night entering and leaving the house?'

'I knew it was Makepeace,' protested Ravenscroft.

'Even though you were unable to see my client clearly in the darkness? I think not. Now let us turn to what happened next. You say that after you saw the thief leaving the premises you and two of your constables gave chase.'

'That is so,' replied Ravenscroft coughing and shuffling uneasily in the witness stand.

'How long were you chasing this thief?'

'For some time.'

'For some time,' sneered Rawlinson. 'Can we be more precise? Was it a few seconds?'

'No, it was longer than that,' replied Ravenscroft conscious that he was falling into the trap and aware that he could do little to prevent it.

'Was it a minute, perhaps ten minutes, maybe an hour – or possibly even the next day?' joked his adversary.

Laughter broke out from several parts of the court.

'Silence!' bellowed the judge.

'It was probably about three minutes,' muttered Ravenscroft.

'What was that?' asked the judge.

'I think the inspector said three minutes, your honour,' smiled Rawlinson.

'Proceed, Mr Rawlinson,' sighed Winslow.

'Thank you, your honour. Now, Inspector, I would like you to think very hard before you answer this next question, as the innocence of my client will depend upon the accuracy of your reply. During those three minutes whilst you and your colleagues were chasing the thief, did you have him in your sights all of the time?'

'Not all the time—' began Ravenscroft, coughing again.

'I see. So there were times during this supposed chase when you lost all sight of the man you were following?'

'I suppose that was quite possible,' he answered, feeling his confidence slowly ebbing away.

'Would you speak up, Inspector? I'm sure your reply could not be heard by certain sections of this court.'

'I said that it was quite possible,' replied Ravenscroft, after clearing his throat.

'Quite possible! I put it to you, that it certainly was, very possible. You and your officers lost sight of the person you were following. You could have been pursuing anyone for all this court knows. Inspector, it may come as a surprise to you to learn that my client was going about his lawful business when the real thief collided with him, dropping the two watches from his hands as he did so before running off into the crowd. Mr Makepeace then picked up the watches and, being a law-abiding citizen was about to hand them into the authorities when he was suddenly apprehended by you and your officers!'

Ravenscroft looked down at his feet, as the laughter reverberated around the court.

'Silence! I will not tolerate such frivolity in this court. I will remove the public if such an outbreak occurs again,' said the judge, beginning to look increasingly bored by the proceedings.

Ravenscroft let out a deep sigh. To have been allocated both Mr Justice Winslow and Mr Sefton Rawlinson on the same day, was a double misfortune indeed.

'Let us turn to another matter. Did you not say to my client when you apprehended him, for a crime which he had not committed: "got you again, Nigel. You won't escape justice this time. You are going down for a very long time, my old friend, and you will never see daylight again." Do you remember saying those words, Inspector?'

Ravenscroft knew that Rawlinson was enjoying himself at his expense and wished that he could get the wretched business over with as soon as possible. He looked across at Makepeace, who was grinning up at the gallery. 'I cannot remember exactly what I said.'

'Come now, Inspector, did you, or did you not say, "Got you again Nigel. You are going down for a very long time and will never see daylight again"?'

'I don't remember saying he was going down for a very long time—'

'I put it to you, Inspector, that you had already made up your mind that my client was guilty of the crime you had just witnessed, and that your judgement in this case was severely flawed,' glared Rawlinson.

'That is not so,' protested Ravenscroft, coughing once more.

'In fact, you wanted to put my client away for a very long time and you did not care how you did it!' shouted Rawlinson.

'That is incorrect—'

'This so called information, that you say you received and acted upon,' said the barrister, suddenly changing his line of questioning, 'what information was that?'

'I cannot say.'

'Cannot say – or won't say?'

'The information was given to us in confidence. I cannot divulge my source,' protested Ravenscroft.

'Come now, Inspector. Are you trying to make us believe that you had inside knowledge that this offence was about to take place? I think the court will conclude that this is all nonsense. I put it to you that there never was any inside information, and that you were so anxious to send my client to prison for a very long time, that you did not care how you achieved that objective?'

'That is just not so,' said Ravenscroft, shaking his head, and feeling as though he had just fallen down a large well and was unable to see any daylight that might aid his escape.

'Your honour,' said Rawlinson, drawing himself up to his full height and addressing the judge, 'Your honour, I put it to you, that there is simply no case for my client to answer. Inspector Ravenscroft has stated that he could neither see who entered or left the premises where the burglary took place, and that he and his men lost sight of the thief during the following chase. In fact, he has admitted that the man he arrested may not have been the real thief at all! Furthermore, he is clearly prejudiced against my client and is prepared to go to any lengths to ensure an unsafe conviction. I would submit to your honour that there is only one action that you should—'

'Yes, yes, Mr Rawlinson. You have made your point,' said Mr Justice Winslow, with annoyance, 'Case dismissed! The prisoner is free to go.'

Cries broke out from the gallery, as a smiling Makepeace shook hands with his brief.

A dejected Ravenscroft stepped out of the witness box.

'Next case!' ordered the judge.

'Crown versus Norrice!' shouted the usher.

As Ravenscroft began to leave the court, he made way for a small boy who was being escorted towards the dock.

'George Norrice you are charged with having a silver crown in your possession. How do you plead?' yelled the usher above the ensuing noise.

'I ain't guilty, sir. It were the lady who gave it me. . . .'

Ravenscroft closed the door of the court behind him and, avoiding the collection of criminals, barristers and onlookers who thronged the corridors of the Old Bailey, stepped out into the bright sunshine, and sought to distance himself from the events of the morning as quickly as possible, striding forth into the streets of London.

Later that afternoon, Ravenscroft made his way slowly up the old creaking staircase that lead to his superior's office. A note had arrived at lunchtime stating that he was to present himself there at 3.30 precisely. No doubt the Yard had heard about the events of the morning. He was not looking forward to the next few minutes.

Reaching the landing, he paused to recover his breath and to prepare himself for the ordeal ahead, before knocking purposefully on the door.

'Enter!'

Ravenscroft made his way into the room.

'Ah, Ravenscroft, it's you. Take a seat, man.'

'Thank you, sir,' he replied, trying to sound optimistic.

'Heard about this morning, Ravenscroft; a shambles from start to finish.'

'We were unfortunate—' he began, knowing that the commissioner would not be interested in his excuses.

'It does not look good if the Yard is made to look like fools. I am far from pleased. You should have been sure of your evidence before it went to court, man.'

'We were up against Mr Sefton Rawlinson, sir.'

'All the more reason to have ensured that your case was watertight. Not the first time this has happened, Ravenscroft. No, don't interrupt, when I'm speaking. This is the third time this year when your evidence has been thrown out of court. This incompetence just won't do. It brings the Yard into disrepute and does not convey the right image that we are seeking to establish.'

'No, sir,' said Ravenscroft, looking down at the floor and recalling the other times when he had sat in this same dreary old room being rounded on by his superiors.

'I've also been having a look at your crime figures. They leave a lot to be desired, I can tell you. Since you came back from Malvern last year, your performance seems to have taken quite a tumble, not that your success rate was all that good then, or indeed for the year before. Perhaps this is all becoming too much for you? Quite frankly, I am beginning to wonder if it's not about time you retired. Have you ever considered retiring, Ravenscroft?'

So that was what all this had been leading up to. The Yard obviously wanted to ease him out, to make way for a younger man.

'Never considered it, sir,' he lied, seeking to sound as convincing as possible.

'Between you and me, Ravenscroft, I can tell you that there are plans, well advanced, to pass an act through Parliament in the next year or so, allowing for those officers who want to take early retirement to do so. On fairly reasonable terms as well, I believe. I think you would be seriously advised to consider taking up such a generous offer when it becomes into operation.'

'I'll consider my options, sir, when the time comes. Will that be all, sir?' he said, beginning to get to his feet and seeking to escape the claustrophobic confines of the room as quickly as possible.

'Not quite,' said the commissioner, studying a sheet of paper before him.

Ravenscroft wondered what he was going to be reprimanded for now; what lack of enterprise on his part had they now unearthed to chastise him with.

'Had a letter from the Dean of Worcester Cathedral; gentleman who goes by the name of Touchmore or Touchstone. Can't read his signature, but apparently you met him when you went to Malvern last year and cleared up those murders. Speaks very highly of you; can't imagine why. Apparently someone has run off with one of their priceless books from the cathedral library. Librarian has also gone missing. Asks if we could spare you to go down there and solve the case.'

'Surely the local police will have carried out investigations?'

'Seems some work has been done, but they have failed to make any headway. This Touchmore fellow thinks that you are the man for the job.'

'But, sir, we've a lot on at the moment,' protested Ravenscroft, secretly hoping that his objection would be overruled.

'Granted. There is this Nichols murder to deal with. Some prostitute in Whitechapel who's been stabbed to death. Rather nasty by all accounts. I've got Inspector Spratling on the case. He seems to be managing well. I think we can spare you. No, you take yourself off to Worcester. You'll need to tread carefully in regard to the local force, however. Fellow called Henderson is in charge. He's a prickly customer by all accounts.'

'If that is what you want, sir.'

'What I want, Ravenscroft, is for this case to be solved as professionally as possible,' said the commissioner leaning forward and fixing his eyes on him. 'The Yard's reputation is at stake. We can't afford any more mistakes, like today. Take as long as you like – and don't let the Yard down this time.'

'I'll do my best, sir,' said Ravenscroft standing to his feet.

'I sincerely hope so,' muttered the commissioner looking down at his papers.

Ravenscroft closed the door behind him and made his way down the staircase. As he walked across the courtyard, the idea of leaving London began to grow increasingly more attractive with each step that he took. To be able to put the streets of Whitechapel, the corridors and courts of the Bailey, the rooms of the Yard and the summer heat of London all behind him for a few days, maybe even for a few weeks, seemed freedom and opportunity indeed. There would be old friends to meet, and the chance of good food and fine country air to be experienced and enjoyed. The world had suddenly become a more appealing place.

And, of course, there would perhaps be the opportunity to see Lucy Armitage once more, and to renew his favours in that direction.

CHAPTER THREE

WORCESTER

'My dear Crabb. How delighted I am to see you again!'

Ravenscroft had just alighted from the train at the town's Foregate Street Station and had been reunited with his former colleague.

'Pleased to be welcoming you to Worcester, sir,' said Constable Crabb shaking the hand that had been offered. 'May I take your bag, sir?'

'That is most kind of you.'

'I trust you had a good journey, sir?'

'As well as could be expected. Now, Crabb, tell me your news. How is that good wife of yours, and that fine godson of mine, young master Samuel?' asked Ravenscroft, addressing his younger colleague.

'Both remarkably well, sir, thank you.'

'Your wife must be feeding you well. I'm sure you have put on some weight since I saw you last.'

'I believe you are correct in your observation, sir. It is a fortunate man indeed who marries a good cook. This way.'

The two men made their way down the flight of steps and out into the street.

'This is Foregate Street, sir; the main street of the town. I have taken the liberty of booking you into the Cardinal's Hat. They say the food and accommodation are very good there. It's not far, sir, if you would care to follow me.'

Ravenscroft found himself walking along a wide, busy street, full of horse-drawn vehicles, cabs and people going about their everyday business.

'I have managed to let the Malvern Constabulary release me from duty there, to assist you in your enquiries.'

'That is good news indeed, Crabb. I don't know what I would have done without you last year at Malvern.'

'Talking of Malvern, sir, it seems as though our good friend The Reverend Touchmore of Malvern Priory has been elevated to the Dean and Chapter of Worcester Cathedral.'

'I know. Apparently it was he who asked for me to come down here.'

'I see, sir.'

'And I must say, Crabb, it is a relief to leave all the excitement of London behind me for a few days.'

The two men turned off the main thoroughfare, and soon found themselves in a narrow street, where Ravenscroft's senses were assailed by the noise and clamour of the shopkeepers shouting out their latest offers to the crowds as they passed by.

'This area is called the Shambles. Watch where you are treading, sir! Some of the rotten fruit and vegetables find their way into the road, to say nothing of the horse droppings!'

'I see what you mean, Crabb,' said Ravenscroft, stepping quickly to one side to avoid being pushed into a pile of squashed apples by a large woman of assertive tendencies. 'More like London, than Malvern!' he added.

Reaching the end of the thoroughfare, the two men turned left, and then sharply to their right, and soon found themselves in a quieter area, where the old timber-framed buildings jutted out into the street, and the cobbles were uneven beneath their feet.

'The Cardinal's Hat is just down here, sir.'

'Unusual name for an inn.'

'I believe its name has something to do with the pilgrims who lodged there whilst visiting the cathedral. Speaking of which, sir, you can just get a view of it over there, above the roof tops on our right.'

'It looks an imposing building.'

'I have arranged for us to visit the reverend gentleman there in about half an hour. I knew that you would want to commence investigations right away.'

'You thought right, Crabb.'

'Ah, here we are,' said Crabb, stopping and opening the door of the inn.

An elderly man with a ruddy complexion and stout appearance came forward to greet them as they entered the bar. 'Good day to you, sir.'

'Good day to you, landlord. This gentleman is Inspector Ravenscroft from London. He will be staying with you.'

'I'm pleased to make your acquaintance, sir. From London, you say. We don't have many folks from London staying 'ere. On police business, sir?' the landlord enquired.

'That's of a confidential nature, my man,' interjected Crabb. 'See that the inspector gets your best room.'

'All the rooms at the Cardinal's Hat are of the highest quality. Martha, will you take this gentleman up to number five, if you please.'

A young girl emerged from around the corner and picked up Ravenscroft's bag.

'I'm sure you will enjoy your stay at— Oh, I should have warned you about that beam! It's as well to duck when you go through.'

'Thank you,' muttered Ravenscroft, rubbing the top of his head where it had just come into contact with the offending woodwork. 'I'll try and remember next time. On second thoughts, just place the bag in the room, and we will return later.'

'As you wish, sir.'

'Delighted to meet you again, Inspector, and you Constable Crabb. Do please both take a seat.'

The speaker was an elderly clerical gentleman, of rotund appearance and whose round, red face was adorned with a fine set of grey side whiskers. 'As you can see my circumstances have somewhat changed since our last meeting. I had quite expected to spend the remainder of my days ministering to my flock at the Priory in Great Malvern, but then the good Dean, The Reverend Doctor Sanderson, unexpectedly died – I say unexpectedly, he was ninety-one at the time of his demise – but everyone thought he would go on for ever. Then he caught a rather nasty chill and passed away over a weekend. So sudden. The bishop contacted me and invited me to become the new dean and join the chapter of Worcester Cathedral. At first I declined the offer, believing that my true mission was to be found in Malvern, but the bishop was so persuasive, I eventually came to the conclusion that it was my Christian duty to accept such an undertaking,' said the cleric, without pausing for breath.

'You certainly have a very fine house here at the Cathedral Close,' said Ravenscroft looking around the room, with its Regency furniture, ornate decoration and fine paintings.

'Indeed so, although of course I am only the custodian. We are all here on this earth, for only for a brief time, and we have a duty, I believe, not only to safeguard that which has been passed down to us but also to leave something of ourselves for posterity. When I first came here—'

Crabb coughed, as Ravenscroft interrupted the dean's flow of words. 'Your letter speaks of a missing book?'

'Ah yes, the *Whisperie*.'

'*Whisperie?*' enquired Crabb.

'Yes, an unusual title. It was written by a monk, here at Worcester, in the early thirteenth century. I need not say that the book is one of our most priceless relics. Irreplaceable, of course. What makes the work so unusual is its content. You must understand, gentlemen, that up to that time most works were of a religious nature, either drawing upon the script of the Bible, or recounting the activities of the early Christian missionaries to these islands. Then in the year 1216 King John died and his body was conveyed here to Worcester, where he lies to this day in the chancel. Apparently he had quite a liking for the place. John, however, was a very unpopular monarch, by all accounts, and most people were rather pleased when he died. He had heavily taxed many of them for so many years. Not only was the church and the barons taxed, so were the ordinary townspeople, yeoman farmers, merchants and, of course, the Jews. The country was practically ruined by his foreign exploits, and following a revolt by the barons he was forced to sign the Magna Carta, which I am sure you have heard about.'

Ravenscroft nodded and leaned back in his armchair, enjoying the history lesson.

'There were quite a number of rumours spread about the cause of his death, at the time. The accepted version is that he died from eating too much food, although many believed that he had been poisoned by either one of his own barons or by someone – God forbid – who was high up in the church. All these accounts, or rumours, are included in the *Whisperie*, which was written by our unidentified monk at the time of John's funeral. I cannot stress too highly, Inspector, the importance and significance of this work to both the cathedral, and to the nation. It must be recovered at all costs.'

'You say the book was taken from the library?' asked Ravenscroft gazing out of the window, across the Close, towards the cathedral.

'Yes, Worcester Cathedral has one of the finest libraries of medieval books and manuscripts in the country. The collection runs to many thousands, with some of the items dating back to, and before, the cathedral's foundation. Many of the works give a profound insight into the life of the late medieval Benedictine priory, and are all handwritten and beautifully decorated with colourful initial letters and cartouches. They were nearly all lost in a fire that broke out in the vestry sometime in the last century I believe—'

'Where are the books kept now, sir?' asked Crabb looking up from his notebook.

'In the library, which is situated over the vestry, on the south side of the cathedral,' replied Touchmore, taking out a large handkerchief from his pocket and dabbing his brow.

'They are in a secure location?' asked Ravenscroft.

'Absolutely, Inspector; only the librarian and myself have a set of keys which opens the door leading into the library.'

'Are the public allowed to view the library?'

'No. Visitors are only allowed access to the library by prior appointment, and once there are closely supervised by the librarian. Could I offer you gentlemen a glass of sherry?' said Touchmore, rising from his seat behind his desk.

'Not for me, thank you, sir,' said Ravenscroft.

'Nor me, sir, don't touch the stuff,' added Crabb.

'Then you won't mind if I do? I find a glass of sherry taken at this time, strengthens one's resolve for the rest of the day. Now let me see, where were we?'

'I believe we were talking about the disappearance of the *Whisperie*, Dean. When did you first notice that it had been taken?' asked Ravenscroft.

'One of our minor canons came to my office in the morning, to say that he had found the door to the library open, and that there was broken glass everywhere. I immediately went to investigate and found that the cabinet that housed the *Whisperie* had been broken into, and that the book was missing,' replied Touchmore pouring himself a large glass of sherry and resuming his seat.

'I understand that your librarian is also absent?'

'That is correct, Inspector. Nicholas Evelyn has not been seen or heard of since the book was taken. It is all most worrying.'

'Do you think he could have taken it?' asked Ravenscroft.

'At first sight, it would seem most unlikely. He has been librarian here for over forty years. I'm sure that if he wanted to steal the book he would have done so many years ago. Also as he had a set of keys to both the library and the cases, he would not have needed to smash the cabinet to acquire the book.'

'Nevertheless both he and the book seemed to have disappeared at approximately the same time,' said Ravenscroft. 'What can you tell us about Evelyn?'

'I can't tell you a great deal about the man I'm afraid. I have been here less than a year, and during that time have only spoken to him on perhaps three or four occasions. He kept very much to himself, but I suppose that was the nature of his occupation,' replied the dean, replacing his handkerchief.

'So, he was a very lonely man?'

'Yes, I suppose so. I do not remember him attending any of the social or ecclesiastical events of the cathedral.'

'Was he married?'

'No, I believe he lived alone, in lodgings near the old Cornmarket.'

'Has anyone been to see if he is there, sir?' asked Crabb. 'He could have been taken ill.'

'Those were exactly my own thoughts at first, Constable. No, I have been to his lodgings, and checked his rooms, but his landlady has not seen him since the night of the robbery.'

'What else can you tell me about him?' asked Ravenscroft.

Touchmore sipped his sherry and thought for a moment, before replying, 'I can't in all honesty add anything else at all. Dear me, I find it rather sad that I do not know more about the man. I should have taken the time to engage him in conversation and found out more about his concerns.'

'Do not reproach yourself, sir. I'm sure you are a busy man,' said Ravenscroft.

'There is perhaps one thing: I know that the vestry has been concerned that perhaps Evelyn has been finding the job somewhat arduous of late. It was suggested to him that he should consider taking on another, younger assistant, with a view to eventual retirement.'

'And what was his response to this suggestion?' asked Ravenscroft.

'I understand that he became quite annoyed, and rejected the proposal, after which nothing more was said on the subject.'

'Thank you, Dean. I wonder if we might now visit the library?' asked Ravenscroft, easing himself out of the comfortable armchair.

'Of course, Inspector; I understand how important it is for you to view the scene of the crime. If you would care to follow me, gentlemen, we will make our way over to the cathedral.'

Touchmore led the way across the lawns of the Cathedral Close.

'It is certainly an impressive building,' remarked Ravenscroft, as the three men entered through the south doorway.

'It is one of the finest cathedrals in England, Inspector. Ah, I hear the choristers practising.'

The three men stood in silence, listening to the sound of boys' voices drifting down into the nave of the cathedral, and looking upwards at the fine stained-glass windows and impressive arches.

'The boys come from the adjoining King's School. They attend morning and evening services in the cathedral, and often come here, at quiet times in the day, to practise,' informed the dean.

Ravenscroft smiled, as a bewildered Crabb looked around in awe. 'A magnificent building; I had not expected it to have been so large, and inspiring.'

'If you would care to follow me, gentlemen,' said Touchmore leading the way across to an old oak door in one of the walls. 'This will take you up to the vestry, after which another wooden staircase will enable you to reach the library. You will find that the room has been left exactly as we found it. If you will excuse me though, gentlemen, I will not come with you. I have a meeting to attend, and I find the ascent somewhat difficult at my age.'

'Thank you, Dean. I am sure we can manage,' said Ravenscroft.

'Till later then, gentlemen.'

Ravenscroft and Crabb began their climb up the stone steps.

'Well, our Mister Touchmore seems to have done very well for himself,' said Crabb, following behind his superior.

'Good fortune always shines on the righteous – or so they say.'

'No wonder they wanted old Evelyn to retire. These steps are worse than the main street in Malvern!' muttered Crabb.

'Ah, here we are. This must be the vestry,' said Ravenscroft, pausing to steady his breathing.

'Bit of a dusty old room,' remarked Crabb.

'And there are the steps up to the library. You can go first this time, Crabb.'

The two men made their way up the old wooden steps. Eventually they could see a heavy oak door ahead of them at the top of the flight. Crabb pushed open the entrance to the library and they stepped inside.

Ravenscroft took a large spotted handkerchief from his coat pocket and mopped his forehead. 'I must be out of training, Crabb,' he said, between gasps.

'You'll have to go back to Malvern for another water cure, sir,' laughed Crabb.

Ravenscroft gave his colleague a look of disdain.

'There are certainly plenty of books up here. Rows and rows of them,' said Crabb.

'Well, whoever broke in here, certainly made a mess of the place. Broken glass everywhere,' said Ravenscroft walking over to the case. 'Mind where you tread, Crabb. This was obviously where the *Whisperie* was kept, and it looks as though this candlestick was used to break the glass, as it is lying here in the case.'

'I have just found this discarded candle on the floor nearby,' said Crabb.

'So it looks as though the robbery took place at night. It is surprisingly quite light in here with the sun coming in through the windows. I noticed the candlestick on the desk over there also contained a candle, so whoever broke in, lit some of the candles so that he could carry out the deed,' said Ravenscroft examining the broken case.

'Seems as though our Mr Evelyn is in the clear then?'

'Maybe, but I tell you something odd, Crabb. This case is still locked, but the door to the library is unlocked. There is no way a thief could have got through that door other than by using a key. But this then raises the question: if he had a key to the room, then probably the thief would also have had a key to the case, so why smash the case if he had a key?'

'Perhaps there are more than two sets of keys?' suggested Crabb. 'Or maybe the thief stole the set of keys from Evelyn?'

'If that was so, why smash the case?'

'Perhaps Evelyn forgot to lock the door when he left that night, and the thief just walked in and smashed the case?'

'That could be a possibility, but there is another strange thing. Whoever smashed open the case with the candlestick risked damaging the book. The stick itself might have landed on it and some of the smashed fragments would almost certainly have cut the pages. The point in taking the book was that it was a rare item. Whoever took it would not have wanted to run the risk of damaging it. Also look at the way the stick lies in the cabinet: I would say just where it landed. The thief would have had to remove it in order to recover the book. Tell me, Crabb, if you had used this stick to break open this case to get at the book, how would you have done it?'

Crabb thought for a moment. 'I would have raised the candlestick like this to break the glass, but would have kept hold of it and probably discarded it on the floor afterwards.'

'Precisely; you would not have risked the stick crashing into the case and damaging the book, you would have kept hold of your weapon.'

'So what do you think happened, sir?'

'I believe that whoever was here that evening, used the keys to open the door of the library, and the case; then he removed the book before locking the case and using the candlestick to break the glass. The thief then left in a hurry, failing to lock the door behind him.'

'This is all rather suspicious, sir.'

'I don't think we can rule out the possibility that it was Evelyn himself who not only took the book but also smashed the case afterwards.'

'But why go to all that trouble, when he could have just taken the book anyway?' asked Crabb, looking perplexed.

'Perhaps he wanted it to look as though someone had broken in and taken the item.'

'But if he planned to abscond with the book, surely he would not have been bothered what the authorities would think?'

'Maybe he planned to arrive for work the following day, make believe that he had just discovered the theft, and by raising the alarm would hope to leave himself in the clear?'

'But he did not return the following day,' added Crabb.

'No,' said Ravenscroft deep in thought. 'He did not. I wonder why.'

'He probably thought better of it when he reached home. Thought he would run off with the book after all, while he could,' suggested Crabb.

'Perhaps; well, I don't think there is anything else here for us. Just look at his desk. See if there are any notes or letters, or anything else he might have left that may be of interest.'

'Right, sir,' replied Crabb, beginning to search through the desk, as Ravenscroft busied himself by walking between the library shelves, admiring the rows of books there, and pausing now and then to examine some particular work which attracted his attention.

'Nothing, sir,' said Crabb, looking up from the desk, after a few minutes.

'Then let us make our way down.'

The two policemen retraced their steps to the vestry, and after a brief look around there, began their descent to the ground.

'This is interesting,' said Ravenscroft, crouching down on one of the steps. 'See here, part of a used candle. I wonder whether our thief dropped it in haste, on his way down? If so, he would have been plunged into darkness. Fortunately we have the daylight from the slits in the wall. At night it would have been completely dark.'

'Lucky he found his way to the bottom without falling and breaking his neck.'

Upon reaching the ground floor, Ravenscroft and Crabb set off to explore the rest of the cathedral.

'Some building this!' remarked Crabb.

'Indeed, but it was not all built in a day. The cathedral was obviously built in stages, each generation seeking to continue the work that had been begun by others. Today we can only marvel at such dedication and determination,' said Ravenscroft, pausing to examine one of the monuments in the chancel.

'King John, gentlemen!'

Ravenscroft turned round to see who had spoken to them.

'I see you have found our monument to wicked King John. You must be Inspector Ravenscroft? Let me introduce myself: Matthew Taylor, choirmaster of this noble edifice, at your service.'

The two men shook hands. Ravenscroft observed that the speaker was a young man of untidy appearance and wayward hair. 'I am pleased to make your acquaintance, Mr Taylor. This is my associate Constable Crabb.'

'I hear you have come from London to help us recover the old *Whisperie*.'

'We can but try,' said Ravenscroft. 'We are also looking into the disappearance of the librarian.'

'Ah, old Evelyn; you think he ran off with the book?' smiled the younger man.

'We are keeping an open mind.'

'I doubt that he is your thief, Inspector,' replied the other, in a casual, light-hearted manner.

'Oh, why do you say that, sir?' enquired Ravenscroft.

'The man was as dull and as cold as that stone over there – completely lacking in any form of imagination or initiative. Such an act as bold as that of the stealing of the *Whisperie* was beyond his enterprise.'

'You did not think much of Mr Evelyn then?' asked Ravenscroft, intrigued to learn more from the young choirmaster.

'To tell you the truth, Inspector, I don't think that I ever exchanged more than a dozen words with him. He was the sort of person who always seemed to be there, like one of the old tombs, merging into the background. I always thought it best to ignore him. He was rather a sad person I suppose. No, Mr Ravenscroft I think you will have to cast your net a little wider.'

'And where do you suggest we "cast our net", sir?'

'Far be it for me to cast aspersions or blight anyone's character by rumour and whisper, Inspector. But I suppose you might begin in the direction of Dr Silas Renfrew.'

'Silas Renfrew?' asked Crabb.

'Antiquarian and scholar of this parish; he lives in a rambling old house up towards Fort Royal. He has plenty of money at his disposal, and has a fine collection of old books and manuscripts, by all accounts. He was always visiting the library here. I know he particularly admired the *Whisperie*. He spoke to me about it once, saying he would gladly like to possess it if it ever came on the open market. Perhaps he took it to enhance his collection.'

'I thank you, Mr Taylor. We will be interviewing Dr Renfrew during our enquiries.'

'Well, if you will excuse me, gentlemen, I have yet another dreary choral rehearsal to conduct at the King's School. I leave you in the safe hands of the blessed saints, Wulfstan and Oswald.'

'Who?' asked Crabb.

'Dear me, Constable, you must really do your homework. They were both early bishops of Worcester. If it was not for them, there would be no cathedral and we would not be standing here today. That is Wulfstan over there, and Oswald is on the other side,' said Taylor, pointing to two stone shrines that lay on either side of the chancel. 'Until we meet again, Inspector.'

Ravenscroft nodded, as the choirmaster set off at a brisk walk down the main body of the church.

'Which one is Oswald?' asked Crabb, looking down at the worn effigy. 'This one seems to have been knocked about a bit.'

'It was probably vandalized at the time of the Civil War. Interesting character our Mr Taylor,' said Ravenscroft, beginning to make his way down the aisle towards the nave of the cathedral.

'He seems very young to be the choirmaster.'

'He also seemed quite anxious to tell us about Renfrew.'

The two men made their way out of the cathedral and into the Close.

'Where to now, sir?' asked Crabb.

'I think I should pay my respects to your Superintendent Henderson at the station here in Worcester, and then perhaps we will visit the librarian's lodgings and see what we can find there. But first, if I am not mistaken, Crabb, someone is intent on attracting our attention.'

'Good day to you, sir, we were rather hoping we would catch you before you left the cathedral. You must be the policeman arrived from London.'

The speaker was a tall, thin, elderly lady. Two other ladies of similar appearance stood behind her.

'I am indeed. My name is Inspector Ravenscroft, and this is my colleague, Constable Crabb.'

'Allow me to introduce myself. Miss Mary Ann Tovey,' said the elderly lady nodding in Ravenscroft's direction.

'Miss Tovey,' replied Ravenscroft.

'And this is my younger sister, Emily.'

'Inspector,' smiled the lady of that name.

'Miss Tovey.'

'And this is my youngest sister, Alice Maria,' said the lady, completing the introductions.

'We live in the house, just over there,' said the first Miss Tovey, turning round and indicating one of the Georgian buildings behind her. 'Number five.'

'We live at number five,' repeated the second Miss Tovey.

'Number five,' added the third.

'A fine building,' said Ravenscroft, wondering why the three sisters had sought to engage him in conversation.

'It was left to us by our late father. He was a schoolmaster at King's School for forty years, until his untimely death thirty years ago,' said Mary Ann.

'He was the schoolmaster at King's School, you know,' said Emily.

'Until he died thirty years ago,' added Alice Maria.

'I am very sorry,' said Ravenscroft, not knowing quite what to say to the three elderly sisters who now faced him.

'We saw him that night,' said the first Miss Tovey.

'Saw who, my dear lady?'

'Why, the person you are looking for, Inspector, the librarian, Nicholas Evelyn.'

'Nicholas Evelyn,' repeated her younger sister.

'The librarian,' added the third.

'When did you see him exactly?' asked Ravenscroft, as Crabb took out his notebook.

'I was just retiring to bed for the evening, when I saw him creeping along the side of the building in a rather furtive manner, as if he was up to no good. I remember it was exactly eleven o'clock, because I had just heard the church clock strike and I always retire exactly at that time of night,' said Miss Mary Ann in an excited manner.

'Exactly at eleven o'clock,' said the second sister.

'And I saw him as well, Inspector,' added the youngest sister, anxious not to be excluded from the conversation.

'You say that he was acting in a furtive manner?' asked Ravenscroft, addressing the eldest sister.

'Yes, Inspector. It was as if he did not want to be seen. He went in through the door over there.'

'Through that door,' said the second Miss Tovey, pointing to the cathedral.

'Was Mr Evelyn in the habit of coming back to the cathedral late at night, ma'am?' asked Crabb.

'Not usually. That's why we thought it so odd,' said Mary Ann.

'Very strange indeed,' added Alice Maria.

'Did any of you ladies happen to see him come out of the cathedral?' asked Ravenscroft.

'Why yes. I remember looking at the clock. It was a quarter to twelve exactly,' replied the elder sister.

'I saw him as well, Inspector,' said Miss Emily.

'He was very secretive,' added her younger sister.

'How do you mean, secretive?'

'He kept looking around him, to see if anyone had noticed his presence there,' said the elder sister.

'Did you see what happened next, ladies?' asked Crabb, making notes in his book.

'Yes. He made his way across the lawns there, before he went down the steps at the end, towards the river. We all thought it rather strange that he should be going down to the river at that time of night,' replied Miss Mary Ann.

'It was very dark,' added her younger sister.

'Did you see whether Mr Evelyn returned later?'

'No, Inspector,' replied Mary Ann, a puzzled expression on her face.

'Well, this is all very interesting,' said Ravenscroft, smiling. 'You have been most helpful, ladies.'

'I am glad we have been of assistance,' said Miss Mary Ann, looking rather pleased.

'We always try and help the authorities as much as we can,' remarked Miss Emily.

'I do hope you find Mr Evelyn – and the book,' said Miss Alice Maria.

'We will endeavour to do so,' said Ravenscroft.

'You know where we are, Inspector, if we can be of any further assistance, please do not hesitate to call upon us,' said the eldest Miss Tovey.

'Perhaps you would care to take tea with us, when you can spare the time,' said the second sister.

'You would be most welcome, and your constable as well, of course,' added the third sister smiling, as they began to turn away.

'That is most kind of you, ladies. If you will excuse us now, I wish you good day.'

'Good day, Inspector,' said the eldest sister, a remark that was repeated by her two companions.

Ravenscroft and Crabb watched them as they walked back, towards the house across the green, deep in conversation with one another.

'Well, they certainly seem to know what is going on,' remarked Crabb, closing his notebook.

'It is fortunate for us that they were so observant. So we now know that it must have been Evelyn who returned to the cathedral that night to steal the book.'

'Why did he just not take it during the daytime?'

'Because he wanted it to look as though someone had broken in during the night and taken it. If he had smashed the glass during the day, there was always the possibility that someone in the distance might have heard the sound of the glass breaking, or that he would have been caught in the act by someone suddenly entering the library. No, he had to undertake the robbery at night, when he knew he would be alone and undisturbed.'

'Why did he then go down to the river, at that time of night?' asked Crabb, looking puzzled.

'Perhaps he was meeting someone. He might have kept an appointment with someone who wanted the book. Let's follow in his footsteps and go down there and see what we can find.'

'Just the river, I should think, sir.'

'Nevertheless, I would be most interested to see whether there is a towpath, and to see where it goes.'

'I think one of our constables is looking for us, sir. I'll give him a shout. Over here!' said Crabb, gesturing to the officer.

'Ah, there you are, sir. You must be Inspector Ravenscourt?' said the breathless constable.

'Ravenscroft,' corrected the detective.

'Begging your pardon, sir, Superintendent Henderson sends his compliments and has asked me to see that you get this note, sir.'

'Thank you, my man,' said Ravenscroft, taking the piece of paper and reading its contents.

'Something serious, sir?' enquired an anxious Crabb.

'Apparently they have recovered a body from the River Severn down at Upton. They think it might be Evelyn. We are to go to Upton right away and meet Henderson there,' replied Ravenscroft, refolding the piece of paper.

'This way, sir, I've got a trap waiting,' said the constable.

'Then we'd best be on our way, Officer.'

As the group of three men made their way out of the cathedral precincts, they failed to notice the forlorn hooded figure, who gazed down upon them from the ramparts of the tower of the great building.

CHAPTER FOUR

'There is no doubt, I suppose, that it is Nicholas Evelyn?' asked Ravenscroft, staring down at the body on the river-bank.

'Everything seems to fit his description, sir,' answered the constable.

'Blessed if I see how you can tell, after the fellow has been in the water for the past few days,' remarked Crabb.

'When was the body discovered?' continued Ravenscroft.

'Early this afternoon. A fisherman found the body at the side of the river. Apparently he had been swept into the bank by that tree over there.'

'Tell me, Constable, this is the River Severn, which I believe flows through Worcester and down here to Upton, before eventually making its way to Bristol?'

'That is correct, sir. Next place after here is Tewkesbury, then Gloucester.'

'So it seems most likely that either Evelyn fell into the river at Worcester whilst it was dark, or that someone killed him. Either way, the body then made its way down here to Upton.'

'Seems most likely, sir, as you say,' replied the constable.

'Where is Superintendent Henderson?' asked Ravenscroft.

'Over there, sir, in the inn. Shall I tell him you have arrived?'

'Not for a while. Tell me has anyone looked in the pockets of the deceased man, or examined the body?'

'I don't think so. Tell you the truth, I don't think anyone quite liked the idea of taking a close look at him!' said the constable shaking his head.

'Well, Constable, I think we need to,' said Ravenscroft taking out his handkerchief as he bent down towards the corpse. 'The body seems to have quite a number of cuts and marks on the head and face. Someone could have hit him on the back of his head I suppose, or the wounds could have been caused by the body hitting various obstacles on his way down the river. There is no way of telling. We need to turn him over so that I can remove his coat. Can you help me, Constable?'

Ravenscroft held the handkerchief up to his nose with one hand, whilst using the other to assist the constable in removing the garment, Crabb being content to remain at some distance. 'Thank you, Constable, now let us see what is in his pockets. A few coins, a handkerchief – ah, this is what we are looking for Crabb – a set of keys on this ring.'

'Could be the keys to the library, sir,' suggested Crabb.

'Almost certain I would say. You take charge of them, and when we return to Worcester we will see if they fit. There seems to be nothing else of interest on his person. No sign of the book.'

'Could have fallen out of his pocket?'

'If that is the case, the *Whisperie* is now lying on the bed of the River Severn!'

'Then we shall never recover it, sir.'

'I don't think we should reconcile ourselves to that assumption just yet. We know that Evelyn in all probability took the book, and that when he left the cathedral he walked down the steps to the river. Why go down there at that time of night? I fancy that he must have been going to meet someone – in which case he could have given the book to the person whom he had arranged to meet,' replied Ravenscroft, deep in thought.

'Then that person killed him and threw him into the river,' added Crabb, after a moment or two.

'Perhaps – or he lost his footing on the way back and fell in the water.'

'Poor fellow,' said Crabb mournfully. 'To have worked in the cathedral for forty years and to have met his end like this seems a great shame.'

'What we need to find out, Crabb, is who it was that Evelyn was meeting that night. Then we might be able to find out why Evelyn took the book, and who now has it.'

'I think we should go and pay our respects to Superintendent Henderson, sir,' suggested Crabb.

'Of course, over there you say?'

The two men made their way over to the old timber-beamed inn situated a few yards further along the towpath. As they neared the building they were met by the sound of laughter and loud voices.

'I should go steady, sir,' said Crabb looking, down at the ground sheep-
ishly.

Ravenscroft gave Crabb a perplexed look, before pushing open the door
to the inn. Five or six men were standing round the bar.

'—and I said to the snotty-nosed corporal, clean your bloody rifle or
the damned Russians will roast you alive!'

The speaker was a late-middle-aged man of military bearing, dressed in
a long overcoat, who was leaning on the bar with one elbow, whilst holding a glass of whisky in his other hand. His companions burst out laughing at his last remark.

'—and so this silly idiot of a man turns to me, puffs himself up like an
overblown melon and says who the bloody hell is giving me orders?'

More laughter ensued from the group.

'And who the devil might you be, sir?' said the speaker, suddenly noticing Ravenscroft's arrival. 'We have no comment to make to the papers at
this stage,' he said, turning away to the bar.

'I'm not from the local newspaper; I'm Inspector Ravenscroft from the
Yard. I'm looking for Superintendent Henderson of the Worcester
Constabulary.'

'Are you indeed? Well, you have found him: I'm Henderson,' said the
speaker, giving his companions an amused glance.

'I am pleased to make your acquaintance, sir,' said Ravenscroft, stepping forward.

'So you're Ravenscroft. All the way from London, you say. Can't see
why they should have sent for you. We are more than capable of dealing
with the case.'

'I was asked to come down here by the cathedral authorities.'

'Were you, by Wellington! Dammed insult I call it. It's a bad reflection
on the local force when they have to call in outsiders. Dammed rude of
you to have started your investigations before paying your respects,'
snapped Henderson, his moustache bristling.

'I'm sorry, sir,' said Ravenscroft, looking down at the floor of the bar.

'Er, still, I suppose it is not your fault. I expect you were only obeying
orders, as they say. Got to do what the Yard tells you. Well seeing as you
are here, you might as well join me in a tincture, Ravenscroft.'

'Not while I am on duty, sir, thank you.'

'That's high and mighty of you, Ravenscroft!'

'We'll see you later, Reggie,' said one the drinkers, making his excuses and preparing to leave.

'No need to go, gentlemen. That fellow we pulled out of the river ain't going anywhere.'

'Nevertheless, Reggie, time we were going,' said another of the group.

'See you later, gentlemen. The inspector and I will resume our conversation outside,' replied Henderson, clearly irritated by his junior's arrival.

Ravenscroft stepped out of the inn where he was confronted by an anxious Crabb. 'I see you have met with the superintendent then,' whispered the constable, before standing to attention, as the door of the inn opened once more and Henderson stepped forth.

'You've had a look at the body then, Ravenscroft?'

'Yes, sir.'

'Well, what do you make of it?' asked the superintendent, in an annoyed tone of voice, and walking back briskly towards the body on the side of the river-bank.

'He has obviously been in the water for a few days. Whether he was murdered, or just lost his footing—' began Ravenscroft, attempting to keep up with his superior.

'If you ask me, Ravenscroft, I'd say the fellow probably had too much to drink, lost his footing and fell in the river.'

'We found a set of keys on him, which would suggest that he is Evelyn, the librarian.'

'I see,' said Henderson approaching the body. 'I see. Did you find the book on him?'

'Afraid not, sir.'

'Not surprising. It looks to me as though someone just broke into the library and stole the book. Smashed the case; no consideration!'

'Have you come up with any information that might lead us to the culprit, sir?' asked Ravenscroft, as tactfully as he could.

'No, we have not!' snapped Henderson. 'That's your job. The force has plenty of more important things to deal with at the moment than to spend our time trying to recover some old religious book! I've got the races to organize on Pitchcroft next week. You get on with it. Find out who took the book, Ravenscroft.'

'Yes, sir.'

'And keep me fully informed. I want to be kept up to date with progress in this case. Can't afford to offend the cathedral.'

'Yes, sir, of course.'

'And you, Constable, see that the undertaker is called. Can't have this fellow lying here all day! Damn sightseers will be arriving soon! Good day to you, Ravenscroft.'

'Good day, sir.'

Ravenscroft and Crabb watched their superior officer stride off across the grass towards his waiting cab.

'So that was Superintendent Henderson,' remarked Ravenscroft, breathing a sigh of relief.

'I tried to warn you, sir. Apparently he used be a major in the army before he was elevated to the local constabulary. They say he fought in the Crimea. The men are not all that keen on him, by all accounts.'

'Oh, why is that?' asked Ravenscroft.

'Rather too fond of the bottle,' said Crabb, rubbing the side of his nose.

'I take your meaning, Crabb. Well, I think that is all we can do here for today. Time I returned to Worcester to try the fare at the Cardinal's Hat. We'll meet again in the Cathedral Close at nine in the morning.'

Ravenscroft slept badly. The unfamiliar surroundings, a particularly unappetizing supper, and the sounds of a late night drunken reveller outside the hostelry all conspired to keep him awake until the early hours of the morning. He rose at seven and, after dressing and partaking of some early morning refreshment, he set off to explore the streets of the town.

He retraced his steps of the previous day, back along Friar Street and the Shambles, and through the main thoroughfare, until he reached the railway station. He then turned down one of the side roads to his left, and eventually found himself on the towpath on the banks of the Severn.

He looked along the river-bank, past the bridge and the warehouses, towards the mighty cathedral. To Ravenscroft, the building seemed to tower over all that was before it, declaring its importance and dominance over the affairs of the town. He began to wonder what events it had witnessed down through the centuries, and what secrets it retained within the confines of its walls.

As he made his way along the towpath, he passed a number of boats, the occupants of whom were busily engaged in unloading various cargoes, and transporting the sacks and boxes to a large warehouse on the side of the quay. He then walked beneath the shadow of the cathedral until he reached a set of steps, which he knew would almost certainly take him up to the precincts of the building. Ravenscroft paused and looked out across the river. This must have been where Evelyn had made his way that night before he had met with his unfortunate death – but which way had he then turned after he had walked down from the cathedral? If he had taken the route back towards the bridge, he might then have made his way up towards the town, but if this had been his intention, Ravenscroft concluded, it would surely have been quicker to have turned into the town from the cathedral in the first place. The more he considered the possibilities, the more it seemed probable that Evelyn would have gone in the other direction, taking the path that led away from the cathedral and the town. If that was the case, where was it that Evelyn was going at such a late hour?

Ravenscroft decided to follow the towpath. After a while the outer stone walls of the cathedral precincts ended and he passed an inn overlooking the river. Perhaps Evelyn had met someone there that night?

He continued on further, passing a number of derelict buildings and one or two fine houses on his way, until he reached the entrance of the Birmingham to Worcester Canal, where a boat was awaiting its turn to enter the lock gate. Could Evelyn have met with someone on one of the boats perhaps? The possibilities appeared to be endless. Whoever it was who Evelyn had met that night, had killed the poor man and thrown his body into the Severn. As Ravenscroft looked down at the murky waters, he resolved that he would send Crabb to call at the inn, and also to make enquiries at the lock gate, to see whether anyone could remember seeing Evelyn that night.

He decided it was time to return to the cathedral and, after retracing his steps along the bank of the river, he made his way back up to the Close.

Finding a seat on the green, he sat down and looked at the range of buildings that ran round the cathedral precincts. There was the house where the Tovey sisters lived, and Touchmore's imposing residence as befitted his status as the Dean of Worcester Cathedral.

Deep in thought, he suddenly felt something running into his leg, and looking down found a metal hoop at his feet. He picked up the object. A small boy, not more than six or seven years of age was running towards him, closely followed by a woman who was endeavouring to keep up with him.

'Please, sir, can I have my hoop back?' asked the boy looking across at him with appealing eyes.

'Of course you can,' smiled Ravenscroft. The boy reminded him of another, younger boy he had seen the previous year. That child had been playing with his toys, and had a mother to care for him.

'I'm so sorry, sir. Will you please forgive my son?' The speaker was evidently the child's mother. Ravenscroft observed that she was simply dressed, plain in appearance and in her mid-twenties. 'Of course, it is no problem, I can assure you. It is good to see the little fellow enjoying himself,' he replied.

'I bring him here, as there is more space for him to play. Where we live, near the Cornmarket, there is nowhere he can go and play, and it's too dangerous by the river. We usually manage to come here every day for a few minutes, before I start work.'

'Please take a seat,' offered Ravenscroft, sensing that he might be able to gain some local information from the woman, 'I'm sure your boy will manage to entertain himself, while you recover your composure.'

'That is most kind of you, sir. I don't think I have seen you here before?'

'No. I live in London.'

'London! My word, I've always wondered what London must be like. I imagine all the people there are very busy, and very rich,' said the young woman taking her place on the seat.

'Well, everyone is certainly busy, but not many people there are rich,' smiled Ravenscroft.

'The Queen, she lives there. She must be very rich?'

'She is indeed.'

'Have you seen the Queen, sir?'

'I saw her once, and only briefly. She came by in her carriage.'

'My! I should like to have seen her,' said the woman sadly. 'She must be very grand. And what brings you to Worcester? Oh, I'm sorry. People say I am always asking questions about things that don't concern me.'

'I don't mind answering your question. I'm a detective. I have come down here to investigate the disappearance of the librarian at the cathedral.'

'Oh!' exclaimed the woman.

'You knew Mr Evelyn?' asked Ravenscroft.

'Why yes, sir. He lives in the same lodging-house as me and my boy. We have rooms on the ground floor, and he has rooms on the top floor. He is always good and kind to us, sir. Whenever he sees my boy he often pats him on the head and gives him a farthing.'

'That is very good of him.'

'And now everyone says he's missing.'

'You have not seen him since the night he disappeared?'

'No. Be careful, Arthur. Don't go to near the houses!' she cried out to the boy.

'Did Mr Evelyn mention that he was going away?'

'No. He said nothing to me about going away.'

'Did he ever say anything about a book called the *Whisperie*?' asked Ravenscroft leaning forward.

'*Whisperie*. My, that's a funny name. No, I don't think Mr Evelyn ever mentioned anything about a *Whisperie*.'

'Was he in the habit of receiving visitors to his rooms?'

'Oh no, sir; he always kept very much to himself. We used to laugh and say you could set your watch by the time Mr Evelyn went out to work. He always left at half past eight in the morning, and came home at exactly half past six in the evening. Six days a week; it was always the same.'

'Did he ever go away, to stay with friends perhaps, to travel, or go on holiday?'

'No. I don't think so. He always seemed to be there. He didn't seem to go out much in the evenings either.'

'He seems to have lived a very lonely life.'

'Yes, I suppose he did, but you speak as though something has happened to him.'

'You mentioned that you come here every day,' said Ravenscroft, changing the subject and leaning back in his seat.

'Yes, before I start work.'

'And you always sit on this seat?'

'Yes,' replied the woman, a puzzled expression on her face.

'When you have been sitting here, have you ever seen Mr Evelyn perhaps talking with someone?'

'No, I don't think so. He was always at work by then, I suppose.'

'And where do you work?' enquired Ravenscroft, curious to know more about the woman he had engaged in conversation.

'At that house over there, across the Green,' she replied, pointing at one of the large imposing buildings. 'I'm a parlour maid. I work for Sir Arthur Griffiths. He is the Member of Parliament for the town. He is a very important man,' she added proudly.

'I'm sure he is – and you must consider yourself fortunate that you work in such a fine house.'

'I do indeed. Sir Arthur is often away in London, but when he is here, he always seems to be busy, entertaining and such like. We are kept very occupied.'

'You have worked there long?'

'For about eight years, sir.'

'You must like it.'

'Yes, there is always plenty to do. Sir Arthur lives there with his only daughter, Miss Griffiths, she has charge of the house.'

'It is a pleasant residence, overlooking the cathedral. I would certainly like to live in such a house,' said Ravenscroft smiling.

'One day my son will live in such a house,' she replied looking away. Ravenscroft thought he could detect a note of sadness in her voice. 'Well, sir, you will have to excuse me. It is time I took my son to school, before I commence my duties for the day.'

'Of course,' said Ravenscroft rising to his feet. 'Thank you for talking to me – and you are?'

'Ruth Weston, sir.'

'Well, Mrs Weston, perhaps we may—'

'Miss, sir. Miss Weston.'

'I'm sorry. Miss Weston. I have enjoyed our conversation. Perhaps we might talk together again?'

'Yes, I am generally here at this time each morning. I hope you find Mr Evelyn.'

'Good day to you, Miss Weston,' replied Ravenscroft.

'Arthur, come here. It is time for school.'

Ravenscroft resumed his seat and watched the woman taking her child's hand. He followed them with his eyes as they left the cathedral grounds. He resolved to call upon the Member of Parliament in the near future. Perhaps someone in the household might have additional information regarding Evelyn and the night in question. The more he learned about the reclusive librarian, the more the man intrigued him. Evelyn had appeared to have lived such a dull existence, almost to the point of boredom. What had then suddenly driven a man of such regular, sober habits, to commit a deed which seemed so alien to his whole personality? What force could have caused such a dramatic change?

'You look deep in thought, sir.'

'Ah, Crabb, I did not see you there,' said Ravenscroft, looking up at his constable.

'I trust you slept well at the Cardinal's Hat?'

'Not particularly well, thank you. But what news of the keys we recovered from the body?'

'They appear to fit both the doors to the library, and the cases. No doubt about it: they were Evelyn's keys all right,' answered Crabb, taking his seat beside Ravenscroft.

'It was just as we supposed. I have just been talking with the parlour maid who works in that house over there, a Ruth Weston, who apparently resides in the same lodging house as our friend Evelyn. She describes him as being a very lonely man of regular habits, who entertained no one, and who kept very much to himself.'

'Seems to confirm very much what the dean and the choirmaster said.'

'We need to find out where the librarian went to that night, after he left the cathedral. I took a walk along the towpath this morning, and I am convinced that when he went down the steps, he turned left and made his way in the direction of the canal. There is an inn on the way, where he might have met someone. I want you to spend the morning interviewing people at the inn to see if they saw anything that night.'

'Right, sir.'

'Then I want you to go further along the towpath, to where the river and the canal join. If there are any barges there, interview the occupants – see if they saw anything on the night he disappeared. Then meet me back here at one o'clock.'

'Yes, sir. And where will you be?'

'I think it is about time I called on Dr Silas Renfrew, to find out more about this missing book. Perhaps he might be able to tell us more about Nicholas Evelyn, and why he suddenly chose to steal the *Whisperie*.'

INTERLUDE

LONDON

'You appear to have done well, Monk,' said the woman in black, leaning forward in the darkness, straining to catch a glance of the man from beyond the candle.

'It was not difficult. I just had to wait my time. I knew she would be easy,' replied the voice in a dry, matter-of-fact tone.

'You made sure that no one saw you?' she asked anxiously.

'I would not be sitting here now, had I not been so careful,' he retorted.

'I am sorry. I should not have questioned your ability in this matter,' she said quickly, anxious not to cause offence. 'Tell me how it was done?'

'Bucks Row; it was dark. She was easy. I held her head back against the wall, then I drew the blade across her throat,' he said without emotion.

'The papers said you slashed her stomach?'

'You object to my methods?'

'No, of course not; that wretched woman deserved to die,' she replied bitterly. 'Tell me, did she cry out, or express any words of remorse before she died?'

'Women like that know nothing of remorse. I squeezed her throat; looked into her eyes and saw the fear there; she had no chance to speak.'

'I see. I would have liked some atonement,' she said, sadly.

'The woman must have hurt you a great deal,' he stated.

'I told you there were to be no questions regarding my motives in this concern,' she said quickly, becoming annoyed by his enquiries. 'It is enough for you to know that the woman gravely wronged my family some-time in the past. Now she has paid the ultimate price. You have kept your side of the bargain. That is all I could have asked for. Now, I will fulfil my obligation. Here are the twenty sovereigns we agreed upon.'

She placed the small bag of coins down on the table, expecting a hand to emerge from the darkness of the room to take up the reward.

'You do not count the coins?' she asked presently, wondering why he had not taken it.

'I have no cause to doubt your word. I trust our arrangement. There is only one thing that concerns me.'

'Ask.'

'You addressed me as Monk. That is not my name.'

'I would not expect you to go by your real name,' she said.

'It is a name of convenience,' he laughed.

'I know what it is like to assume another identity, to slip unnoticed into the shadows, to observe, and yet not be seen.'

'You must never ask who I am, or ask to see my face, if our work is to continue.'

'That is agreed,' she replied, observing the determination and threat within his voice.

'I prefer the dark. You need have no fear that anyone will ever see me. The police are stupid; they will never catch me. I have a number of disguises – and I know the alleyways and backstreets better than any of them. I will always be long away, before they even discover my handiwork. I am well aware of your inner desires, my dear lady. I know your secret and true purpose. There will be no betrayal on my part.'

She found something both frightening and reassuring about the coldness and precision of his voice.

'But should you ever attempt to see my features, discover my true identity, or even try to follow me, you will know that our arrangement will end, and that I will take all available steps to protect myself. It will be as though you had never lived. No one will have known of your existence. I trust I make myself clear on this point?'

'Of course, your identity is of little concern to me,' she replied, growing concerned by the increasing anger in his voice.

'Then we are two of a kind. You seek to conceal your identity beneath your veil, whilst I prefer the darkness of the shadows. You and I are in great need of each other.' He paused for a moment. 'You said there would be others?'

'I have the name of your next victim.'

'She is of the same tendency?' he asked.

'Yes, she is a common prostitute. Her name is Chapman. Annie Chapman.'

'And where is this Chapman to be found?'

'She usually resides at Crossinghams – when she has earned enough from her casual encounters, to pay for her bed for the night. It is a cheap lodging house. You will find it situated in Dorset Street.'

'I know of the place. I must congratulate you upon your research,' he replied, a note of sarcasm creeping into his voice.

'I do not need your words of false encouragement,' she said.

'The sum will increase this time,' he said suddenly, ignoring her last remark.

'Of course, I will pay you forty sovereigns when you have carried out the deed. I trust that is a satisfactory arrangement?'

'It will suffice.'

'This time I will pay you an extra ten sovereigns, if you can carry out an additional service,' she said, slowly sensing his greed, and drawing closer to the candle, so that she could almost feel the warmth of its solitary flame.

'Go on.'

'I would have her rings. Bring me her rings, as a keepsake, and I will reward you with the extra money.' She was beginning to find the room and the darkness oppressive, and wished the interview would end.

'It will be done.'

'We will need to meet afterwards. I will be away from London for the next ten days. I have business to attend to,' she said, rising quickly from her chair.

'That is understood. We will meet here at the same time exactly, in two weeks.'

'That will give you enough time?' she enquired.

'More than enough. No doubt the newspapers will keep you informed of my success.'

'Then I wish you good night.' She turned and made her way towards the door.

'Enjoy your stay in the countryside. They say that Worcester is pleasant at this time of the year.'

She opened the door, and quietly left the room, betraying nothing.

The solitary light, swinging in the evening breeze, guided her way down the steps and across the courtyard. Her desire now was to leave the area as soon as possible, now that the arrangements had been made, and to return once more to her other world.

But why had he mentioned Worcester? How could he have known? She had been so careful to give nothing away – and yet. . . .

CHAPTER FIVE

WORCESTER

Ravenscroft alighted from the cab at the end of the drive, and gazed up at the house before him.

'Shall I wait for you, sir?' enquired the cabman.

'No. Thank you. I will make my own way back,' replied Ravenscroft, paying his fare.

'Right you are, sir.'

He watched as the cab turned and began its return journey down the London road towards the centre of Worcester, before making his way up the drive. The house certainly looked imposing with its long, fine, wrought-iron veranda and matching white balconies, and its sweeping views across its lawns. He drew back the large knocker and struck the door, hearing the echoes from inside the building.

'Yes?' enquired a tall, well-built man with a swarthy complexion.

'I would like to speak with Dr Silas Renfrew.'

'And who are a you?' replied the speaker, in what Ravenscroft judged to be an Italian accent.

'I am Inspector Samuel Ravenscroft. If you would be so kind my man, I would be obliged if you would present my card to your master.'

The man glared at Ravenscroft, then took the card and stared down at it, as if trying to make out the letters there. Ravenscroft coughed, and shuffled his feet impatiently.

'You, a'wait here,' replied the servant eventually, before closing the door abruptly in Ravenscroft's face.

A sudden noise made him turn. A large peacock was making its way

56

across the lawn, its fine plumage displayed behind him.

The door reopened. 'My master will a'see you, now,' said the Italian, indicating that Ravenscroft should enter the building.

He stepped inside and found himself in a large hall. As he stood on the black and white tiled floor, he looked across at the large marble statue of a naked man which stood on a plinth at the bottom of a winding staircase.

'David. Very fine, I think you will agree. Florentine; fifteenth century. One of only two known examples of the artist's work concerning this subject,' said a voice emerging from one of the rooms.

'It is certainly impressive,' said Ravenscroft.

'Oh, Inspector, it is far more than that. But let me introduce myself. Doctor Silas Renfrew, a refugee from your late forlorn colony,' said the American owner of the voice, smiling and extending a hand.

'I am pleased to make your acquaintance, sir,' said Ravenscroft, feeling his hand being shaken vigorously in a tight, encompassing grip. He had expected the antiquary to have been much older, perhaps reserved and eccentric in manner, whereas the man who now addressed him appeared to be not much older than himself, was of a well-kept appearance and possessed an outgoing personality.

'Would you care to follow me into the library, Inspector? Can I offer you a whisky – or of course, you English prefer tea.'

'Nothing for me, sir, thank you.'

'That will be all, Georgio,' said Renfrew opening the double doors of a room at the rear of the hall.

The manservant gave a slight bow, before giving Ravenscroft a suspicious glance as he left the room.

'Do come in, Inspector.'

Ravenscroft found himself in what was evidently the library, for three sides of the room were entirely covered from floor to ceiling with rows of books. He also observed a large oak desk covered with yet more books and piles of papers. A number of glass cabinets were situated at various intervals on what appeared to be an ornate, eastern, hand-woven carpet. Doctor Silas Renfrew was obviously a man who placed a high value on the accumulation of knowledge.

'Please take a seat,' said the American indicating one of two comfortable old leather armchairs which had been placed before the open fireplace. 'I'm afraid you will have to take me as you find me.'

Ravenscroft nodded and seated himself.

'I knew, of course, that it would only be a matter of time before you arrived,' said Renfrew exhibiting a slow, methodical drawl.

'Then you know, sir, that we are investigating the disappearance of both the librarian, and the *Whisperie* from the library of Worcester Cathedral. I believe you know the work, sir.'

'I do indeed, Inspector; one of the finest books in the cathedral library.'

'Perhaps you would be so kind as to tell me more about the work.'

'Written around the time of King John's death in 1216, by an unidentified monk, and highly decorated with rich ornate initial lettering. A work of unique splendour, full of wonderful rumours and whispers concerning the death of the late king, hence its title – the *Whisperie*,' said Renfrew with enthusiasm, as he took the other seat.

'What value would you place upon it?' asked Ravenscroft.

'My dear Inspector, some works are so unique that it is almost impossible to estimate their value.'

'And the *Whisperie* would fall into that category?'

'Almost certainly.'

'Would I be correct in assuming that it would only be a collector, such as yourself, who would be interested in purchasing such a work, should it ever be offered on the open market?'

'Undoubtedly. No self-respecting museum would wish to be implicated in the theft of such an item – but if you are suggesting that I might be tempted to purchase the work should it be offered to me by the thief, then my answer would be no. I would have no desire to tarnish my reputation.'

'But other collectors, perhaps, would be less circumspect?'

Renfrew said nothing, but merely shrugged his shoulders.

'I understand that you were in the habit of visiting the cathedral library. Why was that, sir?'

'There are many fine medieval works in the collection, and as a scholar as well as a collector, I often had recourse to consult several of the items there. It is my ambition eventually to publish the definitive work on English early medieval church documents.'

'I see,' replied Ravenscroft. Clearly Renfrew was out to impress him with his learning. 'You no doubt consulted the *Whisperie*.'

'Of course; many times in fact. As I said before, Inspector, the work is unique. It will feature highly in my book.'

'No one has approached you yet, sir, offering the book for sale?'

'Certainly not.'

'And if such an offer were to be made?'

'I would purchase the book, inform yourself of the identification of the culprit, and then return it to its rightful place in the cathedral.'

Ravenscroft was beginning to find Renfrew's smile and casual manner somewhat disconcerting. 'Tell me about the librarian?' he asked.

'Nicholas Evelyn.'

'You spoke to him a great deal?'

'He was not a man with whom one could easily converse.'

'Could you elaborate further, Mr Renfrew?'

'I found him accommodating enough. Apparently he had worked in the library for over forty years. His knowledge of the collection was extensive. His conversation however, was very limited. He never went out of his way to enquire into the nature of my research, and seemed to prefer the sanctuary of his own desk, to sharing the fruits of my findings with me. In fact, I always had the impression that he rather resented me being there. He struck me as being rather possessive about the collection.'

'Did he ever mention the *Whisperie*, in general conversation?'

'No. I don't believe he did.'

'Can you think of any reason why he would have stolen the book?' asked Ravenscroft.

'No. I cannot, Inspector – unless he was paid to do so.'

'Oh, why do you say that, sir?'

'People generally steal for one of two reasons: either to profit by the theft by selling their gains on to a third party, or because they want to keep the item for their exclusive use.'

'And which of these two categories would Evelyn have fallen into?' asked Ravenscroft.

'Evelyn does not seem the kind of man who would fall into the first group, but I cannot see any reason why he would want to take the book for himself to enjoy alone. After all, he could see it every day of his working life. Have you considered the possibility that someone else took the book?'

'We keep an open mind, sir,' said Ravenscroft, becoming a little annoyed by his host's methodical, well-thought-out, answers.

'We must all do that, Inspector.'

'You never mixed socially with Evelyn outside his work, perhaps visiting his lodging?'

'Why would I need to do that, Inspector? But no, I never saw him outside his place of work. I did suggest to him once, however, that he might like to come up here and view my collection.'

'And did he ever take you up on your offer?'

'No. A great pity. I think he would have found the collection interesting. I never mentioned it again – after his lack of interest, that is.'

'I have to tell you that Evelyn is dead. We recovered his body from the river yesterday,' said Ravenscroft suddenly, hoping that such a disclosure might penetrate the other's certainty.

'I suppose that was always a probability,' replied Renfrew, showing no emotion.

'Why do you say that, sir?'

'If the man had taken the book, then he might well have been acting for another – and that other person could have killed him.'

'You would have made a fine detective, sir. There was no sign of the book upon his person.'

'Then it is to be hoped that it is not lying at the bottom of the River Severn,' smiled Renfrew.

'Tell me, sir, how long have you lived in Worcester?' asked Ravenscroft, changing the subject.

'Three years.'

'You live here alone?'

'Except for my manservant, Georgio – he tends to all my needs – and my cook. I find that a French cook is one of life's great essentials.'

'And why did you choose Worcester?'

'Because of the collection, at the cathedral, for my research,' smiled Renfrew again.

'Of course. Well, I won't take up any more of your time. You have been most helpful. If anyone should approach you concerning the book, I would be obliged if you would contact me straight away,' said Ravenscroft rising to his feet.

'Certainly, Inspector. I am sorry I could not have been of more assistance to you. But I would be negligent in my duty as a host, if I did not show you some of my favourite treasures before you leave. I can see Inspector Ravenscroft that you are a man who appreciates fine art, if I am not mistaken.'

'I have a few minutes—' began Ravenscroft.

'Excellent! Come over here, Inspector, and I will show you something which I am sure you will appreciate.'

Renfrew led the way across to one of the display cabinets. 'This is an early known copy of *The Canterbury Tales* by Geoffrey Chaucer, a work of such richness of characterization and humour. Written in Middle English,' said Renfrew, pointing to a book lying inside the closed cabinet. 'A work that was to have a profound influence on all works of fiction that were to follow on later.'

Ravenscroft nodded and looked down at the intricate writing.

'Almost impossible to read, unless one has a knowledge of the language of the period. Next to it is a page from the *Lindisfarne Gospels*. The original work was thought to have been written around AD 700. This translation into English was made two hundred and fifty years later.'

'Over nine hundred years old,' remarked Ravenscroft.

'Again, it is a work of such outstanding beauty and significance, laying the foundations for Christian writers for centuries to come. A work which is beyond value,' enthused Renfrew.

'And what is this work?' asked Ravenscroft, indicating an open manuscript, lying within the case.

'I thought your eye would be drawn to that sooner or later. That is part of the *Worcester Antiphoner*, a composite liturgical work dating from the late fourteenth century, handwritten by the monks here at Worcester, and based upon the Officer Antiphoner, Calendar, Psalter and Hymnal of the century before.'

'A priceless work?' enquired Ravenscroft, beginning to find the tone of his host somewhat condescending.

'Of course, Inspector. You cannot put a value on such a unique manuscript as the *Worcester Antiphoner*. But I sense the workings of the police mind. You are saying to yourself – how has this man acquired such a work? Surely it should be part of the cathedral library? Did he pay Evelyn a large sum of money to lift the work for himself? Will this man stop at nothing to acquire priceless works of art?' said Renfrew smiling and making light of the matter.

'I must confess that such a thought did cross my mind.'

'Then let me put your thoughts at rest, Inspector. The work was not taken from the library by Evelyn, and sold to myself for a large sum of money, although it is true that I had to sell a great many of my American stocks to pay for it. I acquired it in auction in New York, approximately five years ago, when I was still resident in America. I can produce the sale documentation and provenance should you so desire.'

'That will not be necessary, sir. Perhaps I should be going,' said Ravenscroft, tiring of the American's literary treasures, and anxious now to leave.

'Oh, Inspector, just one more item, which I prize above all other, and which you will surely appreciate,' said Renfrew leading the way across towards another glass-case where two large volumes could be seen. 'Tell me what you notice about this?'

Ravenscroft leaned forwards and looking down at the printed writing on the open volume, began to read the words there.

And then he falls, as I do. I have ventured,
Like little wanton boys that swim on bladders,
This many summers in a sea of glory,
But far beyond my depth: my high-blown pride
At length broke under me, and now has left me,
Weary and old with service, to the mercy
Of a rude stream that must for ever hide me

'Well done, Inspector. I see you have a feeling for the great bard. You are looking at the *First Folio* of Shakespeare's works. The lines you have just read, are spoken by Cardinal Wolsey in the play, *King Henry VIII,* following his downfall and dismissal by the king. The piece begins with the words – "Farewell! A long farewell, to all my greatness!" – rather appropriate I think you would agree. Foolish indeed is the man of God who ventures into the world of politics and deception! But I see I have kept you for too long from your investigations. Please forgive my enthusiasm. Please feel free to return when you have more time. I will be more than delighted to show you some more of my children.'

'You are most kind sir.'

The two men shook hands as the door opened and the manservant entered, leaving Ravenscroft wondering as to how the Italian had known that his departure was imminent.

'Georgio, show Inspector Ravenscroft out.'

Ravenscroft followed the servant across the hallway, cast a final look at the statue and stepped out in the late summer air.

'And how was your visit to Doctor Renfrew, sir?' asked Crabb, as he and Ravenscroft supped their mugs of Worcester ale at the Old Talbot.

'Quite interesting, but also very revealing,' replied Ravenscroft.

'In which way?' said Crabb, helping himself to a large chunk of cheese.

'The man is an American scholar. He lives alone in a large rambling house on the edge of Worcester, except for an Italian manservant and a French cook. Says he has been living here for the past three years whilst undertaking research into the documents at Worcester Cathedral. He possesses, what appears to be a large collection of early English books and manuscripts including one rare item, the *Worcester Antiphoner*, which I am sure should be part of the cathedral collection, although he claims he purchased the work at auction in New York five years ago.'

'Do you think Evelyn could have sold him the book?'

'If Evelyn took the book, it would seem logical that he would first offer it for sale to Renfrew, although that might seem a little too obvious,' replied Ravenscroft, cutting up a piece of ham and placing it on his fork.

'We could make a search through his collection?' suggested Crabb.

'We could, but I don't want to alarm him just yet. Anyway if he had the book, I'm sure he would not have left it lying around for someone like myself to discover. He will have hidden it where no one could find it.'

'I suppose you're right. Remarkably good cheese this.'

'I can't say I particularly warmed to our good doctor. He is the kind of man who enjoys showing off his knowledge, feeling secure behind a cloak of learning. I felt he knew all the questions I was going to ask, long before I asked them, and his answers seemed very precise and well thought out, – too well thought out perhaps.'

'Sounds a suspicious sort of character to me, sir.'

'Although he did contradict himself, once, however,' said Ravenscroft, deep in thought and ignoring Crabb's last remark. 'When I first asked him if he would purchase the *Whisperie*, should it be offered to him, he replied that he would not, as it would damage his reputation. Later though, when I asked him again, he replied that he would purchase the work but would then hand it back to the cathedral. It is probably nothing. Now, Crabb, tell me how you got on with your investigations this morning?'

'Well, sir, I first enquired in the Old Diglis to see if any of their customers could remember Evelyn meeting anyone there the night he disappeared, but I'm afraid no one could recall seeing anyone of his description visiting the inn then, or upon any other occasion. However most of the regulars were not there so it could be worth while our returning again this evening.'

'I take your point, Crabb. And what did you find out at the canal?'

'Again, no one can recall seeing him, although several of the barges there that night will be halfway to Birmingham by now. Certainly the lock keeper cannot remember seeing anyone resembling Evelyn.'

'I don't think he got as far as the canal that night. If he had arranged to meet anyone by appointment, it must have been either at the Old Diglis or by the banks of the river.'

'You are probably correct, sir. What is our next line of enquiry?'

'After we have eaten this excellent ham and cheese, I suggest we go and pay a visit to Evelyn's rooms. We may be fortunate enough to find something there that might just assist us in our investigations.'

The two men looked up at the old black beamed building, which bore the name Glovers in faded letters above the door.

'This must be the place. Evelyn apparently had rooms on the top floor,' said Ravenscroft, banging his fist on the studded door. Receiving no reply, he repeated the action.

'All right, I'm coming. Give an old woman a chance, can't you? I ain't got three hands, has I?' shouted a voice from behind the door.

The two policemen exchanged glances as they heard the sound of a key turning in the lock. Presently the door opened a few inches to reveal a blotchy red nose and two tired-looking eyes.

'Yes, what do you want? We're full up. We got no rooms, at present; plenty of regular lodgers.'

'We are not after a room—' began Crabb.

'Then why are you wasting my time?' growled the face.

'We are policemen, madam, investigating the disappearance and death of one of your lodgers, a Mister Nicholas Evelyn. Can we come in?' asked Ravenscroft smiling.

'Dead, you say! Evelyn dead! God bless us all! You best come in then,' replied the old woman opening the door wider. The two policemen stepped into the darkened hallway where Ravenscroft found himself speaking to an elderly stout woman with a red complexion and thinning untidy hair, who was wearing a dirty apron, a pair of slippers and a dress, that he estimated had clearly seen better days.

'Dead,' she repeated.

'I'm afraid so. His body was recovered from the Severn yesterday. He had been in the water for several days. I am sorry if this has come as a shock to you. You are. . . ?' asked Ravenscroft.

'Mrs Glover. Mr Glover passed on twenty-seven years ago, he did.'

'I am sorry to hear it,' said Crabb.

'Bit late now!'

'Can you tell me how long Mr Evelyn had lived here?' asked Ravenscroft.

'He were 'ere, when old Glover bought the place thirty-five years ago,' muttered the old woman, shuffling further along the hallway.

'Did he always have the same rooms?'

'On top floor. Never wanted to move.'

'I wonder whether we might examine Mr Evelyn's rooms?' asked Ravenscroft.

'Don't know why you want to do that for. Thought that churchman had done that before you. He didn't find anything.'

'Yes, I believe the Dean, The Reverend Touchmore, did call to see if Mr Evelyn was ill, shortly after his disappearance. Tell me, Mrs Glover, was Mr Evelyn ever in the habit of receiving visitors in his rooms?'

The old woman thought for a moment. 'No, he never had no visitors. You best come this way then, if you want to see his room.'

'No one at all?'

'Never. No one ever called on him. Not in the last thirty-five years anyway.'

'He was a man who kept very much to himself then?' said Ravenscroft following behind the old woman, who began to haul herself up the stairs.

'Suppose so.'

'Do you know whether Nicholas Evelyn had any relatives at all?'

'None that I knows about,' replied the landlady, becoming short of breath.

'Do you know where he came from, before he came to Worcester that is?' asked Ravenscroft observing the peeling wallpaper on the walls.

'Don't know. I never asked where he came from.'

'When you supped together, did he ever say anything about his past, or about people he knew?'

'Don't provide supper. Lodgers look after themselves.' Mrs Glover paused on the landing, holding the side of the banister whilst taking in deep breaths.

'Are you all right?' enquired a concerned Ravenscroft.

'This is as far as I go. I can't manage the other two flights, on account of me leg. Follow the stairs up, as far as you can. Door ain't locked.'

'Thank you, Mrs Glover, I'm sure we can manage,' replied Crabb.

Ravenscroft and Crabb made their way up the two remaining flights of stairs, until they reached a small landing, with a door facing them. 'Our Nicholas Evelyn was a man who liked to climb up stairs,' said Ravenscroft pushing open the door.

The room in which the two men now found themselves, was of an untidy but compact nature. A single bed ran the length of one wall, with an attic window above, which looked out across the crowded tenement buildings of Worcester. A table and chair were situated in the centre of the room, the former being littered with old books and papers; a further few books were to be found on a small bookcase near the door.

'So this is where our librarian spent his evenings, in this lonely uninviting room, at the top of an old rambling lodging-house, in the centre of Worcester,' said Ravenscroft beginning to examine the books on the table.

'You would have thought he would have wanted to move somewhere better,' said Crabb.

'One thing I have learned about our friend, is that he was a creature of habit. It would have been completely out of character for him to have disturbed the equilibrium of his daily routine. I suppose the room also suited him, being near his place of work, and the view above his neighbours must have meant that he could have kept an eye on everything that was happening below him. Have a look through those papers on the desk, Crabb.'

'What are we looking for, sir?'

'I don't really know at this stage – just anything which is out of the ordinary; something that does not perhaps fit in with everything else. His books seem dry fare, mainly medieval history, and books about old books and manuscripts,' said Ravenscroft walking across the room to where another half-open door led into an even smaller room. 'This must be where he washed and dressed,' he said, observing the bowl and stand, and the few clothes hanging on the rail.

'These papers seem to be mainly about books and manuscripts,' said Crabb.

'Go through them and see if there is any mention of the *Whisperie*,' instructed Ravenscroft, examining the contents of a small chest of drawers. 'It looks as though our librarian only had one change of clothes. He didn't appear to eat much either, just the remains of some bread on this plate, and a piece of hard cheese.'

'Perhaps he had his food brought in?' suggested Crabb. 'Or he dined out a lot.'

'More likely he just bought food back to his rooms when he needed it. Give me half those papers.'

The two men spent the next few minutes going through the librarian's papers, before finally Ravenscroft threw them down on the table, a look of frustration across his face. 'Nothing! No mention of the *Whisperie*. No letters or anything of a personal nature. Don't you find that strange, Crabb? We have here a man who appears to have had no friends, and no past. A man, in fact, whose life was the same from one day to the next.'

'Not my kind of life,' said Crabb.

'Nor mine. It is as if he found comfort from his drab, ordered life. Do you know what I think, Crabb? I think something occurred in his life a long time ago, something which was so dramatic and upsetting, that it drove him to this life, where he could forget all that which had happened to disturb him.'

'He could have been engaged to a lady perhaps, and she jilted him at the altar, or she died shortly after they were married?'

'It could have been something like that, but our Evelyn does not look to have been the marrying type. Whatever it was, he buried it underneath these layers of order and drabness, where he could feel secure and cut off from the world. But then something happened one day, quite recently I would think, that threatened to disturb all this – something which reminded him of his past, and drove him to commit an act that was to be totally out of keeping with his character, and was to lead to his eventual death.'

'That is all very profound, sir, if you don't mind my saying so,' remarked a puzzled Crabb.

'What was it that drove him out of this room that night, to commit such an outrage? If only we could discover the answer to that question, then we might be able to find out who killed him and eventually recover the book,' said Ravenscroft pacing up and down the room.

'That is true, sir.'

'Well, Crabb, it does not seem as though we will find the answer here, much though I would have hoped. Best make our way downstairs and pay our respects to Mrs Glover once more before we leave. I find this room rather sad and oppressive the longer I have to remain in it,' said Ravenscroft, moving away from the table, and suddenly catching his boot on the edge of the waste-paper bucket. 'There are some pieces of torn paper in here. Tip them out on to the desk,' he instructed, looking down at the contents of the container.

'Right, sir.'

'See if we can fit the torn pieces together. It might be something important.'

The two men manoeuvred the fragments of paper around.

'It seems to be some kind of message.'

'I can just about read it. Evelyn seems to have screwed up the paper first, before reading it again, and then finally tearing up the note into small pieces. Ah, here we are—'

Tonight. Midnight. Leave book in usual place. You are released

'What on earth does that mean, sir?'

'It seems to indicate that after stealing the book, Evelyn is told to leave it in a prescribed place. Clearly the person who wrote this note was planning to collect the book later.'

'Yes, sir, but what does it mean by "you are released"?' enquired Crabb.

'Yes, of course!' exclaimed Ravenscroft. 'By stealing the book, and by giving it to another, Evelyn was fulfilling some kind of pledge, and was being allowed to go free.'

'Perhaps he was just being paid, and had fulfilled his side of the bargain?'

'I don't think so. He does not appear to have been the sort of person who sought wealth and riches. No, I think he was being blackmailed. Someone had discovered his dark secret, and was threatening to disclose it to the church authorities unless—'

'He stole the *Whisperie* for them!'

'Exactly!'

'But we are no further forward in discovering what that secret was?'

'I agree, but we now know that after stealing the book that night, Evelyn went down to the river with the direct purpose of leaving the book somewhere – "the usual place" – evidently a place where things, messages perhaps, had been left before.'

'Why didn't this person just ask Evelyn to steal the book for him, and then hand it over? Why go to all the business of sending messages and such like?' asked a bewildered Crabb.

'Because our blackmailer – for want of a better word – did not want Evelyn to know who he, or she was.'

'Ah, I see now.'

'Now we must find out where this place was. My guess is that it is somewhere between the base of the cathedral steps, and just off the towpath, and before the entrance to the canal. We need some men to search that area thoroughly. The book might still be there. Our black-mailer might not have collected it yet. Go back to the station and see if you can round up some men, I'll meet you all at the bottom of the steps.'

'Right, men, line up here and listen to what the inspector has to say.'

'Thank you, Constable Crabb. All of you will no doubt have heard about the theft of a book from the cathedral library some nights ago, and the recovery of the body of the librarian from the river,' said Ravenscroft addressing the four uniformed policemen who now faced him. 'We believe that after the librarian came down these steps he made his way along the towpath, and out towards where the canal joins up with the river at Diglis. Somewhere between the two places he hid the book. We don't know exactly where. As we go along the towpath, I will send each of you inwards away from the river. We are looking for a hiding place, somewhere small where the book might still be hidden. If you find a parcel of any kind, recover it, and bring it to me. Is that clear?'

'Yes, sir,' answered the constables in unison.

'Then, let's set to it, men.'

The party set off. Eventually, after clearing the outer walls of the cathedral precincts, Ravenscroft brought the group to a halt, by some waste ground. 'You two search this ground thoroughly. I want every stone turned over.'

'Like looking for a needle in a haystack,' muttered Crabb.

'We must at least try while there remains the outside possibility that the book might still be hidden. Here, you go and look in that empty building over there,' replied Ravenscroft, instructing one of the remaining two men. 'And then make your way inwards towards the inn.'

'Right, sir,' replied the constable.

The rest of the party continued on its way, until they reached another building, where Ravenscroft despatched the final officer. 'You and I, Crabb will proceed further on. There are several other places that need investigation.'

The search for the *Whisperie* continued into the late afternoon. Occasionally one or more of the constables would rejoin Crabb and Ravenscroft, who would then send them off to search in another direction.

'We seem to be getting nowhere, sir, if you don't mind my saying,' said Crabb, wiping his brow with his handkerchief.

'I think I am inclined to agree. We seem to have reached the canal and have turned up nothing. If the book was out there, it must have been taken long ago.'

'Oh dear, sir. I think we may be in trouble,' said Crabb, looking down at the ground.

'Ravenscroft! What the deuce is going on?' shouted a familiar figure striding in their direction.

'Good afternoon to you, sir,' replied Ravenscroft. 'We think the *Whisperie* might be hidden out here somewhere.'

'The blazes it is! What the devil do you mean by taking some of my men, and tying them up all afternoon here on some useless search? Don't you know that I need every man I can get to prepare for the Races?' growled Superintendent. Henderson.

'I'm sorry, sir, that was my doing,' said Crabb.

'Constable Crabb was only acting on my orders, sir,' said Ravenscroft quickly.

'Well you've overreached yourself this time, Ravenscroft. I told you that you were to keep me fully informed about developments in this case.'

'Yes, sir, I'm sorry,' replied Ravenscroft feeling like a naughty school-boy being addressed by his irate teacher.

'Damned insolent, I call it! Dammed insolent, taking my men without permission!'

'I felt we had to act quickly, sir, if we were to recover the book. Acting upon information obtained this afternoon—'

'Information? What information?' snapped Henderson.

'We found the remains of a note at Evelyn's lodgings, instructing him to leave the book in a prearranged hiding place.' replied Ravenscroft, hoping to pacify his superior's anger.

'And just where is this place?' asked Henderson, glaring at his junior officer.

'I believe Evelyn hid the book somewhere between the cathedral and the canal.'

'Good God, man! You could be searching from now till next Christmas! You're wasting your time and I'm damned if you will waste any more of my men's time on this wild goose chase!'

'Over here, sir!'

The speaker was a uniformed constable who was waving his hands in the air in an excited fashion.

'Excuse me,' said Ravenscroft, running over to what appeared to be the remains of an old building.

'I think I've found something.'

'Well done, Constable.'

'It was this piece of cloth, sir. It was lying on the ground. Then I found this.'

Ravenscroft knelt down.

'Well, man, what can you see?' asked Henderson, peering over Ravenscroft's shoulder.

'This slab seems to cover a recess of some sort, in the bottom of the wall of this old building, making a kind of cavity,' replied Ravenscroft, sliding the stone across. 'This was undoubtedly the place where the *Whisperie* was placed that night. Evelyn must have used the cloth to wrap around the book, and whoever later recovered the *Whisperie* decided to discard it.'

'That's all very well, Ravenscroft, but where is the blessed thing now?' growled Henderson.

'Taken, sir! Taken!'

CHAPTER SIX

Ravenscroft sat on the seat in the cathedral grounds, his thoughts return-ing to the events of the previous day. He was unsure which was the most unsettling – the wrath of his superior officer, or his failure to recover the lost book. The former had caused a severe dent in his professional repu-tation, whilst the latter meant that he and Crabb had to begin all their investigations all over again. Then he remembered that small attic room, in the centre of Worcester where Nicholas Evelyn had lived out his meagre, sad existence for nearly forty years, until the revelation of some disclosure from his past had driven him to commit such a desperate act which had resulted in his demise. How was he ever to discover the librar-ian's secret, and would he ever be able to recover the lost book? And it was still not clear whether Evelyn had been murdered, or that he had simply lost his footing in the dark and fallen into the river by accident. It seemed as though the cathedral was not yet anxious to give up its secrets.

He rubbed the top of his head where he could feel the bruise caused by his failure to remember the beam in the bar of the Cardinal's Hat that morning. Watching a large pigeon searching for food on the ground in front of him, he could not help but feel that perhaps this day was not going to be one of his best.

He had half expected to have seen Ruth Weston and her son on the green, but had been disappointed even in this expectation. In a few minutes Crabb would be joining him; then he would try and think of some new line of enquiry that they could follow, and perhaps slowly they would edge nearer towards the truth.

Looking up he saw the three Tovey sisters closing the door to their house, and walking along the pathway towards where he was seated.

'Miss Tovey,' said Ravenscroft, rising from his seat, 'Miss Emily. Miss Alice.'

'Good morning, Inspector. Is it true what we have heard about poor Mr Evelyn?' asked Miss Mary Ann.

'They say he drowned in the river,' remarked Miss Emily.

'Poor Mr Evelyn,' added Miss Alice Maria.

'I'm afraid, ladies, that you are correct. We recovered Mr Evelyn's body from the Severn, the day before yesterday.'

'Oh how sad. And have you found the book yet, Inspector?' asked the eldest sister.

'Alas, no.'

'Oh dear me.'

'Tell me, ladies, on the night you saw Evelyn entering and leaving the cathedral, did you notice anything else unusual?' asked Ravenscroft, feeling as though any possible line of enquiry was worth pursuing.

'I don't think so. Can you remember anything Emily?' asked Mary Ann.

'No, nothing, Sister,' she replied.

'Nothing at all,' added Alice Maria.

'Did you see anyone else entering or leaving the cathedral at that hour, or anyone else walking across the Close?'

'There was Dr Edwards,' offered the eldest sister. 'He always goes for a walk at around midnight.'

'Forgive me, but who is Dr Edwards?'

'He is the Master of the King's School,' replied Mary Ann.

'Did you see where he was going, or where he had come from?' asked Ravenscroft, sensing that perhaps his new line of enquiry was about to unfold.

'He came up the steps from the river.'

'Just a few seconds after Mr Evelyn had walked down them,' added the middle sister enthusiastically.

'They must have passed each other at the bottom of the steps,' interjected the youngest sister.

'I see, ladies. That is most helpful. Did you see where Dr Edwards went next?'

'He made his way back to his house,' replied Mary Ann.

'It is over there,' said Emily pointing to a large Georgian building.

'I'll pay Dr Edwards a visit. He may remember seeing something that night. Thank you for your observations, ladies.'

'I'm glad we have been able to help. Aren't you going to ask us about the monk?' asked the eldest sister.

'The monk. What monk?' asked a puzzled Ravenscroft.

'The monk who came out of the cathedral,' said Mary Ann.

'Shortly after Mr Evelyn came out of the cathedral,' said Emily.

'Just after Dr Edwards went into his house,' nodded Alice Maria.

'Did you see where he went to?' he asked, beginning to think that perhaps today was going to prove more interesting than he had first dared to hope.

'He went down the steps.'

'Down towards the river.'

'And tell me, could you see who this monk was? Did you recognize him at all?'

'Oh no, he had his monk's hood up, covering his face,' replied the eldest Miss Tovey.

'Are there a number of monks who still worship in the cathedral?' asked Ravenscroft.

'Oh yes. There are a number who still carry out the services,' said Mary Ann.

'I see. Was there anything unusual about him, perhaps in the way he walked, that reminded you of anyone who has business in the cathedral? Can you remember anything at all? Did he move quickly or slowly?'

'I don't think he reminded us of anyone,' replied Mary Ann.

'He moved quite quickly,' said Emily.

'Yes, he was quite quick, as though he wanted to catch up with Mr Evelyn,' added Alice Maria.

'Good morning, sir. Ladies,' interjected a smiling Crabb, arriving on the green.

'I hope we have been helpful, Inspector?' enquired the eldest sister.

'You have been most helpful.'

'You will let us know when you have recovered the book?' asked Emily.

'We should so like to know,' smiled the youngest sister.

'Of course, you will be the first to know,' said Ravenscroft raising his hat.

He watched them as they walked across the green towards the town, busily engaged in conversation with one another.

'Well, sir. You seem a bit brighter this morning, if you don't mind me saying so,' said Crabb.

'The Tovey sisters have just informed me that on the night in question, they saw Dr Edwards, who is the Master of King's School, out for his usual nocturnal walk, and that he probably encountered Evelyn at the bottom of the steps down by the river. Furthermore the sisters also saw one of the monks leaving the cathedral and heading down towards the river, shortly after Evelyn had left.'

'Do they know which monk it was?'

'Alas no. Apparently he didn't remind them of any of the regular monks, although they admit they could not see his face.'

'Could have been anyone dressed up as a monk, to disguise his appearance,' suggested Crabb.

'That is a distinct possibility.'

'Well, sir, where shall we start today?'

'I think we will call on the Master of King's School first, after which we will make enquiries in the cathedral regarding this mysterious monk.'

The two men walked across to the master's house and rang the doorbell.

'Good day to you. I am Inspector Ravenscroft and this is Constable Crabb. We would like words with your master, if you please,' said Ravenscroft, addressing the maid who had opened the door to them.

'I'm sorry, sir, but Dr Edwards is not here at present.'

'Could you tell me where I might find him?'

'He could be at the school, sir, although at this time of day you are more likely to find him with the choir in the cathedral,' replied the maid.

'Thank you. Then that is where we will go.'

Ravenscroft and Crabb made their way back across the close and entered the cathedral. As they stepped into the cool, dark interior they heard the sound of boys' voices in the distance, and to Ravenscroft it seemed as though they had entered another world, leaving the sunlight and sounds of the town behind them, forsaking that existence for the ageless sanctity of peace and reassurance of the cathedral.

The two men stood in silence, adjusting their eyes to the half light, each not wishing to disturb the serenity of the occasion.

Suddenly the singing came to an abrupt stop, and was replaced by a man's voice. Ravenscroft and Crabb made their way up the nave of the church towards the choir stalls.

'No! No, boys! That just won't do. I dread to think what poor Thomas Tallis would think of your feeble attempts to master his work if he were alive today. Mr Taylor, I am sure the choir can do better than this?'

The speaker was a late-middle-aged gentleman, whose learned appearance included a flowing white beard, and a pair of half-moon spectacles perched on the end of his nose.

'We are trying our best Dr Edwards, I can assure you. I can hear a boy talking in the back row! Tadcaster be silent and report to my study after choir. Now on the third beat,' instructed the choirmaster raising his hands in the air.

Ravenscroft indicated to Crabb that they should find a place on one of the rows of seats, and the two men listened in awe, as the boys' voices rose upwards towards the great window at the far end of the cathedral.

'Much better, boys. That was much better. I think that will be all for this morning. Mr Taylor if you please,' said Edwards, in what Ravenscroft discerned as a Welsh accent.

The boys began to move away from the choir stalls, talking as they did so.

'Silence!' bellowed Edwards in a voice that seemed to echo round the cathedral. 'Remember where you are!'

The choirboys silently began to make their way down the nave, Matthew Taylor the choirmaster, following on behind them, a collection of music sheets under his arm.

'The boys sing well,' said Ravenscroft, addressing the master.

'When they are in a mind to exercise restraint,' said Edwards.

'I believe you are the Master of King's School?'

'I am indeed. Doctor Geraint Edwards at your service. Can I be of any assistance to you? You have a son you would like to enrol? Perhaps you would care to view the school? I am sure my—'

'Alas, Dr Edwards I have no sons to place in any school. No, I am investigating the death of the librarian here, and the disappearance of a valuable book from the library.'

'Ah, then you must be the famous London detective we have heard so much about?'

'I am certainly from London, but I cannot claim to be in any way famous,' said Ravenscroft, smiling and shaking the master's hand. 'This is my associate Constable Crabb. I wonder if you could spare us a few minutes of your valuable time?'

'Of course, Inspector, anything I can do to be of assistance.'

'How well did you know Nicholas Evelyn?'

'I hardly knew the man at all. I knew he was the librarian of course, but other than that we had very little contact with one another, except when one or two of the more senior boys undertook research in the library. He always seemed the kind of person who kept very much to themselves,' replied Edwards removing his spectacles and cleaning them with his handkerchief.

'So we have discovered,' added Ravenscroft.

'I have been the master here at King's for the past twelve years, and during all that time must have only spoken to him on perhaps three or four occasions.'

'I understand, sir that you are in the habit of taking a late night walk every evening?'

'Yes that is correct, Inspector. I usually find that a late night turn of the cathedral precincts clears my mind of the business of the day before retiring.'

'Were you undertaking your usual walk on the night the librarian disappeared?' asked Ravenscroft.

'I was indeed.'

'What time was that, sir?' inquired Crabb making notes in his pocket book.

'Sometime between half past eleven and twelve o'clock,' replied Edwards replacing his glasses.

'That was rather late to be out, sir,' said Ravenscroft.

'I had been working on some papers late into the evening. I usually like to go out about half past ten or so.'

'Did you go down by the river?'

'Yes, I believe I did, but what is all this to do with the disappearance of the librarian?' asked a puzzled Edwards.

'During your walk, Dr Edwards did you encounter anyone?'

'I don't believe so.'

'It is very important, sir. Whilst you were down at the river-side did you hear or see anything unusual at all? Was there anyone else down there?'

persisted Ravenscroft.

'No, Inspector, I saw no one – although – yes, I remember now. I was about to make my way up the steps from the river when someone collided with me.'

'Did you happen to see who it was?' asked Ravenscroft.

'No. He just muttered some words of apology, and then continued on his way along the side of the river. If I remember correctly. I think he went in the Diglis direction,' replied Edwards, scratching his head.

'Doctor Edwards, do you think the man could have been Evelyn?'

'I don't know, Inspector. It was very dark and he had his face covered, but I suppose it could have been Evelyn, although I would not like to swear that it definitely was him.'

'Tell me, Doctor, when you reached the top of the steps and made your way back to your house—'

'You seem particularly well informed with regard to my movements, Inspector Ravenscroft,' said Edwards, becoming slightly annoyed.

'The three Miss Tovey sisters saw you come up the steps, and return to your house.'

'Ah, that would explain things. There is not much that those three sisters miss regarding the affairs of the cathedral and its inhabitants. But I think you were going to ask me whether I saw anyone else during my travels – and the answer is no.'

'You did not see a monk leaving the cathedral?' asked Ravenscroft.

'I have already said that I saw no one else that night,' replied Edwards firmly.

'Thank you, Dr Edwards. You have been most informative.'

'Glad to have been of service, but if you will now excuse me gentlemen, I have a Latin class to take.'

'Of course, sir,' said Ravenscroft, then adding, 'we may have need to speak with you again,' as the master strode down the nave.

'I think we may have annoyed him, sir,' said Crabb closing his note-book.

'That's as may be, but we are investigating a possible murder, and the disappearance of a valuable book. Now, it is my intention to call upon Sir Arthur Griffiths. He is the Member of Parliament for Worcester and resides in one of the houses in the Close. Can you go to the Worcester Library and find out all you can about him? There are no doubt a number of reference books you can consult. Whilst you are there, you might as well see if you can find any entries for the Master of King's, Dr Geraint Edwards. I will see if I can locate any of the monks who frequent the cathedral. One of them might be able to recall the events of the night Evelyn disappeared.'

'Right, sir. You might even be able to find out which one of them was prowling around the cathedral that night.'

'We can but hope, Crabb. I'll see you in the Old Talbot at lunchtime.'

'I look forward to some more of their excellent cheese, sir,' said Crabb.

Ravenscroft made his way around the near empty cathedral, pausing now and again to study one of the worn effigies, or to read one of the numerous plaques, that had been placed by succeeding generations, on the walls of the building. Now that the choirboys had left, he found the silence of the holy place almost overpowering and, looking upwards at the mighty roof, he felt the sudden insignificance of his own transient existence.

'My son.'

The voice made him turn.

'I did not mean to startle you.' The speaker was a tall, thin, elderly monk.

'I was admiring the Chantry,' said Ravenscroft.

'Ah, Prince Arthur's Chantry. You know the story?'

'No. I'm afraid not.'

'Prince Arthur was Arthur Tudor, eldest son of King Henry VII and brother to Henry VIII. Unfortunately he died before his father, and therefore never ascended the throne. Had he survived, there would probably have been no Henry VIII and no English Reformation. The whole course of English History might have been totally different – no Mary Tudor or Queen Elizabeth, perhaps not even the Stuart succession. Strange how these things turn out.'

'Indeed so,' replied Ravenscroft, observing that the monk spoke in a quiet, almost musical tone of voice.

'But I sense that your interest lies not completely in admiring the cathedral architecture.'

'You are correct in your assumption. I have been called in by the cathedral authorities to investigate the disappearance of the *Whisperie*.'

'Then you must be Inspector Ravenscroft. My name is Jonus, Brother Jonus.'

'I am pleased to meet you,' said Ravenscroft shaking the other's hand. 'Are there many monks still associated with the cathedral?

'There are only a handful of us left now, but we still seek to worship here, and to uphold a number of the ancient services. Would you care to take a walk with me round the cloisters, Inspector?'

'That would be most welcome,' replied Ravenscroft.

'I understand that you have found the body of the librarian,' said the monk leading the way.

'Yes, we recovered Nicholas Evelyn from the River Severn.'

'The poor unfortunate man, I will include him in my prayers tonight.'

'You knew him well, Brother Jonus?'

'As well as one can know another. He was a very private man.'

'So we are given to understand.'

'He was also a very sad man.'

'Why do you say that?'

'He seemed to be haunted by something from his past.'

'Do you know what that was? Did he ever confide in you? I know that you are not permitted to disclose anything that might have been said to you in the way of a confession, but—'

'No, Inspector, he never sought to speak to me. I knew, of course, that he was greatly troubled, and I prayed that he might one day seek to relieve himself of his burden – but he did not, and now it is too late. I hope that God will forgive him, and that his soul may now rest in peace. Ah, here we are at the cloisters.'

There was something in the monk's quiet way of speaking, and the religious man's calm dignity, that Ravenscroft found reassuring. 'Did you see him at all in the cathedral that night?'

'I did not see him, Inspector Ravenscroft, but I was aware of his presence.'

'Could you explain further?'

'It is my custom to offer up prayers in one of the side chapels each night, before the other monks enter the cathedral at twelve to conduct the midnight mass. I was in the chapel as usual. I could sense that he was passing by on his way up to the library.'

'You did not think it strange that he should have been out at such a late hour?' asked Ravenscroft, as they began their walk.

'We are a cathedral, Inspector, and as such we must accommodate all those who wish to come and worship here, no matter what time of day or night they choose to seek salvation.'

'Then the doors are not kept locked at night?'

'The main doors at the entrance to the cathedral are generally locked after nine in the evening, but it is always possible for someone to enter through one of the many other side entrances to the building.'

'Tell me, Brother, did you also see – or rather sense – when Evelyn left?'

'Yes, it was some minutes before twelve o'clock.'

'And what did you do then?'

'I continued with my devotions until I joined the other brothers for the midnight mass.'

'This is important, Brother: do you know whether all the brothers were there that night for the service?' asked Ravenscroft eagerly.

'I believe so.'

'But you are not sure?'

'There are only six of us left now. I would have known if one of my other five brothers was missing. Why do you ask?'

'A person, wearing a monk's habit, was seen leaving the cathedral shortly after Nicholas Evelyn left. We believe that this person could have followed Evelyn down to the river.'

'I see,' said Brother Jonus deep in thought. 'Well I think I can give you my assurance that it was not one of my brothers – and I saw no one else in the cathedral that night.'

'You saw no one at all?'

'No one, Inspector.'

'Is there any way that someone could have entered the cathedral, unnoticed, earlier in the evening, before your arrival?'

'That is a possibility.'

'It would have quite easy for such a person to have remained hidden for some time?' asked Ravenscroft.

'There are certainly many places within the cathedral where such a person might be concealed.'

'Could someone acquire a monk's habit similar to your own?'

'We usually have two spare robes hanging in a cupboard in the Chapter House,' replied Brother Jonus.

'I wonder whether we could go there now, to see whether one of them has been taken.'

'Of course, Inspector, if you would care to follow me.'

Ravenscroft followed the monk out of the cloisters, and the two men made their way across to the Chapter House. Entering the room, Jonus opened the door of the cupboard – to reveal a single robe hanging on one of the pegs before them.

'It seems you are right, Inspector.'

'You would definitely say that one of these robes has been taken?'

'We always have two hanging here. Of course it is possible that one of the brothers might have taken it, to replace his own if it were soiled. I could make enquiries should you so wish.'

'I would appreciate that, Brother Jonus. You have been most helpful, but I must leave you now, if you will excuse me. If anything else occurs to you, I would appreciate it if you would get in touch with me.'

'Certainly, Inspector: I do hope that you will be able to recover the lost book, it means so much to us all here in the cathedral. You see it is part of our legacy, and it is our duty to see that it is cared for and passed down for future generations. It is as though we have all lost a child,' said Jonus.

'I will certainly do my best to find and return the *Whisperie*,' replied Ravenscroft with confidence.

'When you have time my son, it will be good for us to speak again. You know where to find me. I sense that there is something disturbing you. It often helps to confide in another,' said Brother Jonus, giving a gentle smile as he closed the door to the Chapter House.

'Thank you, Brother Jonus. I will remember that,' replied Ravenscroft as he walked away, deep in thought.

'Well, Crabb, tell me the fruits of your research at the local library this morning?' asked Ravenscroft, helping himself to a large slice of ham at lunch at the Old Talbot.

'Quite a great deal concerning our Member of Parliament; not so much about Dr Edwards,' replied Crabb, taking out his pocket book.

'Tell me about Edwards first.'

'Born 1828 in Cardiff. Educated at some private school in Bangor – the name of which I can't pronounce – then studied for a degree in Latin and Mathematics at Cardiff University, after which he undertook a number of teaching appointments in Wales, before becoming assistant master at Monmouth College. He was appointed Master of King's School twelve years ago, and has a wife and two grown-up children. He has also written three books on Latin grammar, and a book about Welsh Druids. That's about all. Pretty dull fish, if you ask me, sir.'

'And Griffiths?'

'Sir Arthur Granville Sackville Boscawen Trevor Griffiths – quite a mouthful that, sir – born in 1840, second son of Gaspard Boscawen Griffiths of Chester. Educated at Rugby School before going on to Queen's College, Oxford where he gained a degree in History and Politics. Whilst at Oxford he was President of the Oxford Union. He is a member of two London clubs – The Athaneum and Carlton. Also owns another house in London, in Kensington Gardens, I believe. First contested Tunbridge Wells for the Tory Party in 1865, where he was unsuccessful, but later contested Worcester, which he won in a by-election in 1870, and has remained the member ever since. He was knighted three years ago, for services to the party.'

'Any family?' asked Ravenscroft.

'There was a wife, Cecily, but she died about ten years ago. He does not appear to have remarried, and there is one child still alive from his first marriage, a daughter, I believe.'

'Yes, Ruth Weston, the parlour maid, mentioned her. She apparently runs the house for her father. Did you find anything else?'

'No, sir. I think that's about all. Oh, I did take the trouble to look up your Dr Silas Renfrew whilst I was at the library. Born in New York in 1842, son of wealthy American parents; he came over to England about four years ago. He has quite an important collection of early English books and manuscripts, and has written one or two of books on the subject. Belongs to a number of learned academic and literary societies in both America and London,' concluded the constable.

'Well done, Crabb.'

'And how was the rest of your morning, sir?'

'I had a good look round the cathedral, and encountered one of the monks, a Brother Jonus, who remembers Evelyn both entering and leaving the cathedral on the night the book was taken. However, he cannot recall anyone else being there at the time – but we did find that one of the monk's habits had been taken from a cupboard in the Chapter House.'

'So whoever killed Evelyn and took the book from its hiding place, disguised himself as a monk, so he would not be recognized?' remarked Crabb taking another drink of his ale.

'It seems that way.'

'But why kill Evelyn, once he had the book?'

'Because he wanted to make sure that Evelyn would not talk about his role in the theft. Also he wanted to create the impression in the eyes of the world, that Evelyn had taken the book, and that it had been lost in the river when Evelyn was drowned.'

'Very clever, seems we are dealing with quite a ruthless person!'

'And we have to find out who this person is, so that we can recover the book. Drink up, Crabb, it's time we called on the household of our Member of Parliament, to see if its occupants can shed any more light on this matter.'

A few minutes later found the two men making their way across the Cathedral Green, until they arrived at an imposing Georgian residence, the outside of which bore a brass plaque bearing the words – SIR ARTHUR GRIFFITHS, MP.

Crabb rang the doorbell.

'Good afternoon, my name is Inspector Ravenscroft. This is Constable Crabb. Is your master at home?' said Ravenscroft, addressing the maid who opened the door to him.

'I'm afraid Sir Arthur is busy at the moment, sir. Perhaps you would care to make an appointment and call back later?' replied the girl.

'Could we see Miss Griffiths? I understand she is the lady of the house. Perhaps you would be kind enough to give her my card,' said Ravenscroft, taking it from his pocket and giving it to the maid. He had half expected that Ruth Weston would have attended to them, but then he concluded that Sir Arthur would probably have more than one maid in such an imposing residence.

'If you would care to wait in the hall, sir, I will see if Miss Griffiths is free to see you.'

'Thank you. Could you say to your mistress that the matter is of great importance.'

Ravenscroft and Crabb stepped into the hall, as the housemaid walked away with Ravenscroft's card on a round silver tray.

'Well, this looks a fine place and no mistake,' whispered Crabb looking around the hall with its ornate furniture and fine paintings. 'Worth a shilling or two this lot, I'd be bound.'

'Our Member of Parliament certainly seems to have done well for himself,' replied Ravenscroft smiling, as he looked at a set of hand-coloured political satires on one of the walls.

The sound of a man's voice could be heard talking in low tones from behind one of the doors.

'Sir Arthur?' said Crabb in a whisper.

'Possibly,' replied Ravenscroft.

'Always makes me feel uncomfortable, places like this,' said Crabb in a slightly louder voice.

'Miss Griffiths will see you now, sir,' said the maid, returning from the drawing-room. 'If you would care to follow me, gentlemen?'

The two policemen followed the maid into the room.

'Inspector Ravenscroft, miss, and er—' began the maid.

'Constable Crabb.'

'—and Constable Crabb, miss.'

'Gentlemen, do both please take a seat.'

Ravenscroft observed that the speaker was of a tall, thin stature, her black hair contrasting with her pallid complexion. He estimated her age as being not much above twenty.

'Thank you, Miss Griffiths. I very much appreciate you seeing us with-out an appointment,' he began, seating himself on one of the drawing-room chairs, as Crabb took out his pocket book and stood by one of the bookcases.

'I am sorry that my father cannot see you. He is a very busy man, as I am sure you will appreciate. He is with someone now in his study, one of his constituents, I believe. How can I be of assistance to you?' she replied somewhat nervously.

'You have probably heard about the death of the librarian at the cathe-dral, Miss Griffiths, and the disappearance of one of the old books from the library. We are making enquiries into both these concerns. As your house overlooks the Green, and has a fine view of the cathedral, I would be obliged if you would answer a number of questions for us.'

Their hostess smiled, but said nothing.

'Nicholas Evelyn, the librarian: did you ever have cause to speak with him?' asked Ravenscroft.

'No. I knew of him, of course. I have often seen him entering the cathedral in the mornings, but I have never spoken to him,' she answered, a puzzled expression on her face. 'I think the same would apply to my father,' she added, placing her hands neatly in her lap.

'Have you ever visited the library, Miss Griffiths?' asked Ravenscroft.

'No, I don't believe that I have ever done so. My father and I always worship at the cathedral on Sundays, of course, but we never visited the library. We had no reason to do so.'

'Can I turn to the night of the theft of the *Whisperie*. Did you happen to see anyone entering or leaving the cathedral late that evening?'

'No, I usually retire at just after nine. My room is at the back of the house.'

'So you would not have seen anyone, miss?' asked Crabb, looking up from his notebook.

'I have just said, Constable, that my bedroom does not face on to the cathedral,' she replied firmly.

'Was your father here that night, or in London?' asked Ravenscroft, quickly giving Crabb a brief sideways glance.

'He was here in the house. I believe he also retired, shortly after myself.'

'And his room, Miss Griffiths, where is that located?'

'My father's bedroom is also at the rear of the house. He will probably only confirm what I have just told you. I don't really see the point of any of these questions, Inspector.'

'We have reason to believe, Miss Griffiths, that Mr Evelyn, the librarian, was killed that night, at approx twelve o'clock, and that whoever killed him was seen emerging from the cathedral dressed as a monk at around that time.'

'I'm sorry for poor Mr Evelyn, but as I have told you, Inspector, we had both retired to bed earlier that night,' replied Miss Griffiths, showing signs of irritation at Ravenscroft's questions.

'As you just said. I wonder if we might have a few words with your servants. They might have seen something that night, and be able to help us in our investigations,' said Ravenscroft smiling, and seeking to placate the lady of the house.

'I'm sure that will not be necessary. I will make enquiries myself and inform you of the results. Now, if you will excuse me, I have some important correspondence to attend to,' said Miss Griffiths standing up and ringing the bell at the side of the fireplace.

'I will also need to have a few words with your father,' said Ravenscroft also rising to his feet.

'I have told you, Inspector, that my father had retired early for the night. I cannot see what good it will do you to interview him. My father is a very busy man, and is generally fully engaged both here and when he is in London. I can answer any questions you may need to ask in the future.'

'Well, thank you, Miss Griffiths,' said Ravenscroft, realizing that his hostess was anxious that he should leave, and that there would be little point in trying to continue with the interview.

'Sarah, would you show the inspector out,' said Miss Griffiths addressing the maid who had entered room.

'Good day to you,' said Ravenscroft.

As the two men made their way across the hall, Ravenscroft observed that the door to the study was slightly ajar.

'—I am sure, Mrs Marchmont, that we can be of assistance to you, in your affairs,' said the voice of a man, whose back was to the door.

Ravenscroft caught a brief glimpse of a lady seated on a chair, as he passed by.

'This way, sir,' said the maid opening the front door.

Ravenscroft and Crabb made their way out of the building, and strode quickly across the Green.

'My God, sir, you look as though you have just seen a ghost,' said Crabb, hurrying to keep up with his superior.

'I have Crabb. That woman in the study with Sir Arthur—'

'Mrs Marchmont, he said.'

'Mrs Marchmont. When I saw her in Malvern last year she went by another name. Her real name is Mrs Kelly!'

CHAPTER SEVEN

'Tell me about your Mrs Marchmont, or rather Mrs Kelly,' asked Crabb, as the two men sat drinking ale later that night at The Old Diglis.

'Well, Crabb, it's a very sad business. You may recall when we were investigating those murders in Malvern last year, I told you that I had met a woman on the train, who was dressed entirely in black,' said Ravenscroft.

'She wore a veil over her face if I recall. Evidently a widow,' interjected Crabb.

'I discovered that both her husband and her young son had recently died and were buried in the churchyard at Malvern Priory. It was there that I met her one day, and eventually learned the sad fate of her family. Her husband had been used to travelling up to London for a few days each month, on business, and it transpired that he was rather prone to indulging in extra-marital activities with certain young women of the night in the Whitechapel area of London.'

'That's your area, is it not, sir?'

'It is indeed. I know it well. The place is filled with villains of every age, race and sex. There are people there who would steal the very clothes off your back or, worse still, murder you in some dark alleyway if they thought you were carrying money on your person. To escape its miserable streets, to experience the civilized pastures of Malvern and Worcester is paradise indeed! But to return to our Mrs Kelly: after a while, her husband fell ill and eventually died, probably as the result of picking up some sexual disease from one of those loose women. By the time of his death, he had already passed on the disease to his wife, and then their new born son became ill, and she had to nurse him through a long and painful illness before he, too, died.'

'Poor woman,' muttered Crabb.

'Indeed. To nurse a sick husband through months of illness is one thing, but to see a son die and not be able to do anything to relieve his suffering, must be an agony too hard to comprehend. I remember she was quite bitter about everything – and with good reason – and that she swore that one day she would seek her revenge on the women of Whitechapel for the wrongs they had committed. I tried to reason with her, but must confess I felt utterly at a loss what to say, and before I could speak she strode away from the churchyard suddenly and that might have been the last I saw of her, except for one further encounter.'

'You saw her again? In Whitechapel?'

'The day I left Malvern and returned to London, I remember l was just outside Paddington Station when suddenly a woman rode off in a cab after telling the man to take her to Whitechapel.'

'And have you seen her since, in Whitechapel that is?'

'No – and I must admit that I have not given her any more thought, until today, when I caught sight of her in the study of Sir Arthur Griffiths' residence. I tell you, Crabb, it came as quite a shock to see her again, after all this time, and in the very house we were visiting.'

'I wonder why she is now calling herself Mrs Marchmont?' asked Crabb. 'After all, you said her real name was Kelly.'

'I have no idea,' said Ravenscroft, taking another sip from the tankard.

'Perhaps she has just changed her name, so that she can put the past behind her. Start a new life, like.'

'Do you know, Crabb, I think you might be right. And if that is the case, then who are we to deny her that relief, after all she has suffered?'

'You don't think she is mixed up in any of this business at the cathedral, sir?'

'Highly unlikely, I would think. What need would she have of a medieval book?'

'What do you think she was doing at Sir Arthur Griffiths' house?'

'She was probably seeking his advice on some matter. He is, after all, the local Member of Parliament,' replied Ravenscroft.

'Begging your pardon, sir, but are you certain that it was this Mrs Kelly that you saw? It could have been someone else. After all, you did say she wore a veil most of the time that you saw her.'

'That is true, but on our second encounter she did raise her veil and I saw her face quite clearly – and the bitterness engrained there. No, I am sure that she and Mrs Marchmont are the one and the same woman. Anyway, enough of our Mrs Kelly, we must be careful not to be deflected from our investigations. Be so good, Crabb, as to get us a refill for these tankards, and whilst you are over there ask the landlord if he would be so good as to join us.'

After exchanging a few words with the landlord at the bar, Crabb returned to Ravenscroft. 'He says he will bring them over in a minute. What did you think of our Miss Griffiths then, sir?'

'I am quite fascinated by her. She was very reserved; nervous even. I think she was very relieved when we left,' said Ravenscroft.

'She seemed very protective towards her father, not letting us see him.'

'I think we must insist on seeing Sir Arthur. He might have seen something that night. We cannot go on her assumption alone.'

'Here we are, gentlemen. Two more tankards of our finest Worcester ale,' said the landlord, placing the vessels down on the table before them.

'And very good ale it is too, landlord,' said Ravenscroft lifting one of the tankards to his mouth.

'How can I help you, sir? Your colleague said you wanted to speak with me.'

'Yes. We are investigating the disappearance of both the librarian, and a valuable book from the cathedral,' began Ravenscroft.

'Ah, I thought so. I told my wife as soon as you came in that you were the law.'

'I had not thought we were so conspicuous, after me changing out of uniform and all,' said Crabb.

'On the night the librarian disappeared, we believe he made his way along the river-bank, just outside your premises. We were wondering whether you remember seeing him at all?'

'I don't remember seeing anyone out of the ordinary,' replied the land-lord.

'Did Mr Evelyn ever come into the inn? He was an elderly gentleman, thin, grey hair, had a bit of a stoop, very retiring, kept very much to himself,' said Ravenscroft.

'No. Don't recall seeing such a person. We gets mainly our locals in here. I'm sure I would have noticed anyone out of the ordinary.'

'Thank you. You have been most helpful. One final question: did you happen to see anything or anyone falling into the river on the night the librarian disappeared – or perhaps heard a loud splash? Probably around twelve o'clock?' asked Ravenscroft.

'I can't say, sir. I'll check with the wife, see if she heard anything. She has a far better memory than I have.'

'Thank you, we would be most obliged.'

'Seems as though we have drawn a blank there,' said Crabb.

'Evelyn must have met his attacker by the river, after placing the book in the hiding place in the old ruined building. I am more than ever convinced that Evelyn did not meet the person who was blackmailing him until his very end.'

'Poor man.'

'Look over there, Crabb. Do you see that rough fellow drinking at the other end of the bar? He seems to be consuming a great deal of liquor tonight,' said Ravenscroft.

'He could do with a shave and a good wash, if you ask me. Don't like the look of that scar down the side of his face. Looks as though he came off the worse in some fight or other,' said Crabb, taking a pull on his ale.

'Probably just come off one of the barges. And here I think is our good landlord returning.'

'Gentlemen, I have had a word with my wife. She swears she heard a loud splash in the river. Just after twelve, she thinks. She remembers taking a look out of the window, but she didn't see anyone out there on the towpath and thought no more about it. We get lots of noises being near the river. Always something, or someone, falling in the water. We used to get quite alarmed when we came here fifteen years ago, but now we don't take much notice.'

'Thank you, landlord,' said Ravenscroft.

The publican returned to the bar.

'Where do we go from here, sir?' asked Crabb.

'To tell you the truth, I am at a loss, but one thing I am certain about is that there is a lot more for us to unearth about the cathedral and its inhabitants, before we can arrive at a solution to this case.'

'Come on. Give us another tankard!' shouted the man at the bar.

'I think you have had more than enough for tonight, Billy,' said the landlord, giving a sideways glance in the direction of the two policemen.

'Who says I've had enough? I can pay. I've got plenty of money. Pour me one,' continued the man, in a slurred voice.

'I've told you, Billy, you've had your fair share tonight. Why don't you go home and sleep it off?'

'Don't want to go home. Here's a crown, another one I say!'

'He's not short of money,' whispered Crabb.

'Sorry, Billy, can't do it. It's more than my reputation at stake. Get yourself home, and take your money with you,' said the landlord, again casting a glance in their direction.

'Don't you tell me to go home! Pour one for me, and for everyone here tonight!' said the man, suddenly lunging forwards and grabbing the landlord's shirt.

'I think our landlord could do with some assistance. Time we intervened,' said Ravenscroft.

'Leave him to me, sir. I'll see him off,' said Crabb, rising from his seat.

'Give me a drink, or I'll poke yer eyes out!' growled the man.

'Now then, Billy, leave off there,' said Crabb, walking over to the bar and placing his hand on the other's shoulder.

'And who the devil might you be?' said Billy, turning round and shaking off Crabb's hand.

'I'm Constable Crabb from the local constabulary. If you don't leave off drinking this minute and take yourself home, I'll have to arrest you and you'll spend the rest of the night in the cells.'

'Bugger you! You ain't no peeler. You ain't got no uniform on!' growled Billy.

'Watch your language, my fellow. Just pick up your money and go,' instructed Crabb.

The man suddenly threw a punch at Crabb, who dodged quickly to one side, leaving his attacker to crash into one of the tables. 'Come on. Get yourself home, or it's the cells for you, my lad,' said the policeman, in a firm voice.

Billy picked himself up off the floor, steadied himself and brushed the sleeve of his tattered jacket.

'Best do as the policeman says, Billy. You come back tomorrow night and we'll have a drink together then,' said the landlord.

'Right you are, captain,' said Billy giving a mock salute. 'Steady as she goes. I'll be all right, captain. I've got my lady. She'll see me all right.'

Ravenscroft smiled as the old sailor made his way out of the bar.

'Sorry about that, sir. Don't know what's got into old Billy tonight. He's usually well behaved. Seems to have come into some unexpected money,' said the landlord straightening up the table.

'Must be one of the hazards of your occupation,' said Ravenscroft.

'Don't I know it! Worcester isn't a bad place, but some of the folks round here don't know how to hold their liquor.'

'Does Billy often come in here?' asked Crabb.

'He's one of my regulars. He earns his money by transporting cargoes up and down the Severn in an old barge called the *Mayfly*. He'll be all right in the morning, when he's slept it off.'

'Well, Crabb,' said Ravenscroft standing up, 'I think my bed at the Cardinal's Hat calls, and I am sure that lovely wife of yours would like to see you back home. Meet me tomorrow morning at nine, and we will see what the new day brings.'

'Good morning, sir.'

'Good morning, landlord,' said Ravenscroft about to take another sip of his coffee.

'Perhaps you would like to read the morning paper, sir,' said the land-lord of the Cardinal's Hat.

'Thank you.'

'Report of some terrible murder in London on the inside pages, might be of interest to you, sir.'

Ravenscroft opened the newspaper and began to read.

TERRIBLE MURDER IN EAST END OF LONDON

We have received reports from the London newspapers of a terrible outrage committed in the Whitechapel District of London. The victim has been identified as Annie Chapman, age 47, and is described as being about 5ft tall, of stout appearance, with dark wavy brown hair, blue eyes and thick nose. A member of the unfortunate classes, she frequented Crossingham's Lodging-house in Dorset Street, prior to her murder.

The body was discovered by one John Davis, a carman employed in Leadenhall Market, at around 6.00 a.m. on the morning of 8

September, in the back yard of 29 Hanbury Street. He immediately raised some of his neighbours, and the local constable was quickly on the scene. We understand that the body was found lying on its back and that it had been severely mutilated. An inquest is to be held shortly.

This outrage is the second to have occurred recently in this area of London. Our readers may recall that on the 30 August last the body of Mary Ann Nichols was discovered in Bucks Row.

We are given to understand that the police are conducting enquiries and that a number of leads are being taken up. Earlier today. . . .

'Good morning, sir,' interrupted a breathless Crabb entering the inn. 'I think you best come straight away. Apparently your Ruth Weston has disappeared. She has not been seen at her lodgings for the past two days.'

The two men stood outside Glovers Lodging-house waiting for the owner to make her way to the door.

'Oh, it's you,' said Mrs Glover peering through the small gap between the door and its surround.

'My constable informs me that you sent a message to the police station regarding Miss Weston,' said Ravenscroft. 'We understand that she has not been seen for the past two days.'

'Left me with the boy, she has. I don't know what to do with him. He's not my responsibility, is he? I suppose you had better come in then,' muttered the landlady, opening the door wider, so that the two policemen were able to step into the hallway.

'When did you last see Miss Weston?' asked Crabb.

'It were night before last. She went out, about ten, I think it was.'

'Did she say where she was going at such a late hour?' asked Ravenscroft.

'No, why should she? I don't interfere in the lives of my lodgers, as long as they lead respectable lives. You best follow me into here then,' said Mrs Glover pushing open a door at the end of the passage.

'Thank you,' said Ravenscroft, finding himself in a small room, where an old tattered armchair occupied the centre, and numerous china figures fought for every available inch on tops of tables and around the mantel-piece.

'I can't have it, Mr Ravenscourt. All my lodgers keep missing like this. Who's going to pay the rent at the end of the week, I should like to know?' moaned the old lady wiping her blotchy nose on her sleeve.

'I'm sure you will be able to find someone to take over Mr Evelyn's room quite soon, and Miss Weston might well return,' suggested Ravenscroft.

'I'll believe it when I see it,' grumbled the landlady.

'I understand that Miss Weston and her son lived on the ground floor. How long have they been here?'

'About three years.'

'Miss Weston was single, I believe.'

'Yes. I don't usually have single unmarried women with children at Glovers. I've got my reputation to think about.'

'But you made an exception in this case,' smiled Ravenscroft.

'More fool me! Never could resist a sob story. Too kind-hearted I am. Glover said it would always lead to my downfall one day.'

'Did they ever cause you any trouble?'

'Suppose not, till now,' said Mrs Glover, blowing her nose loudly on a large handkerchief.

'Tell me, how many lodgers are there boarding with you here?' asked Ravenscroft casually picking up one of the china ornaments and examining it.

'Here, you put that down! That's early Worcester that is,' said the old woman, alarmed.

'I'm sorry,' apologized Ravenscroft quickly replacing the figure. 'You have a fine collection. It must have taken you a long time to have collected so many fine items. You were about to tell me about your other lodgers.'

'Miss Weston and her son, they have the other two rooms on the ground floor. I have the rooms on the next floor. Lord knows why, with my leg. Then there is Mr and Mrs Bailey, nice young couple they have the next floor, Mr Cranston on the floor above them. He's a commercial traveller. No trouble. Perfect gentleman, although he's not often here, travels around quite a lot – always going up to London and such like, on business. Mr Evelyn was on the top floor. We keeps a good house here at Glovers, we do. Glover would never allow any ne'er-do-wells and such like to stay, and I have followed in his footsteps. All my lodgers are highly respectable people. Yes, we keeps a good house here.'

'I'm sure you do, Mrs Glover. Can you tell me when your other guests will be here? My constable and I will need to have words with them,' said Ravenscroft.

'You'll be lucky. Mr and Mrs Bailey went away two weeks ago, travelling in France, don't expect them back till later in the month.'

'And Mr Cranston?' asked Crabb.

'He went up to London earlier in the week, as usual. He should be back in a day or so.'

'Could you tell him upon his return to contact us Mrs Glover?' asked Ravenscroft.

The old woman shrugged her shoulders.

'Could you also let us know immediately if Miss Weston returns, if you would be so kind. Oh, where is the boy now?'

'He's crying his eyes out in their rooms. I can't get him to stop. I've given him his breakfast, what more does he want? Don't know what I'm supposed to do with him.'

'Can I have a word with him?' asked Ravenscroft.

'Suppose so.'

Mrs Glover opened the door and the two men followed her back along the hallway until they reached the rooms at the front of the property. As they entered, they were met by a young boy whom Ravenscroft recognized from his morning encounter on the cathedral Close, as being Ruth Weston's son.

'Has my mummy come back?' asked the child looking up into Ravenscroft's face, with tearful red eyes.

'I'm afraid not,' said Ravenscroft, kneeling down by the side of the boy. 'Do you remember me?'

'You were at the cathedral that morning.'

'That's right, Arthur. Your mother and I spoke together. I am a policeman, and I am going to find your mother. Did she say anything to you the other evening, before she went out?'

'No.'

'Do you have any idea where she was going?'

The boy shook his head, before lowering his eyes to the floor.

'That's all very well, but he can't stay here. I've got things to do. I'm not used to looking after children,' muttered Mrs Glover.

'Constable Crabb and I will do everything we can to find your mother,

Arthur. I'm sure she will soon return. In the meantime, can you be strong for your mother?' asked Ravenscroft speaking softly.

The boy nodded again.

'Good boy. Has he eaten anything since breakfast?' said Ravenscroft addressing the old woman.

'Don't know. How should I know?' sniffed Mrs Glover.

'Here. Take this shilling. Send out for something for the boy. If you could look after him for the rest of the day I'll give you another shilling when we return this evening,' said Ravenscroft giving the coin to the woman.

'Suppose it might be all right for a few hours, but I can't have the boy for too long. He'll have to go to the workhouse if she don't come back for him.'

'I'm sure it won't come to that, Mrs Glover. We quite understand your predicament. We'll let ourselves out. Goodbye, Arthur.'

As the two men walked away from the lodging-house, Crabb remarked, 'This is a turn up. First Evelyn goes missing, now it's Miss Weston.'

'I hate to say it, but I fear the worst. Miss Weston did not seem the kind of person to abandon her child. She seemed to me to be a most conscientious kind of parent. I wonder where she was going to at such a late hour? She must have gone out to meet someone.'

'You don't think she is mixed up in all this business at the cathedral?'

'To tell you the truth, I don't quite know what to think. It seems more than a coincidence, however, that both Evelyn and Ruth Weston lodged there. We will need to interview the others as soon as possible,' said the inspector deep in thought.

'The Bailey couple have gone to France.'

'Then this Cranston fellow, but I suppose we can't do anything there until he returns from London. Right, we must do everything we can to find Ruth Weston,' said Ravenscroft with determination. 'I will write you out a description of the woman, which I want you to take back to the station, and send out to as many local stations as you think fit. Best keep Henderson informed. We don't want to be treading on his toes again. If he can spare any men, send them to walk along the river. I'll go back to Ruth Weston's place of work, and see if anyone there knows why she has gone missing.'

★

Ravenscroft rang the bell of the residence of Sir Arthur Griffiths, and waited for the maid to open the door for him. 'Inspector Ravenscroft. It is imperative that I speak with your master.'

'I'm sorry, Sir Arthur is in London,' answered the maid.

'When did he leave?'

'Yesterday afternoon, sir, shortly after you called.'

'And when do you expect him to return?' asked Ravenscroft.

'Not until tomorrow.'

'Can I speak with Miss Griffiths?'

'I'm sorry, but that will not be possible. She went away with Sir Arthur.'

'I see. Then perhaps you can help me. I understand Ruth Weston works here as a parlour maid.'

'That is correct, sir.'

'Did she present herself for work yesterday?'

'No. To tell you the truth, cook and I are rather concerned about her.'

'It wasn't her day off yesterday?'

'No, sir.'

'Did she give any indication that she might not be available for work?'

'No, sir,' replied the maid looking increasingly worried.

'And I presume that she has not reported for work today?'

'That is correct.'

'Did you not think it rather strange that Miss Weston has not reported for duty for the past two days?'

'Yes, but when I told Miss Griffiths, she said that we were not to worry; she was probably ill and would return in a day or so. Has something dreadful happened to her? Cook and I are awfully worried. Nothing like this has ever happened before.'

'We are doing everything we can to find her. You have been most helpful. Should Miss Weston return, or if you hear anything regarding her whereabouts, I would be grateful if you would send a message to the police station,' said Ravenscroft.

'Of course, I do hope you find her. What's happened to her young boy?'

'Mrs Glover is looking after him for the time being.'

'The poor mite, he must be missing his mother.'

'I'm sure he is,' said a worried Ravenscroft as he walked away from the house.

★

The church clock struck six as the policemen met together once more under the shadow of the cathedral.

'Nothing, sir, no one has seen or heard anything regarding our missing lady,' said Crabb wearily.

'I've been about the town and cathedral making enquiries, but have met with no success. Sir Arthur Griffiths and his daughter both left for the capital yesterday, and will not be back until tomorrow,' replied Ravenscroft.

'I've sent out her description to all the local stations with instructions to report back to Worcester if they hear anything. Superintendent Henderson seems reluctant to let us have any men, but says he will see if he can release one or two officers to go out in a boat along the river, but not until the morning.'

'Then it seems that we have done all that we can do for today. The longer this goes on, the more concerned I become for Miss Weston's safety. Then there is the young lad to consider. I don't think we can leave him to the mercies of Mrs Glover for another night, but I'm damned if I know what to do with him. The thought of the local workhouse seems an unkind consideration,' said Ravenscroft.

'I've an idea. Why don't I take the lad home with me for the night? Better than leaving him with Mrs Glover. Jennie will give him a good meal. He will be all right with us.'

'Tom, that seems a Christian act and no mistake, but I fear it is a frightful imposition on you and your wife.'

'No imposition. Jennie will be more than pleased to take the lad under her wing. Anyway it's only for a day or so. Happen his mother will return tomorrow, and there will be a proper explanation for all of this.'

'You are a good man Tom Crabb. Let's go and collect the lad and you can make your way back to Malvern.'

They searched for Ruth Weston for three days. Ravenscroft and Crabb had walked the river-bank from Worcester to Diglis and beyond, looking for anything which had been swept into the sides of the water. A boat had been hired and had continued the search down to Upton and onwards to Tewkesbury. Descriptions had been sent to nearby towns, posters had been displayed in prominent places, and even the canal was traversed from Worcester to Tardebigge, and from Hanbury across to Droitwich.

Then, on the fourth morning, the two men had suddenly been called up river to Holt Fleet, where a large sack had been pulled from the murky waters near the lock gates.

Ravencroft's heart felt full of despair as they rode in the cab, through driving rain, and out of the city. A uniformed policeman conducted them down the path that led from the bridge at Holt, towards the lock gates, where the keeper waited anxiously for their arrival.

Ravenscroft untied the rope that had been used at the top of the sack, with trembling hands and, as he had done so, he hoped against hope that his journey might yet prove fruitless. But, as he looked down at the body of the dead woman, and recognized her as the woman he had spoken with in the cathedral grounds, he had turned away quickly and felt a despair beyond comprehension.

It did not take them long to establish the cause of death – the red cord that had been used to kill her was still tightly secured round her throat. A brief examination of her pockets revealed them to be empty. The keeper was interviewed, and declared that he had seen or heard nothing out of the ordinary.

They carried the body into the lock keeper's cottage, where they laid her out on the kitchen table, awaiting the arrival of Crabb's colleagues who would eventually take her to the mortuary. Before they left, Ravenscroft took one final look at the body and, fighting back tears, gently brushed the wet hair away from her face.

As he and Crabb sat together in silence in the cab on their way back to Worcester, each not knowing what to say to the other, Ravenscroft began slowly to realize the enormity of the task which now faced them. He had been unable to discover the murderer of the librarian; the lost book still awaited recovery; he had interviewed many people and had gained little in the way of evidence. Now, he was faced with the incomprehensible death of a second victim: a poor, innocent, defenceless woman who had been killed in such brutal fashion.

And, worst of all, he would now have to travel to Malvern, to inform a young boy that his mother would never be returning home to him.

CHAPTER EIGHT

'Do sit down, Inspector.'

'Thank you.'

Ravenscroft and Crabb seated themselves on the sofa in the drawing-room of the residence of Sir Arthur Griffiths.

'I am sorry I was not able to speak to you when you called upon us the other day. I understand that my daughter was able to answer all your questions.' The speaker was a tall, well-dressed, moustached gentleman.

'Your daughter was able to answer some of my questions,' replied Ravenscroft.

'This is a terrible business. I feel somewhat responsible.'

'Oh, why do you say that, sir?'

'The woman was an employee of mine and as such was under my care and protection,' said Griffiths, brushing a hair away from the knee of his well-pressed trousers.

'How long had Miss Weston been employed here?'

'Eight or ten years, I think. Do you remember exactly, my dear?' said the politician turning towards his daughter.

'She came to us eight years ago,' she replied.

'Do you happen to know from which part of the country she came from?' asked Ravenscroft.

'Worcester I believe. She was a local girl,' replied Sir Arthur.

'It was unusual, was it not, that she did not live on the premises? I believe it is the custom for servants to reside where they are employed,' said Ravenscroft.

'That is often the case, as you correctly say, Inspector, but as you are no doubt aware Miss Weston has a son. It would not be appropriate for her and the child to be housed together under my roof.'

'Miss Weston was unmarried. Do you know who the father of her child was?'

'Good heavens, Inspector! It is not my business to interfere into the personal lives of my servants,' protested Griffiths.

'And yet you still kept her on in your employ. A lesser employer might have dismissed her,' suggested Ravenscroft.

'My father is a Christian gentleman,' interjected Miss Griffiths. 'He does not abandon those who seek his help, in their hour of need.'

'I am sure that is a very commendable attitude, Miss Griffiths.'

'My daughter found lodgings for the girl in the town, and after her confinement she resumed her duties here,' said the MP.

'And how did you find Miss Weston?' asked Crabb, looking up from his pocket book.

'We had no cause for complaint,' said Miss Griffiths, turning away and looking vacantly in the direction of the window.

'When did you first notice her absence?'

'Shortly before my father and I left for London.'

'Did you not think it rather strange, Miss Griffiths, that Miss Weston had not arrived for work that day?' asked Ravenscroft.

'I thought she was probably ill, and that she would return to work the following day.'

'Look here, Ravenscroft, this is all rather distressing for my daughter,' said Griffiths.

'I am sorry, sir, but these questions have to be asked if we are to apprehend Miss Weston's murderer,' said Ravenscroft, with as much firmness as he could muster.

'This is a shocking business. It is clear that some depraved ruffian from the lower depths of the town has committed this terrible deed. I would expect you to make an early arrest. To expedite matters I am prepared to announce a reward of fifty pounds for information leading to the apprehension of the villain.'

'I don't think that is wise, Father. You have your position to think about. It would not be appropriate if we were seen to be involved in this affair,' said Miss Griffiths, looking anxiously across at her father.

'My dear, you are perhaps right, as usual. I don't know what I would have done without you, all these years since your mother's death. No,

Inspector, by all means offer the reward, but I think it best if you keep our names out of it.'

'As you wish, although it might be best if we did not announce such a reward for a while, until at least after the inquest. Such an announcement will encourage a large number of people to come forward with all tales of fancy and suggestion.'

Sir Arthur nodded his approval.

'May I turn now to the night of the disappearance of the librarian, Nicholas Evelyn. You were here that night, sir?' asked Ravenscroft.

'I was, Inspector.'

'At what time did you retire?'

'It was just after ten, I believe.'

'And your bedroom is at rear of the house?'

'I have told you this already, Inspector,' interjected Miss Griffiths nervously fingering the lace handkerchief in her lap.

'It's all right my dear, I am sure the Inspector is only performing his duty. Yes my bedroom is at the rear of the house.'

'You were unable then to see anyone either entering or leaving the cathedral later that night?'

'As you say, Inspector.'

'Do you know, Miss Griffiths, if any of the servants saw anything that night?' asked Ravenscroft.

'I have spoken with the cook and the maid. They retired at around ten. Their rooms are in the basement, so they do not have a view directly out on to the cathedral,' replied the young lady, turning the handkerchief round in her fingers.

'Sir Arthur, were you in any way acquainted with the librarian Nicholas Evelyn?'

'No. I had never spoken to the man,' the politician replied, taking out his pocket watch and looking down at its face. Ravenscroft was beginning to feel that his allotted time was drawing to its conclusion.

'I understand that your duties necessitate your being away in London a great deal?'

'I am there during the week when the House is in session, and even when it is not I have a number of business interests that require my presence there one or two days each week. I stay at one of my clubs when I am up in town. The weekend and the rest of the week is spent here in

Worcester. There are great demands on my time from my constituents,' replied Sir Arthur, in a formal manner.

'That is all for now, Sir Arthur,' said Ravenscroft, suddenly standing up. 'We may need to interview you again after the inquest.'

'I'll see you out, gentlemen,' said Griffiths, rising from his chair, and opening the doors to the drawing-room.

'Good day to you, Miss Griffiths,' said Ravenscroft, as he and Crabb left the room.

'Look here, Ravenscroft, we would be grateful to you if you catch this deplorable villain as quickly as you can. Such a gross violation must not go unpunished,' said Sir Arthur, as the three men stood in the hall. 'But I would be obliged if you would refrain from any further questioning of my daughter. She is not a well woman. The disappearance of her maid has caused her a great deal of distress, if you get my meaning.'

'I understand perfectly,' said Ravenscroft.

'Good man. Knew I could rely on you. Catch this murdering scoundrel and I'll see you all right.'

Ravenscroft smiled. 'Thank you, sir. Oh, just one further question: when I was here the other day I could not help noticing that you were conversing with a Mrs Marchmont.'

'Mrs Marchmont?' said a bewildered Sir Arthur. 'What has she to do with this affair?'

'Can I ask you, what was the nature of her business, if I might be so bold?'

'She is one of my constituents. She was consulting me on a legal matter concerning her late husband's estate, I believe.'

'And were you able to be of assistance?' asked Ravenscroft.

'Of course, that is my function.'

'Thank you, Sir Arthur. You have been most helpful.'

As they walked away from the house, across the green towards the cathedral, Ravenscroft broke the silence.

'And what did you think of the Member for Worcester and his daughter?'

'A very close, canny couple, if you ask me.'

'My sentiments exactly; the daughter seems very nervous and anxious to protect her father at all costs. I observed that on our first visit, when she was not at all willing for us to see him. He, in turn, obviously feels equally protective towards his daughter.'

'He said she was ill.'

'I would agree that she does not look to be in the best of health. I also find it strange that a prominent politician such as Sir Arthur Griffiths, would not have dismissed Ruth Weston, when he learned of her being with child.'

'The daughter said her father was of a Christian disposition. Perhaps she had grown fond of her maid, and did not want to lose her, which is why she lodged at Glovers.'

'You are probably right. Talking of Glovers, it seems more than a coincidence that both our victims were lodgers there. There is more to that lodging-house than first appears. We need to search Ruth Weston's rooms and find out more about the others – the Baileys and this fellow Cranston.'

'Oh it's you, again!' said the blotchy red face, staring through the narrow opening.

'Good day to you, Mrs Glover. May we come in?' asked Ravenscroft smiling.

'Suppose you want to ask me some more questions?' grumbled the old woman opening the door wider.

'We won't take up too much of your time, I can assure you.'

The landlady muttered some words which Ravenscroft could not quite comprehend, before leading the two detectives down the passage and into her sitting-room at the rear of the property.

'Mind me figures,' she said, giving Ravenscroft a warning glance.

'Tell me more about your other lodgers, Mrs Glover.'

'Told you last time, the Baileys are away in France for the month. Won't be back until end of next week at the earliest,' said the old woman, searching through a number of letters perched behind one of the large decorative figures on the mantelpiece.

'How long have they lived here?' asked Ravenscroft.

'Three years. Ah here we are! I got this letter from them earlier this week.'

Ravenscroft took the letter and, after examining the postmark, opened the folded notepaper inside. 'I see it was sent from La Rochelle, dated seven days ago. Says they are enjoying the scenery, weather is fine and they hope to visit Nantes on the way back to England. Thank you, Mrs

Glover, that all seems in order. And Mr Cranston, I presume he has not returned yet?'

'He came in about half an hour ago. I heard his footsteps on the floorboards. He didn't stay long, said he was going out to get something to eat. I told him about Miss Weston, and said you would want to speak to him,' replied Mrs Glover, replacing the letter on the mantelpiece.

'Then perhaps he will return before our departure. How long has Mr Cranston been with you?' asked Ravenscroft.

'About two years.'

'While we are waiting for Mr Cranston to return, perhaps you would allow my constable and I to make an examination of Miss Weston's rooms?'

'Why do you want to do that for?' mumbled the old woman.

'We might find something there to suggest who killed her,' replied Ravenscroft.

'You best come this way then,' sighed the old woman, as she led the way out of the room.

'Tell me, was Miss Weston in the habit of receiving visitors?' asked Ravenscroft.

'Certainly not; lodgers is not allowed visitors in their rooms at any time. We don't encourage that sort of thing here. This is a respectable establishment,' replied the landlady, unlocking the door to the room.

'Did Miss Weston ever mention to you that she was seeing anyone elsewhere?'

'Not as far as I know.'

'Did she receive any letters from anyone?' asked Crabb.

'No. She never got no letters.'

'Thank you, Mrs Glover. We'll take a look round Miss Weston's rooms if we may, on our own. We'll give you a call should we need assistance.'

The landlady gave Ravenscroft a surely look, coughed, and opened the door, before making her way back to her sitting-room.

'Close the door behind you, Crabb,' instructed Ravenscroft, stepping into the room. 'We don't want either Mrs Glover or Cranston coming in here and disturbing us.'

The two men found themselves in the same simply furnished, gloomy sitting-room that Ravenscroft had seen when he had spoken to the young boy after his mother's disappearance. A large table and some chairs were situated in the centre of the room, and there were two worn armchairs and a small bookcase, the shelves of which accommodated a small number of books. The table was covered with a needlework cloth of floral design; a vase of roses occupying its centre, the dying petals of which had fallen on to its surface. Another, smaller room led off the main room, where Ruth Weston and her son had slept.

'Tell me what you see?'

'Plain, rather drab room, sir. Clean and respectable like; nothing out of the ordinary,' replied Crabb.

'There certainly appears to be nothing of a personal nature on display. There is a Bible, one or two children's books, but no photographs or portraits and no correspondence that I can see.'

'No scraps of paper lying around this time to give us any clues.'

'This tablecloth was evidently completed by Ruth Weston. Here, remove the vase of flowers so that I can have a closer look at it,' said Ravenscroft, brushing the fallen petals into a neat pile. 'Our Miss Weston was evidently an accomplished needlewoman. See here how she has managed to embroider the name Arthur in the centre of the design, and how she has interlinked it with her own name, Ruth. It is very cleverly done. It must have taken her hours to complete. I can just picture her sitting here in the evenings, doing her embroidery, whilst her son sits beside her probably drawing in that book.'

'A pretty dull existence, if you ask me,' said Crabb.

'Indeed, but perhaps that is the way she wanted it. To me, the room seems to suggest that its occupants had not been prepared to make their home here; to them it was but a staging place on the way to somewhere else.'

'You've lost me there, sir,' said Crabb looking perplexed.

'It is as though the room is speaking to us, telling us that Ruth and her son were prepared to accept its dull, drab interior, whilst waiting for better days.'

'There are the flowers to consider.'

'Yes, the roses. They are the one bright feature of the room, the one indulgence that Ruth allowed herself, but now even they have faded,' said Ravenscroft looking sadly out of the window, and recalling the last time he had looked down at the body of the parlour maid.

'It's that poor boy I feel sorry for, all alone in the world,' added Crabb.

The two men were suddenly disturbed by the sound of the outer door being opened and closed. Ravenscroft looked across at Crabb and they listened in silence to the heavy footsteps on the stairs outside the room.

'I fancy that may be our Mr Cranston returned,' murmured Ravenscroft.

'Shall we go and have words with him?'

'Give him a minute or two.'

Crabb replaced the vase of dying flowers on the table, as Ravenscroft took a final look round the rooms.

Closing the door behind them, the two detectives made their way up the flights of stairs, until they reached the landing, where Crabb knocked on the door facing them.

'I won't be a moment, Mrs Glover,' called a voice from inside the room.

'It's the police, sir,' said Crabb, knocking on the door again.

There followed a long silence, before the door opened to reveal a well-dresed, middle-aged man with dark, swept back hair, a thin nose and glasses. 'Yes, gentlemen, how can I help you?'

'I am Inspector Ravenscroft and this is Constable Crabb. We are investigating the disappearances and murders of two of your fellow lodgers, Nicholas Evelyn and Ruth Weston. May we come in, sir?'

'I suppose so. Mrs Glover did mention that you would be calling on me, but I don't see how I can help you. I am seldom here,' said Cranston opening the door to a small sitting-room, furnished with a desk, a table and two armchairs.

'Why is that, sir?' asked Ravenscroft.

'I am a commercial traveller for the Worcester Porcelain Company. I travel all over the country to visit our retailers, to show them our latest models and wares,' replied Cranston in a dry, matter-of-fact voice.

'Why do you live at Glovers?' enquired Crabb.

'I have to be in Worcester in order to collect the samples from the company. Glovers is not the best of lodging-houses, as you can see, Inspector, but I find it comfortable and convenient enough.'

'What can you tell us about your fellow lodgers?' asked Ravenscroft.

'Very little, I'm afraid, Inspector. As I said I am away a great deal,' replied Cranston, turning away.

'Nicholas Evelyn?' asked Crabb.

'Hardly ever saw the man. I heard him sometimes pacing up and down in his room, which is above mine, but I never spoke to him. He seemed a reclusive, sad sort of fellow.'

'And Miss Weston and her son?' asked Ravenscroft.

'I suppose I did see more of them. I would sometimes see them going into their rooms, as I made my way out in the mornings, and we would exchange a few words of greeting, but that was all.'

'So you did not mix socially with either Mr Evelyn or Miss Weston,' said Ravenscroft, walking across to the window and peering out at the old nearby buildings.

'I have just said that I hardly knew either of them,' replied the lodger in what Ravenscroft discerned, was an irritated tone of voice.

'So you did, Mr Cranston. Do you know whether either of them received visitors?'

'Mrs Glover does not allow visitors in the rooms.'

'How long have you been here in Worcester, Mr Cranston?' asked Ravenscroft, finding that he was beginning to dislike the man.

'For about three years.'

'And where were you before that, sir?'

'Look, Inspector, I have told you all I know about Ruth Weston and Nicholas Evelyn. I don't think it is any business of yours to delve into my past life,' snapped Cranston.

'We are not delving, sir; merely enquiring. Two people in this lodging house have met with untimely deaths, and a valuable book has been stolen from the cathedral library. These are matters of grave concern. You would oblige me, by answering our questions.'

'I was a commercial traveller for the Wedgewood Pottery Company in Staffordshire, before I came to Worcester,' replied Cranston, sighing and giving them an unwelcoming stare.

'And how long were you with Wedgewood?'

'Six years.'

'Why did you leave?'

'Look, I've had enough of these ridiculous questions!'

'"Why did you leave?' asked Ravenscroft, firmly repeating the question.

'I left because I was offered an increase in salary to join the Worcester Porcelain Company. You can check that with them, if you so wish. Now, I must insist you stop these aimless questions, I have some serious paperwork to complete before tomorrow morning,' said Cranston, crossing over to the door.

'We will be doing just that, Mr Cranston. In the meantime, you would oblige me by remaining in Worcester until our investigations are completed.'

'That, Inspector, will prove impossible. Later tomorrow I must leave for London again. I have appointments with a number of important clients which cannot be put off.'

'Nevertheless, I must insist, sir, that you remain in Worcester, whilst we continue with our enquiries,' replied the inspector, annoyed by the other's objections.

'And I have just said that I cannot comply with your request.'

'You would oblige us, sir.'

'No, Inspector. I will not be remaining in Worcester. If you wish to detain me then you will have to charge me with these murders, or some other crime – otherwise you have no right to prevent my travelling up to London tomorrow to conduct my business affairs. Now I wish you both good day gentlemen.'

The two stared at each other, both seeking to test the mettle of the other.

'Good day to you, Mr Cranston,' said Ravenscroft, suddenly walking out of the door, closely followed by Crabb trying to replace his pocket book in the top pocket of his tunic.

'Well, he was a very unpleasant fellow and no mistake,' said Crabb as the two men walked away from Glovers. 'Pity we couldn't have locked him up in the cells of Worcester gaol for the night. He might have then proved more accommodating.'

'I doubt it. I must say I was sorely tempted to have taken him into custody, but I couldn't for the life of me think of anything I could charge him with. He seems the kind of person who would have a brief on to us before we could turn the key in the lock of his cell. But he certainly knows a lot more than he is letting on, I am convinced of that. It is more than just a coincidence that two of his fellow lodgers are now dead.'

'Perhaps Cranston killed Evelyn. Ruth Weston found out about Cranston's involvement, so he had to kill her as well, in order to keep her quiet,' suggested Crabb.

'Maybe.'

'We could search his rooms, sir. The book might still be there.'

'I doubt it. If Cranston is our killer he would have sold it on to a collector by now.'

'Then your Dr Silas Renfrew would have it.'

'Possibly; but we have too little to go on at present, and would cause more harm than good if we go searching people's houses. Your Superintendent Henderson would be very pleased about that, I'm sure. No, there is something which binds the two victims together, and I feel that our Mr Cranston is involved in it somewhere along the line.'

'Do we check his story, sir?'

'We certainly will, Crabb, or rather you will. Would you go to the porcelain works and see what they can tell us about Cranston? In the meantime, I am going to pay a visit to that warehouse down by the bridge.'

'Good day to you, I am looking for Mr Snedden,' said Ravenscroft, addressing a stout, elderly gentleman who was supervising the unloading of cargo from one of the boats tied up along the quay.

'You are looking at him,' replied the man looking up from his note pad.

'I am Inspector Ravenscroft. I am conducting inquiries into the murder of a young woman by the name of Ruth Weston.'

'I've never heard of her. Here, look where you're putting that sack, Tom,' replied the man, shouting at one of his workmen.

'I would not expect you to have been acquainted with her. We recovered the poor unfortunate woman from the river yesterday at Holt Fleet.'

'I'm sorry for the poor woman, but what's that to do with me?'

'The victim had been strangled, and bundled into a sack before being thrown into the river. The sack bore the name 'Snedden' printed on the outside, and there were remains of grain in the bottom.'

'Who did you say you were?'

'Ravenscroft, Inspector Ravenscroft.'

'Funny, we get quite a number of visits from the police. I don't recall seeing you at all.'

'I'm from London. I'm assisting the Worcester Police in this inquiry.'

'I see. Well, we have got hundreds of them sacks. Use them all the time to transport the grain up and down the river.'

'Do you employ a large number of men to transport the sacks of grain?' asked Ravenscroft.

'We employ about thirty or forty men, mostly on a casual basis, as and when we need them.'

'And where do most of the sacks go to?'

'Generally we send them to the flour mills down at Tewkesbury, though sometimes they are transported upstream to the mills at Bewdley.'

'Can you tell me whether anyone took grain upstream, from Worcester, say about five or six days ago?'

'I will have to look in the ledger in the office.'

'I would be obliged if you would do so.'

'Here, Tom, keep an eye on things for a few minutes,' said Snedden, sighing, and passing over the note pad to the workman.

Ravenscroft followed the owner into the warehouse, where some wrought-iron steps took them into a back office. Here Snedden consulted a large book which lay open on the desk.

'Yes, here we are. The *Mayfly* loaded up five days ago, bound for Bewdley with about forty sacks of grain.'

'And who owns the *Mayfly*?' asked Ravenscroft.

'The *Mayfly* is a barge, run by old Billy from Diglis.'

'Billy you say?'

'Yes, rough sort of fellow. Big scar down the side of his face.'

'I know him. My constable had reason to have words with him the other night at the Old Diglis Inn. Tell me, does Billy operate the boat on his own?'

'Oh yes, with the help of the horse, of course. The *Mayfly* has long seen better days, as has old Billy. Between you and me he's rather too fond of the bottle,' said Snedden closing the ledger.

'But you still employ him?'

'He's cheap – and he does the job.'

'Thank you, Mr Snedden. Just one more question: would the *Mayfly* have reached Bewdley by now?'

'She probably got there yesterday.'

'Would she still be there now?' asked Ravenscroft.

'Most likely, I would think. Knowing Billy he'll hold up there for two or three days whilst he drinks away his fee, before he decides to look around for another cargo on the river.'

'Thank you once again, Mr Snedden,' said Ravenscroft shaking hands with the merchant before making his way out of the warehouse.

'And what did you find out about our Mr Cranston?' asked Ravenscroft as the two men met up again outside the Talbot.

'It is as he says, been employed by Worcester Porcelain for the past three years. He is one of their chief salesmen by all accounts. They seem quite pleased with the amount of business he has secured for the company. They can't remember, however, where he came from. We could contact Wedgewood and see if they remember him,' said Crabb, consulting his pocket book.

'We'll do that later. Right now, we have more pressing business. I thought it strange that Ruth Weston was found at Holt Fleet. If she had been killed here at Worcester, and then dumped in the river, we would have recovered the body downstream towards Upton and Worcester, but as the sack was recovered at Holt, the killer must have taken the body upstream.'

'But why go to all that trouble? Why not just throw the sack into the river here?'

'I believe the killer wanted to put some distance between himself and the scene of the crime. No, our killer was going north on business, and dumped the sack upstream believing that it might not be so easily found in that part of the river. Mr Snedden, who owns the warehouse, confirmed that one boat, or rather a barge in this case, called the *Mayfly*, left Worcester five days ago, bound for Bewdley. Holt Fleet is on the way.'

'So our killer might be still in Bewdley on board the *Mayfly*?'

'That might still be the case. Furthermore, the owner of the *Mayfly* is your old friend Billy!'

'He's no friend of mine. We should have clapped him in the gaol when we had the opportunity.'

'The question is, Crabb, why would Billy want to kill Ruth Weston, if he is our killer? It just doesn't seem to make sense. I don't see how he could be involved with Evelyn's death either, but I guess we won't know the answers to those questions until we have tracked him down. You and I need to get to Bewdley as soon as possible and catch up with him. Let's go back to the station and take the fly there.'

Within minutes the two men had left the confines of Worcester behind them as they travelled northwards through the sleepy villages of Hallow, Holt Heath, Shrawley and Astley, until eventually they arrived at the picturesque riverside town of Bewdley. The sinking sun was producing a golden glow over the waters of the river as Crabb tied the horse to one of the trees along the side of the bank.

'There seem to be quite a number of boats moored up along here,' said Ravenscroft alighting.

They made their way along the banks of the river, trying to read the names on the sides of the various boats and barges, in an attempt to find the *Mayfly*.

'Here we are, sir!' Crabb cried out suddenly. 'The *Mayfly*, wonder she's still afloat the condition she's in.'

'Draw your truncheon. Billy could still be on board and might prove dangerous,' said Ravenscroft stepping on to the barge, and opening the door to the living-quarters.

'Seems to be empty,' said Crabb, following him.

'You'r right, it looks as though our Billy is not at home,' announced Ravenscroft looking round at the old rags and rubbish that littered the floor and bed.

'Probably at one of the pubs, sir, drinking away his wages.'

'This looks interesting,' said Ravenscroft, bending down and holding up a reel of bright red cord. 'If I'm not mistaken this is the same cord that was used to strangle Ruth Weston. If you look closely you can see where a length has been cut off the main reel.'

'Looks as though you were right, sir. Billy certainly appears to be our killer.'

'It seems that way; all the more reason to find the blackguard. He must be in one of the riverside taverns. There is nothing for it, we will have to search each one until we find him.'

They alighted from the boat, and stood on the cobbled path. 'My guess is that he won't have travelled far. There are a couple of inns down that way. We'll try them first, and if we don't have any luck, we can come back and try the ones upstream.'

Crabb pushed open the door of the first inn and the two men stepped into the crowded bar. Ravenscroft enquired of the landlord if he had seen Billy and, receiving a negative reply, they made their way to the second drinking place – where again they drew a blank.

'Back the other way, sir?' asked Crabb. Ravenscroft nodded and the two men retraced their steps to where the *Mayfly* was tied up.

'The Cobblers. Sounds the sort of place Billy might frequent,' said Ravenscroft, standing outside a tavern, from where loud singing could be heard.

They opened the door to a smoked-filled room full of drinkers attempting to keep up with the music being played by a buxom woman on an old piano. Ravenscroft pushed his way through the throng until he reached the bar. 'We are looking for Billy,' he said addressing the barman.

'Why who wants him?'

'So you do know him?' said Crabb.

'Over there!' The barman pointed in the direction of the piano.

Ravenscroft strained to look past the revellers in the smoke and the gloom of the poorly lit room.

'There he is, sir. By the piano!' shouted Crabb, above the din.

'Get the cuffs ready. He might not come willingly,' said Ravenscroft, marching towards the singing sailor.

'Hello, Billy. Remember us?'

The old sailor rubbed his eyes with a dirty hand, and lurched forwards in Crabb's direction. 'You're that bloody peeler who threw me out of the Diglis!'

'We'd like a word with you, outside,' said Crabb, removing the sailor's hand from his tunic.

'The bloody hell you will. I'm 'avin me drink. Go away.'

'Come on now, Billy. It will be best for you if you come quietly,' said Ravenscroft, placing his hand on his shoulder.

'And who the bloody hell are you?' snarled Billy stepping forward and thrusting his grizzled features in Ravenscroft's face.

'I am an inspector with the Worcester Police,' replied Ravenscroft, turning away from the stinking smell of alcohol.

'Are you, by blazes?' said Billy, attempting to throw the remaining contents of his glass in Ravenscroft's direction, but missing and dowsing the piano player instead, much to the delight of the other drinkers.

'Here, you look what you're doing!' she shouted.

A sudden quiet came over the assembly, as everyone stared in the policemen's direction.

'Put the cuffs on him, Crabb,' instructed Ravenscroft in a firm voice, whilst grabbing the shoulders of the offending party.

Crabb sharply snapped the cuffs together around Billy's wrists.

'Now come outside, Billy, nice and peaceful,' said Ravenscroft.

'Here, where are you takin' our Billy?' shouted one of the drinkers.

'You ain't takin' him nowhere!' chorused another, a sentiment that was echoed from various parts of the bar.

'You keep your hands off our Billy!' said an aggressive third voice.

The situation was about to turn ugly, and Ravenscroft knew they would need all their powers as policemen, if they were to walk out of the inn unharmed and with their quarry.

'I am Inspector Ravenscroft. My colleague is Constable Crabb. This man is required for questioning concerning the murder of a young female in Worcester some days ago.'

'I don't care who you are. You ain't taking our Billy!' shouted back the first drinker.

' 'Ere, 'ere!' shouted several others, as the crowd gradually surrounded the two policemen.

'Now look here. I am a police officer and I am walking out of this inn with this man,' shouted Ravenscroft, summoning up all his courage, and looking around at the menacing group.

'The devil you will!' came back a voice.

'If anyone tries to stop us, he will be arrested as well, and will spend the night in the cells.'

'You just try. Bleeding coppers!'

'Crabb, draw your truncheon!' instructed Ravenscroft, as the crowd closed in.

'Oh leave off, you silly buggers!' The speaker was the lady pianist who was busily engaged in mopping up the ale from her ample features. 'This is a respectable inn. We don't want any trouble here.'

'I'll poke their lights out first!' growled one of the drinkers.

'You'll do no such thing, Seth Robinson. For God's sake let 'em go. Come on, let's have another sing song,' she said, resuming her seat and striking up a new tune.

'Crabb, let's get out of here, while we can,' whispered Ravenscroft, relieved by the temporary lull in the proceedings. 'Where's Billy?'

'Lord, sir, he's given us the slip!' replied Crabb, looking frantically around him.

'Quickly, let's get out of here.'

The two policemen thrust their way through the singing crowd, and out into the night air.

'Things were turning a bit ugly in there, sir.'

'And our friend Billy has taken the opportunity to escape. He can't have got far, with those handcuffs on him,' said Ravenscroft. 'Where the devil has he got to?'

'He's over there, sir. On the bridge!'

'Quickly. After him.'

Crabb darted along the towpath, Ravenscroft following on behind.

'Come and get me, you stinking landlubbers!' taunted Billy, climbing up on to the parapet of the bridge.

Crabb ran forward and reached out to grab the swaying figure, who suddenly lunged in the direction of the constable. Ravenscroft raced up on to the bridge and was horrified to hear a loud splash, as the two toppled over the edge into the waters below.

'My God, Tom, are you all right?' shouted Ravenscroft, looking down at the waters and trying to pick out the figures in the darkness. 'Tom! Tom!'

'I've got him!' came back a voice he recognized.

'Hang on, Tom. I can see a rowing boat at the side. I'll be with you as soon as I can,' replied Ravenscroft, racing down the steps at the side of the bridge, quickly untying the rope and flinging himself into the vessel. 'Tom, are you still there?' he shouted, as he rowed frantically into the centre of the river.

'Over here!'

'Hang on, Tom.!' shouted Ravenscroft, redoubling his efforts, as he rowed towards his colleague.

'I can't hang on to him much longer.'

'Can you push him up on to the side of the boat?' said Ravenscroft reaching Crabb, and laying down the oars.

'He's out cold, sir,' he spluttered, pushing the old seadog upwards towards the boat. Ravenscroft grabbed hold of the man and hauled him aboard. 'God, he's a weight. Now give me your hand, Tom, and I'll haul you up as well.'

Ravenscroft reached out for his bedraggled colleague, and gradually lifted him upwards and on to the boat.

'Are you all right, Tom?'

'The villain grabbed hold of me, and I couldn't stop us falling into the water,' he replied, breathless and bedraggled, as he collapsed on to the scat.

'You certainly frightened me. Get your breath back while I take a look at him,' said Ravenscroft, turning Billy over at the bottom of the boat.

'I think he might have hit his head on one of the pillars of the bridge as we went over.'

'There's a nasty gash on top of his head. I'm afraid he's dead,' pronounced Ravenscroft, sitting back.

'Save the hangman a job,' muttered Crabb.

'Pity we didn't have the opportunity to question him when he had sobered up. You sit there and I'll row to the shore and see if we can find the local station.'

As Ravenscroft rowed towards the river-bank, he realized that although it looked as though he had now caught the probable murderer of Ruth Weston, he was still no nearer to understanding why the old sailor had committed such an act. He wondered whether Billy had also killed Evelyn, but if so, for what reason? What would the sailor have wanted with the book? Now that Billy was dead, the questions seemed unlikely to be answered – and the recovery of the *Whisperie* seemed further away than ever.

CHAPTER NINE

'Well done, Ravenscroft.'

'Thank you, sir.'

It was the following morning and Ravenscroft and Crabb had just reported the events of the previous evening to their superior at the station in Worcester.

'Good work indeed. Show the people here that the police mean business, and that no crime will go unpunished!' said Henderson stroking his moustache.

'Indeed, sir.'

'Pity you couldn't get a confession out of the murdering swine before he topped himself.'

'He didn't top himself, sir. He hit his head on the side of the bridge when he fell into the river,' corrected Ravenscroft.

'Yes! Yes, whatever! Result's the same and that's what counts,' said Henderson irritably. 'Suppose he killed Evelyn as well?'

'We don't know that, sir. We still haven't recovered the book.'

'Yes, that damn book. You searched the boat, I suppose?'

'We did, sir, but there was nothing except the red cord that I believe had been used to strangle Ruth Weston.'

'H'm. Probably sold the book on to some collector or other,' suggested Henderson.

'We could get a warrant and search Dr Renfrew's house,' interjected Crabb.

'The blazes you will! Renfrew is a prominent citizen. He'll have the law down on us in no time. No, Ravenscroft, we can't go marching over innocent people's property, without a by your leave. It just isn't on, man.'

'I take your point.'

'Look here, I quite understand if you've had enough of this case and want to get back to London. Now that we know that this Billy character killed Miss Weston and probably Evelyn as well, it's only a matter of time before the book turns up.'

'If it's all the same to you, sir, I would like to continue with the case. We don't know that Billy killed Evelyn, and I'm sure that I will shortly be able to recover the book,' pleaded Ravenscroft, anxious that the case should not be taken away from him.

'Yes, yes, all right then. I suppose a few more days won't hurt. You might turn up something. Must get on now, Ravenscroft; races start tomorrow. Worcester will be full by teatime with every rogue and villain that was ever born under the sun; but we'll be ready for them Ravenscroft, yes, we'll be ready for them,' said Henderson, pulling on his coat and striding out of the room.

'Yes, sir,' said Ravenscroft, as the door banged behind their chief.

'So, we've got a few more days to solve this crime,' said Crabb. 'I suppose there's no doubt that old Billy did kill Ruth Weston?'

'I have no doubt at all. He evidently lured Ruth Weston down to the river-bank late at night, where he strangled her aboard his barge. Then he placed the body in one of Snedden's sacks, and kept it on board the boat until he was able to dump it in the river, further upstream. The question remains, however – why?'

'Money, sir?'

'Exactly!'

'He murdered the poor woman for the money she had on her person?'

'Somehow I doubt that. He would have not known how much money she had in her pockets. Also, it does not explain why she left her son and her lodgings to go walking alone, late at night, down by the river.'

'She could have been meeting someone?' suggested Crabb.

'I think you are probably right. Ruth Weston had an appointment with someone down by the river. Instead she meets old Billy, who is the worse for drink, and who then kills her for what little money she has, unless, of course, unless Billy was paid by a third party to kill her!'

'But why? Why would someone, this third party, want Ruth Weston out of the way?'

'That is what we must find out. My guess is that, by some means or other, she had found out who had killed Evelyn, and the killer then lured her down to the river-bank, where he paid Billy a sum of money to kill her and dispose of the body.'

'Seems highly probable, sir, when you think about it.'

'Unfortunately, we are still miles away from finding out who *is* our killer. I tell you one thing Crabb, I don't like that Cranston fellow. I feel he is hiding a great deal from us. Go to the telegraph office, and send a telegram to the Wedgewood factory in Stoke on Trent, asking them if they can tell us more about him.'

'Right, sir, I'm on my way.'

'I'm going back to the cathedral to have another word with Brother Jonus. Meet me there later.'

Walking into the cathedral, Ravenscroft first encountered Matthew Taylor who was busily engaged in collecting up hymn books from the choir stalls.

'Good day to you, Inspector. I trust you are fully recovered from your night time excursion to the fair town of Bewdley,' said the choirmaster, looking up from his task.

'Yes, thank you. But how did you know—?' began Ravenscroft.

'The walls of this cathedral have ears. Speak always in low tones, or your whispers will find you out!' said the other in a light-hearted manner.

'I had not realized that the news travelled so fast. Did you know Billy at all?'

'Oh, everyone knew old Billy, smelly and as damp as a cowpat! He was often seen late at night staggering past the cathedral on his way back to his old tub. It's a wonder he was ever able to find it, the condition he was generally in, but they always say a drowning rat will often return to the scene of his greatest triumphs. And now the drunken old fool has gone and killed the saintly Miss Weston. Could you please hold these books, Inspector, whilst I gather up the rest?' said Taylor unloading a pile of hymn books into Ravenscroft's outstretched arms.

'Why do you think old Billy killed Miss Weston?'

'How would I know, Inspector? I'm only a poor humble songster, and am completely unaware of the workings of the criminal mind,' he laughed.

'This is a serious matter, Mr Taylor,' said Ravenscroft peering over the top of the increasing stack of books.

'Of course, Inspector. You must excuse my frivolous nature. Now, let me see – why do I think Billy killed Miss Weston? Money! There that's your answer. He killed her in return for money.'

'I had deduced that already,' replied Ravenscroft, annoyed. 'Perhaps you might also be able to suggest, who you believe paid Billy to kill Miss Weston.'

'Paid, was he? Well, yes, I suppose he must have been. There are plenty of candidates. What about Renfrew? My mother used to say, you can never trust an American, all descended from rustlers and deported highwaymen. Then there is my employer, Dr Edwards – although please don't let on that I told you so, or I'll be out of a job. You could try the famous illustrious Member for Worcester, his eminence the mighty Sir Arthur Griffiths, or perhaps one of those Tovey sisters thought they needed some entertainment to liven up the dull evenings,' said the choirmaster, loading yet more books on to Ravenscroft.

'You've left one person out, Mr Taylor.'

'Have I? Dear me, who can that possibly be? No, surely not – but, yes, it must be me! I must be the evil mastermind behind these terrible deeds. I killed Evelyn to get my hands on the *Whisperie*, so I could sell it to the crooked American, thus enabling me to spend my ill-gotten gains on the gambling tables at Monte Carlo! Just follow me over here, Inspector. We stack the hymn books on the table.'

'Mr Taylor, what can you tell me about Ruth Weston?' said Ravenscroft, doing his best to ignore the previous remarks.

'Oh the poor Miss Weston, she was such a plain, simple soul. I often saw the poor woman and her son at Holy Communion. She generally sat over there, amongst the servant classes, some rows back from Sir Arthur and all the other Worcester nobility,' he replied, taking the books off Ravenscroft one by one, and stacking them in neat piles on the table.

'Did you ever notice anyone with her? Did she ever have company?'

'No. They always seemed alone. Rather sad, I suppose.'

'Thank you, Mr Taylor. I'm looking for Brother Jonus.'

'Then you will need to gird your loins: it's a long way up to Heaven,' said the choirmaster, taking the remaining books.

'I'm sorry. I don't understand?'

'Up to the tower. That's where Brother Jonus goes at this time of day.'

'I see, and the way to the tower?'

'You go up the steps over there,' said Taylor, pointing. 'Keep going until you get to the top. That's where you will find Brother Jonus – and that is where you must also stop climbing, otherwise you might fall over the edge!'

'I'll try and remember,' replied Ravenscroft, walking away.

'Until next time, Inspector,' called out the choirmaster.

Ravenscroft made his slow progression up the stairs of the tower, pausing now and again to steady himself against the walls and to ease the congestion in his lungs. Eventually he found himself stepping out from the gloom of the stairway into the bright sunlight of the upper platform of the tower.

'Inspector Ravenscroft, you have come to admire the view,' said Brother Jonus smiling.

'Brother,' replied Ravenscroft, shaking hands with the learned monk. 'I was told I might find you up here.'

'From here you can see not only the whole of Worcester but also the surrounding countryside. You have chosen an excellent day to make the climb. See the course of the river as it flows down to Upton and Tewkesbury, and over there where it joins the Birmingham canal at Diglis. There are the Malvern Hills. Now, if you turn the other way, Inspector, you can see the tents being set up on Pitchcroft in preparation for the races.'

'It is certainly a fine view,' replied Ravenscroft, gradually recovering his breath. He walked across to the edge of the platform and peered down.

'You also have a good view of the green, although if you look down too long it can make you rather dizzy.'

'I see what you mean,' he replied, steadying himself and taking a few steps back from the edge. 'I must admit, Brother Jonus, that heights are not always to my liking. Do you come up here often?'

'Every day if I can manage it. I find that it gives me the peace and quiet that I need to consider the ills of the world.'

'And does the world have many ills?' asked Ravenscroft.

'You would know the answer to that question, Inspector, better than perhaps anyone.'

'I have also found that there is a great deal of kindness and consideration.'

'Indeed there is,' replied the monk smiling. 'And how are your investigations proceeding?'

'You have heard about poor Miss Weston?'

'A terrible thing; I have prayed for her soul.'

'We sought to arrest the perpetrator last night, a bargeman by the name of Billy, but unfortunately he sustained a fatal injury whilst attempting to escape,' said Ravenscroft, shading his eyes from the bright sun.

'How awful.'

'Were you acquainted with either of these two persons, Brother Jonus?'

'Miss Weston would often bring her son to the cathedral grounds in the mornings. I would see her sitting on the seat down there by the tree, whilst her son played on the green. They seemed to be quite content and happy. I believe that she also attended services in the cathedral on a Sunday. She was engaged as a parlour maid in Sir Arthur Griffith's residence.'

'Did you ever notice whether she met anyone, whilst sitting on the green?'

The monk thought hard. 'I don't believe so.'

'Did she ever confide in you?'

'Alas no; I'm afraid I cannot help you there.'

'What about Billy?'

'Ah, Billy, he was different. When he wasn't off on one of his journeys or drinking at the Diglis, he could often be found loitering around the main entrance to the cathedral.'

'Oh, what was he doing there?'

'Begging, I'm afraid. He would try and accost the visitors on their way in and out of the building, asking them for money. It was all quite embarrassing, I'm afraid. Sometimes I would go and give him some food and drink, on condition that he stopped his pleadings.'

'And did he?'

'He was generally quite accommodating. Of course, I was always careful not to give him any money. Occasionally, he would go off delivering some cargo along the river or the canal and we would not see him for several days. Then he would return and spend all his money in the taverns, before becoming destitute once more.'

'Did he ever confide in you, Brother?'

'Yes, on a number of occasions. He was a very unhappy man, I believe. Always sorry for how life had treated him, and how he had missed his opportunity when he had been younger,' said the monk sadly.

'He never mentioned anyone in particular?'

'No. There was no one in his life.'

'Do you not think it is strange, Brother Jonus, that Billy, Miss Weston and indeed Nicholas Evelyn, all led lonely, isolated lives? Billy toiling alone on his old barge, Miss Weston and her son living in unappealing-rooms in Glovers Lodging-house, and Nicholas Evelyn spending all his working life in the cathedral library – living separate existences, day after day, year after year, making no friendships, confiding in no one, and yet each seeming as though they were waiting for some startling event that would free them from the worlds they had created for themselves.'

'I can see, Inspector, that you have given this case a great deal of thought. Perhaps each of us is trying to escape from the world of our own creation. The future can often seem more appealing than the present, but it is the past that defines our immediate state. Sometimes it takes a degree of purpose to break the chains.'

Ravenscroft smiled at the old man's words, and turned away from the sun.

'And what is it that you seek, my son?' asked the monk. 'How is it possible that you might change your world?'

Ravenscroft stood in silence for some moments, knowing that the wise old brother was waiting patiently for him to speak.

'There have been two occasions in my life, when I had the opportunity to change direction. Many years ago there was a young lady, whom I held in great esteem and affection, but at the time I failed to realize the strength of my feelings towards her. Eventually she decided to leave for Australia and I never saw her again. It was only after she had left that I began to acknowledge the foolishness of my indecision, and I began to regret the opportunity which I had missed.'

'It is often the case that we do not realize the value of what we have until we have lost it – but please forgive my interruption. There has also been a recent event that preys on your mind?'

'Last year I had cause to visit Malvern, and whilst engaged in my investigations there, I met a young lady whom I thought the fairest, loveliest creature that I had ever seen. My feelings towards this young lady, were I felt, acceptable to her, and I was able to assist both her and her brother. After the conclusion of the case, I had resolved to offer her my hand in marriage. I wanted us to be together, and for both our lives to change for the better.'

Ravenscroft paused and, clearing his throat, looked away into the distance.

'Unfortunately there were a number of problems that stood in our way. A number of years previously she had formed an attachment to a young gentleman who had used her ill. She had found herself with child and he had deserted her in her hour of need. The child – he is now six years of age – is all of her life. She is very protective towards him and will do nothing that will cause him any harm or upset. That is most commendable. I admire her determination and resolve, and would not in any way seek to come between mother and son. She could not bring herself to acknowledge the strength of her feelings towards me, for fear that the lives of her child and herself might once again be placed in danger. During my investigations I had incurred the displeasure of her brother, whom I had considered for a while as being the guilty person in the crime I was attempting to solve. Although he was eventually proved innocent of any crime, he, nevertheless, did not look upon our possible union with any degree of enthusiasm.'

'And what did you do, my son?' asked the monk.

'I-I walked away. I realized that I had little chance of success so I returned to London, tried to involve myself in my work, and trusted that in time, I would forget all about the woman who had so captured my heart.'

'And did you?'

'For a while, but I soon realized that I could never extinguish what I truly felt and yet I had to accept that I was powerless to alter the situation. Now that I have returned once more to Worcestershire, I find myself turning towards the Malverns and realizing that beyond the hills, there lies a small welcoming town, where everything that I have ever desired lies waiting, but I cannot reach out to acquire that which I desire above all other. So you see Brother Jonus, once this case is over, I will go back to my lonely room, in a dingy street in that forgotten part of London, where the sun seldom penetrates and where I will be alone with my thoughts for company. Is it not a sad tale, Brother Jonus, that I tell? Perhaps in time, I will become like Evelyn and Billy and poor Ruth Weston, forgotten by everyone and deservedly so.'

The two men stood in silence for some minutes, each alone with his own thoughts and memories.

'And yet you know in your heart, my son, that you have the power to change all that,' said the monk slowly.

'How, Brother, how? What is it that I must do? I have no desire to bring harm to Lucy by reappearing in her life. I could not expect her to place me before her own son. That would be so cruel and unjust. I have no right to do it.'

'Perhaps you are more afraid of your own rejection?' suggested the monk. For a moment their eyes met, before Ravenscroft turned away suddenly. 'I must go. I have detained you longer than I should,' he said, walking towards the entrance to the steps.

'Then I wish you well, my son, both with your professional undertaking and with your personal endeavours.'

Ravenscroft turned back and shook the monk's hand before beginning the long descent back down to the floor of the cathedral.

Ravenscroft spent an uncomfortable night. The intermittent noises of the late night revellers outside his bedroom window celebrating the commencement of the Worcester Races, rendered the chance of any sleep almost an impossibility. At two o'clock in the morning a large scale fight that threatened to involve both the inhabitants of the whole of Friar Street and the visitors, accompanied by loud jeers and broken raucous applause, made him despair. When at three o'clock the affray seemed to die down only to be replaced by numerous encores of what he supposed to be Irish songs of a particularly unsavoury nature, Ravenscroft decided that it would be futile to remain in his room a moment longer. He dressed quickly, opened the door of the Cardinal's Hat and made his way through the merry songsters until he reached the calm and peace of the cathedral Close.

Ravenscroft found his usual seat and sat down beneath the dim light of the hissing gas lamp. Most of the buildings in the Close were in complete darkness, except for the dim hall light which shone in the house of Sir Arthur Griffiths. The moon illuminated parts of the great cathedral building, throwing shadows across the grass, thereby emphasizing its age and grandeur.

Drawing his coat closer around him, Ravenscroft stretched out his legs, and rested his head on the back of the seat, before giving a deep sigh of relief that he had at last escaped the ribaldry of Friar Street. Closing his eyes, and feeling the gentle breeze of the night air upon his face, he found his thoughts returning to the day when he had first sat there on the same seat and had encountered Ruth Weston and her son. Now Ruth was dead, leaving her child an orphan except for the generosity of the Crabbs, and, without anyone to care for him in the world. Then he remembered the long climb up to the top of the tower and the words which Brother Jonus had spoken to him. For a moment he recalled peering down over the parapet and seeing again the ground revolving around him, and he felt a cold shiver run down his spine at the recollection of the scene. His thoughts turned to the little cottage in Ledbury where he knew that Lucy Armitage would be found, and wondered whether she might have rid her mind of their past meetings, or yet have retained some affection for him, but then he concluded that he must cast away such pleasant thoughts and false hopes.

Gradually his head became heavier and, as it fell downwards on to his chest, he saw himself again in Silas Renfrew's library and heard once more the casual drawl of the American – '. . . part of the *Worcester Antiphoner*, a composite liturgical work dating back to the fourteenth century . . .' The words kept repeating themselves, going round and round in a never ending spiral, until he broke away only to find his exit barred by the threatening presence of the Italian manservant.

'Here, what are you doing out at this time of night?'

Ravenscroft awoke with a start.

'Oh, begging your pardon, Inspector. I thought you were some vagrant or some other ne'er-do-well.'

Ravenscroft looked up into the face of the intruder of his dreams, and recognized the speaker as one of the constables who had assisted him in his search for the missing book along the banks of the river a few days earlier. 'No, I am not a vagrant. To tell you the truth, Officer, I came out here for some peace and quiet. The noise of the revellers outside the Cardinal's Hat was making it impossible for me to sleep.'

'I know what you mean, sir. The cells back at the station are full of them, drunken Irishmen mainly.'

'How long do the races go on for, Officer?'

'Usually about three days. We'll be glad at the station when it's over and they've all gone back to their homes.'

'What time is it?'

'It's just gone six, sir. Soon be dawn.'

'That is good.'

'Well, sir, I'll leave you to your thoughts. Sorry to have disturbed you,' said the police constable, giving Ravenscroft a salute, before walking back towards the town.

Ravenscroft looked up at the sky, where the new day would soon dawn, stretched his legs and gave a loud yawn. 'The *Antiphoner*' The words kept repeating themselves. 'The *Antiphoner* – a work dating back to the fourteenth century'. Renfrew had said that he had purchased the work at auction in New York some years before, but surely such a precious item as the *Antiphoner* should be where it belonged – in the cathedral library – rather than in a private collection? Had he acquired the work illegally, and if so, had he purchased it from Evelyn?

As Ravenscroft made his way back to the Cardinal's Hat in the hope of securing an early breakfast, he became more and more determined to investigate the origins of the ownership of the *Antiphoner.*

'An excellent breakfast, landlord.'

'Glad it was to your liking. We aim to please at the Cardinal's.'

'I wonder whether it would be possible to move to another room at the rear of the property?' asked Ravenscroft.

'Noise keep you awake?'

'I'm afraid so.'

'Sorry, sir, all our rooms are full; with them all attending the meeting I haven't an inch to spare,' replied his host shaking his head.

'That's a pity,' sighed Ravenscroft. The thought of another night listening to the sounds of drunken revelry held little appeal.

'I tell you what, seeing as you are practically a regular, I'll see if I can get one of those Irish chaps to move into your room and you can have his room at the back.'

'Splendid! I would be most obliged to you,' replied Ravenscroft, feeling somewhat relieved.

'It's not quite as large as you've been used to.'

'That is no matter; just as long as it's quiet.'

'See what I can do, can't promise anything, mind.'

'Thank you, landlord; I would be most obliged.'

'Good morning,' said Crabb, entering the dining-room. 'My word, the town's busy today; hundreds of them making their way to the races. Superintendent Henderson will have his hands full.'

'I know. Most of them have been celebrating the prospect of their winnings outside my window most of the night.'

'Bad was it, sir? If things get too unpleasant, you could always come and stay with Jennie and me,' offered Crabb, helping himself to a piece of uneaten toast.

'That's uncommonly generous of you, but I've asked the landlord to find me a quieter room. If he has no success, I might well take you up on your offer. How is that little lad, young Arthur?'

'Still upset, sir, with the loss of his mother, as you would expect. Jennie does her best to comfort the lad as best she can.'

'I'm sure she does. He is fortunate to be looked after by such kind people.'

'Well, what is our plan for today?' asked Crabb.

'When I was at Renfrew's I saw an old manuscript called the *Worcester Antiphoner*. It was very early – possibly fourteenth century. The sort of book that rightfully belongs in the cathedral, and yet Renfrew claimed he had purchased it some years ago at auction in New York before he came to this country. We need to go back to the cathedral library. There may be records there which would indicate that the cathedral once owned the work, in which case we would have grounds to recover it, and that would then give us an excuse to make a search of Renfrew's premises for the *Whisperie* at the same time. Also, we need a reply from Wedgewood regarding Cranston. There is something I don't quite like about that fellow and, as he lodged with both Evelyn and Ruth Weston, he remains a strong suspect. Right then, Crabb, let us be on our way.'

Ravenscroft strode out of the Cardinal's Hat, narrowly avoiding the low beam as he did so, with Crabb helping himself to the remaining piece of toast as he followed.

Entering the cathedral through the main entrance, they encountered Reverend Touchmore, who was busily fixing a notice to the board. 'Good morning to you, gentlemen. I hear that you have apprehended the murderer of poor Miss Weston.'

'We have indeed, Dean, but unfortunately the villain died before he was able to tell us anything regarding Evelyn and the *Whisperie*,' replied Ravenscroft.

'That is very unfortunate, as you say, Inspector.'

'Tell me, Dean, what do you know about the *Worcester Antiphoner*?'

'The *Antiphoner*? Ah, yes. Quite a remarkable work I believe. It should be somewhere in our collection, although I must admit that I have not seen the manuscript myself,' replied Touchmore.

'We think the work may have been lost some years ago,' said Ravenscroft.

'Good heavens! I do hope not – first the *Whisperie* and now the *Antiphoner*. This is all very disturbing.'

'We would like access to the library, if you would be so kind.'

'Yes, of course, Inspector. I have the key here. Dear me. This is very upsetting,' said the Dean, shaking his head and handing over a large key.

'Thank you, sir, we will of course keep you fully informed.'

They made their way up the two flights of stairs, until they arrived at the door to the library, where Crabb unlocked the door.

'I had forgotten how steep these steps really were,' said Ravenscroft breathing hard, and mopping his brow. 'I pity old Evelyn having to climb them every day.'

'I see someone has swept up all the broken glass. Now, with such a vast collection, there must be some kind of index system. A ledger or some cards, or some such like. Look over there. I'll take this side.'

The two men set to work. After a few minutes Ravenscroft lifted down a large ledger from one of the shelves. 'Ah, here we are. What does this say on the front? *Index to the collection*. Now let's see,' he said, placing the large book on the desk and turning its pages. 'Fortunately the manuscripts and books appear to be listed in alphabetical order, which should make things easier. Letter 'A' is at the beginning. 'Ac. Am. Here we are – An. This is where the *Antiphoner* should be.'

'It does not appear there, sir. Can't have been part of the collection then,' said Crabb shaking his head.

'At first sight it would appear that your assumption is correct,' said Ravenscroft, running his fingers along the edge of the page near the spine of the book. 'But it is just as I thought. A page has been removed. If you run your finger along the edge here, it is quite rough. I think someone has cut out the page which gave details of the *Antiphoner* so that anyone who tried to look up the entry would find it not there and assume that the book had never been in the cathedral collection in the first place.'

'Very clever, sir.'

'So the *Whisperie* was not the first item to have been taken: the *Antiphoner* had also been stolen earlier!'

'Then either Renfrew or Evelyn must have taken it.'

'It looks like it. Either way, the work now appears to be in Renfrew's collection. Of course, the manuscript could have been taken some years ago, and found its way to New York where Renfrew purchased it. I think we need to have urgent words with Dr Silas Renfrew and find out how exactly he acquired the item.'

Fifteen minutes later they alighted from their cab, outside the gates of Renfrew's drive.

'Wait for us here, my man,' instructed Crabb.

The two men began walking up the driveway towards the imposing residence.

'No good you asking there,' said a voice from the garden.

Ravenscroft turned and saw a man with a garden fork in his hand, and a pile of weeds at his feet.

'I am Inspector Ravenscroft and this is Constable Crabb. We are calling to see Dr Renfrew.'

'No good there, as I just said. Master has gone away and shut up house.'

'I see. When did he go?'

'It were day before yesterday. Took Georgio with him, and sent the cook home. So it's no use you knocking. All locked up,' said the gardener, wiping his brow.

'Do you know when he will be back?'

'Don't rightly know. End of week perhaps.'

'I suppose you don't have a key,' asked Ravenscroft.

'No. Master took all the keys with him. Anyway, it would be more than my job is worth to let you in, even if I had a key, which I don't!'

'I quite understand. Thank you,' said Ravenscroft walking away.

'Shall I say you called?' shouted out the gardener.

'No. We will come back later in the week when Dr Renfrew has returned.'

They mounted their cab, which swung out into the main road, to begin its descent back into Worcester.

'We could get a warrant, sir.'

'I don't think Superintendent Henderson would allow us to do that, especially as we have no positive evidence that Renfrew stole the *Antiphoner*.'

'We could always break in, sir.'

'Constable Crabb, I don't think I heard that,' smiled Ravenscroft. 'That would go down especially well with our superiors. No, we will just have to wait until he returns. Meanwhile, there is still more to find out about Cranston. He, too, may be in London, but it will not stop us from continuing with our enquiries. The birds may have flown Crabb, but remember that in time, they always return to their nests!'

INTERLUDE

LONDON

The small light flickered at the top of the steps as she made her way slowly upwards, treading carefully, not wanting to stumble in the darkness. She knew that he would be there, that he had carried out his task and that her vengeance could continue.

'Come in!' said the distant voice, as she pushed open the creaking door. 'Shut the door and take a seat.'

It was the same dry, cold, clinical voice, with which she had grown familiar.

She made her way across by the light of the wavering flame on the table and sat down.

'You were not followed?'

'I kept to the dark alleyways; I was not observed. You have done well,' she said, placing a small pouch of coins on the table.

'Chapman was easy. There was plenty of time in the yard.'

'You have the rings I asked you for? The newspapers mentioned that they had been taken.'

'On the table, in the packet,' instructed the voice.

She reached for the packet, opened it and tipped its contents on to the table. 'Three brass rings.'

'You have the extra payment?'

'I have included it with the rest.'

'Good. You wish me to continue with my work?' The words came quickly and without emotion, as she had expected.

'Of course, the name of your next victim is Elizabeth Stride. She lodges at 32 Flower and Dean Street. You will find it easy enough. I would desire you to bring me her ear-ring. I will pay you fifty sovereigns as before. I trust these terms are acceptable.'

'They are, my lady.'

'Then I will return exactly one week after you have carried out the deed,' she said, collecting up the rings and replacing them in the packet.

'That may not be possible.'

'Why is that?' she asked anxiously, fearing that Monk might not be prepared to carry out all that she desired.

'I have other business to attend to.'

'I see.'

'Give me the name of one other. There may be an opportunity to remove her as well. Two on one night! Now that would be a challenge indeed!'

'It would surely be too dangerous—' she began.

'I will be the judge of that!' the voice snapped, 'The fools have not caught me yet, and they never will. Give me the names of the others.'

'There are to be two more. I will give you the name and address of your fourth victim, but not the last – she is the main cause of my hatred. I would have you prepare something different for her.'

'As you wish.'

'Catherine Eddowes. She lives with an Irish porter called John Kelly in Flower and Dean Street, but they are away from London at present, probably harvesting. You will have to wait for her return.'

'I understand.'

'Bring me any item from her person – a ring, ear-ring, or bracelet, perhaps. I will leave the choice to you.'

'And the price?'

'As before, fifty sovereigns' she suggested, but knowing that he would want more.

'Fifty sovereigns is acceptable for the first; I require a hundred for the second,' he said coldly.

'It is too much,' she protested.

'Then you must find some one else to continue the work. Take your rings and go!' he shouted.

'You know that I cannot do that,' she replied, growing afraid of the increasing anger in his voice.

'There are plenty others who will carry out what you desire, but they will not do it as well. There is also the risk that they will be caught, and the trail will lead back to yourself,' he said, the anger subsiding.

'You have thought of everything, as usual,' she sighed.

'Then you will pay?'

'It is agreed.'

'Then our meeting is at an end, my dear lady.'

'When shall I return here?' she asked, rising out of the chair.

'You will not return here ever again. Enquiries are being made. Precautions must always be taken: I am not prepared to take the risk.'

'Then how am I to contact you?' she enquired.

'You will not. I will know of your whereabouts and will make arrangements to meet you for one last time. That is when you will pay me, and tell me the name of your final victim.'

'I see. Then it must be so.'

'Perhaps you will then be at peace?'

'My work will be completed, that is all,' she said, walking over to the door. 'That is all I desire.'

'Good day to you, my lady,' – the words of farewell were said in mocking tone.

She closed the door behind her and made her way down the wooden steps, taking in the night air in deep gasps. Tomorrow she would be free to leave the capital, to escape from the world of sin, degradation and pain – and to seek once more the temporary sanctuary of the county town of Worcester.

CHAPTER TEN

WORCESTER

'Good morning, sir. I trust you slept well?'

'Slightly better, thank you, Crabb, although a cave might admit more light into its interior than the darkened box that passes for a room in this establishment, but at least it is at the rear of the property and hence reasonably quiet,' replied Ravenscroft, pouring himself another cup of coffee from the silver jug.

'Never mind, sir. The races finish tomorrow, so perhaps the landlord will let you have your old room back.'

'One would hope so. Help yourself to some of the toast. There is more than enough for one person.'

'Thank you, I don't mind if I do. Jennie always cooks me a good break-fast before I leave in the morning, but I must admit that by the time I arrive in Worcester, I'm ready for another bite,' said Crabb eagerly help-ing himself.

'I think you have some news?' smiled Ravenscroft.

'Oh yes, sir. Nearly forgot. We've had a telegram back from Wedgewood,' he replied, taking out the item in question from the top pocket of his tunic and passing it over.

'Sorry to inform you, have no record of anyone called Cranston work-ing for company,' said Ravenscroft, reading the telegram. 'Well, it seems as though our Mr Cranston was lying when he said he had previously worked for Wedgewood. I wonder why?'

'He evidently had something to hide, sir.'

'It would appear so. Perhaps he said that he had worked for

137

Wedgewood, so that they would take him on here at Worcester,' suggested Ravenscroft.

'You would have thought that they would have taken up his references,' said Crabb helping himself to a second piece of toast.

'Employers don't always bother, although I would have thought that in this case they would have done so. After all, being one of the chief sales-men for the company must be an important position. We will need to question Cranston upon his return.'

'So, sir, what can we do today? What with Cranston, Renfrew and Griffiths all out of town, it seems as though our investigations have come to a halt.'

'Far from it, I want you to go back to the Worcester library and see if they have any information regarding auction rooms in New York. I know it's a bit of a long shot, but they may have American directories and such like. If you find any, make a note of their names and addresses.'

'Right, sir, and may I be so bold as to ask what line of enquiry you will be following?'

'I will be doing something which I should have done long ago.'

'Oh, and what might that be, sir?'

'I shall be taking morning coffee with the Tovey sisters!'

'Oh, do come in, Inspector.'

'Thank you, ladies,' said Ravenscroft stepping into the hallway.

'Please, come into the morning-room,' said Mary Ann.

'Thank you,' he replied walking into the room.

'Do, please take a seat,' said Alice Maria smiling.

'Perhaps you would take coffee with us?' asked Emily.

Ravenscroft seated himself in one of the elegant Regency chairs, as Mary Ann rang the bell and gave instructions to the maid to bring in the coffee. The room in which he found himself was comfortably furnished with fine mahogany furniture, paintings and ornaments. He thought he could detect a slight aroma of lavender in the air. 'You have a fine view of the cathedral' he remarked.

'We can see everything from here,' said the youngest sister.

'We heard about poor Miss Weston,' said Mary Ann sadly.

'She used to sit on that seat every morning,' stated Emily, 'watching her little boy play on the green.'

'Whatever will happen to the poor child now?' asked Alice Maria, anxiously.

'Do not distress yourselves, ladies. One of my constables has taken the boy home and his wife is caring for him at present,' replied Ravenscroft.

'But what will happen to the poor boy after all this is over?' asked Mary Anne.

'He can't be taken to the workhouse. Surely not,' said Emily, a worried expression on her face.

'We must see what transpires, ladies,' said Ravenscroft trying to sound as reassuring as he could.

The maid entered the room, bearing a large silver tray upon which stood four cups and saucers, and a large jug.

'Do please help yourself, Inspector,' said Mary Ann.

'You are most kind,' said Ravenscroft pouring out a cup of coffee.

'I believe you caught the unfortunate man who committed the dreadful crime,' said Emily.

'Yes. It appears that it was a bargeman by the name of Billy who killed Miss Weston.'

'How awful!'

'Two deaths in such a short time!'

'Worcester is usually such a quiet, respectable place.'

'I realize that all this must have been quite distressing for you ladies, but I am sure once we have recovered the *Whisperie*, Worcester will return to its former quiet, law-abiding ways.'

'Why was poor Miss Weston killed? Why should all this have come to pass?' asked Mary Ann, a worried expression on her face.

'I wish I could answer that question ladies, but unfortunately at the present I am unable to do so, but I think it is only a matter of time before the full truth will be revealed,' said Ravenscroft with confidence.

'It has been such a terrible time,' said Miss Alice Maria.

'Not since that poor boy died all those years ago in the cathedral—' began Miss Emily.

'Shush, my dear, I'm sure the inspector will not want to know about that,' said Mary Ann quickly reprimanding her sister.

'It was all such a long time ago,' added Alice Maria.

'On the contrary, I would be obliged if you would enlighten me further,' said Ravenscroft leaning forwards in his chair.

'How long ago was it, Sister?' asked Emily.

'1851. Yes it was 1851. I remember the year exactly. It was the year Father took us all up to London to see the Great Exhibition,' replied Mary Ann.

'You mentioned something about a boy dying in the cathedral?'

'The poor boy killed himself!'

'He was found hanging from a rope one morning.'

'He was one of the choirboys.'

'You say one of the choirboys committed suicide in 1851. Thirty-seven years ago. Did they ever find out why he killed himself?' asked Ravenscroft anxious to learn more.

'No. I think there was an inquest,' said Mary Ann.

'But they said they could find no reason as to why such a young boy should have killed himself,' added Alice Maria.

'How old was he?' asked Ravenscroft.

'Thirteen I think,' said the eldest sister.

'No, no, my dear, I think he was fourteen,' corrected Emily.

'No sister, I remember distinctly the coroner saying he was just twelve,' interjected Alice Maria shaking her head.

'Do you happen to remember the name of the boy?' asked Ravenscroft replacing his coffee cup on the small table at the side of his chair.

The three sisters fell strangely silent for a few moments, as each tried to remember the name of the boy.

'No matter, ladies,' said Ravenscroft presently.

'I'm sorry, Inspector.'

'Please don't worry. Perhaps you would be kind enough to let me know if you recall the name of the poor unfortunate boy. You say he was a choirboy. Then he would have been a pupil at King's School,' asked Ravenscroft.

'All the choirboys are pupils of the school,' said Alice Maria.

'Then I may be able to find out more from Dr Edwards and from the school records. Thank you, ladies, for the coffee,' said Ravenscroft rising from his seat.

'I do so hope that we have been of some assistance to you, Inspector?' said Mary Ann.

'You have been most helpful.'

'Do please call and see us again,' said Alice Maria.

'I certainly will. Good day to you, ladies,' said Ravenscroft taking his leave, his mind occupied with thoughts of the choirboy who had taken his life thirty-seven years ago and wondering whether this new line of enquiry would prove to have any bearing on the events he was currently investigating.

'Well, Crabb, what did your research at the library reveal?' asked Ravenscroft, as they stood outside the entrance to King's School, later that morning.

'I discovered that there are no less than five auction houses in New York. I have their names and addresses here. Shall we contact them, sir?'

'It might take too long. No, at the present we will wait for Renfrew's return and see what he has to say about the purchase of the *Antiphoner*. At present I am more interested to learn about this choirboy who hanged himself all those years ago.'

'Can't see how it can help us with our investigations,' replied Crabb, pulling the bell at the side of the door.

'At the present, neither can I, but I feel it is a line of enquiry that may prove of value to us.'

'Good morning to you, gentlemen,' said the porter opening the door.

'We would like to see Dr Edwards, if you please,' said Ravenscroft.

'Certainly, sir, I will see whether he is free. Who shall I say has called?'

'Inspector Ravenscroft and Constable Crabb. We have spoken to Dr Edwards before. I am sure he will remember us.'

'If you would care to wait in the hall, gentlemen,' said the elderly porter eying them with a degree of suspicion, before shuffling off down a long passageway.

Ravenscroft and Crabb waited silently, passing the time in examining the various portraits and photographs, of past masters and recent boys, that hung on the walls.

'Doctor Edwards will see you now, gentlemen. If you would care to follow me,' said the porter returning.

The two detectives followed the servant until they reached a door which was opened to reveal a book-lined study.

'Good morning, gentlemen,' said Edwards in his loud Welsh voice.

'Good morning to you, Dr Edwards,' said Ravenscroft, shaking hands with the headmaster.

'Please do sit down. How can I help you? I think I told you all I knew about the night I met Evelyn, when we last met, Inspector. I'm sure that I have nothing further to add,' said Edwards.

'I have come to see you on an entirely different matter. I have just learnt that in the year 1851 a choirboy from this school committed suicide and I was wondering whether you could throw any light on the matter?'

'Good heavens. 1851. That was long before my arrival here.'

'We appreciate that, sir. You arrived in. . . ?'

'1876.'

'When you came to King's did anyone mention anything about the incident?' asked Ravenscroft.

'How have you come by this knowledge?' asked Edwards. Ravenscroft thought he could detect a degree of caution creeping into the schoolmaster's voice.

'The Tovey sisters recalled the incident to me. Apparently their late father had been a teacher here at the school.'

'So I believe, although he had died many years before my own arrival here. I must confess, Inspector, that this is the first time anyone has spoken to me about such an incident. Certainly no one mentioned it to me when I arrived twelve years ago, but then there was probably hardly anyone on the staff who would have been here as long ago as 1851,' replied Edwards removing his spectacles and breathing on them before wiping them on a cloth which lay on his desk.

'I see,' said Ravenscroft.

'Perhaps the Tovey sisters' memories are at fault. They could be confused. Age can play many tricks. Maybe the incident happened elsewhere or at an earlier date,' suggested Edwards, replacing the glasses on the end of his long nose.

'They seemed quite certain, although I must admit that they could not remember the boy's name. Does the school keep records?' asked Ravenscroft.

'It does, going back many years. There might be something here,' said the master rising from his seat somewhat reluctantly, and walking over to one of the large bookcases. '1851? Let me see. 1840. 1845. 1850. Yes, here we are, 1851,' he said, taking down a large volume from the shelves and laying it upon the table. 'If you would care to go through it, gentlemen, you might find something. You don't mind if I carry on writing a few letters?'

'Not at all,' replied Ravenscroft, opening the volume.

For the next few minutes the two policemen worked in silence, turning over the pages of the school records, whilst Edwards busied himself with his correspondence.

'Nothing at all!' announced Ravenscroft, sighing and closing the volume.

'Perhaps the Tovey sisters had the wrong year?' suggested Crabb.

'No. They were most insistent that the year was 1851. They remembered it because their father took them to see the Great Exhibition.'

'Well, gentlemen, it appears that the school can be of little assistance to you in this digression from your investigations,' said Edwards, in a tone which Ravenscroft felt almost bordered on sarcasm.

'Thank you for your time, Dr Edwards.'

Edwards looked up briefly from his writing, and gave Ravenscroft and Crabb a casual glance as they left the room.

'Well, no luck there. I thought Edwards was a bit off hand.'

'He was probably not too enthusiastic our searching through the school records,' replied Ravenscroft.

'Perhaps your Tovey sisters invented the whole story,' suggested Crabb as the two men walked away from the school.

'No. I consider it the more likely that the school did not enter details of the incident because they felt it reflected badly on them. If there was such an incident, they obviously thought it better to forget that it ever happened at all.'

'You could be right. But if the school has no record of the incident, what are we to do?'

'The Tovey sisters said there was an inquest. It could be that the local paper sent a reporter to cover it. Take me to the library, Crabb. Let us see if they have any back copies filed away.'

'Constable Crabb, you are becoming almost a regular visitor,' remarked the librarian looking up from his desk as the two detectives entered.

'This is my inspector,' said Crabb.

Ravenscroft and the librarian shook hands.

'Well, gentlemen, how can I be of assistance to you?'

'We understand that you might keep back copies of the local paper here in the library,' asked Ravenscroft.

'Yes, we have bound volumes of the *Worcester Guardian* going back many years. They are bound in half-yearly volumes. Was there a particular year that you would like to examine?'

'1851,' said Ravenscroft.

'The year of the Great Exhibition,' added Crabb, trying to be helpful.

'If you would care to take a seat, gentlemen, I won't keep you long,' said the librarian, before disappearing into a back room.

The two men busied themselves in looking at the books on the shelves, before the librarian returned a few minutes later bearing two large volumes which he placed on the table. '1851,' he announced. 'I'll leave you to it, gentlemen. Just call me when you have finished.'

'Thank you,' said Ravenscroft, opening one of the volumes. 'You take the second half of the year in that one, Crabb. See if there is a report of the coroner's inquest into the death of the choirboy.'

As they turned over the pages of the bound weekly newspaper, the only noise which disturbed their research came from the tall grandfather clock which ticked regularly in the corner of the library.

'Absolutely nothing!' said Ravenscroft closing the volume shut after what had seemed more than an hour. 'Absolutely nothing. There are reports of quite a few inquests, but nothing that faintly resembles the death of a young boy.'

'No luck here either,' added a dispirited Crabb.

'You know, I am beginning to think that both you and Dr Edwards are correct in your opinions, and that those Tovey sisters invented the whole business just to confuse,' said Ravenscroft, a look of annoyance on his face.

'Never mind. The boy's death probably has nothing to do with the case anyway.'

'You could be right. However, there is just one more avenue still left open to us. Call the librarian Crabb.'

Crabb made his way out of the room, returning a few moments later with the custodian of the books. 'I understand that your search has been unsuccessful?' said the librarian.

'It would appear so. We were searching for a possible report into the death of a young choirboy in the year 1851, but it would seem that the newspaper failed to cover the story,' said Ravenscroft.

'Ah, that would be the young boy who hanged himself.'

'You know about the incident?' inquired Ravenscroft optimistically.

'Yes, I attended the inquest. I had just arrived in Worcester and everyone was talking about the poor boy. I had the afternoon free from my duties, and so decided to attend the inquest.'

'Please, go on,' urged Ravenscroft.

'Well, sir, I can't recall much about the actual inquest. It was a long time ago, but I do remember the coroner saying that on account of the boy's age and given the circumstances of his demise, all reporters were asked to remove themselves and were forbidden to print any details relating to the case,' said the librarian scratching his head.

'So that is why there is no report in the paper,' said Crabb.

'Exactly. So the Tovey sisters did not invent the story, after all. Tell me, do you remember anything else about the inquest, – such as the name of the boy, why he killed himself, anything at all?' asked Ravenscroft.

'I'm sorry, I can't help you any further. The memory is not what it was,' said the librarian after some moments.

'You have been most helpful. There is, however, one more thing that you might be able to help us with. Would you happen to know whether the Coroner's original records were kept, and if so, where they might be?'

'Oh, they'll be over at the County Court offices, if they are still there. I believe quite a few of the records were destroyed some years ago in a fire, but you could be fortunate.'

'Then that is where we shall go next. Thank you once again for your valuable assistance,' said Ravenscroft before leaving, a new sense of purpose in his stride.

A few minutes later the two men found themselves in the outer annexe of the County Court buildings. Crabb rang the bell in the gloomy, dank room.

'Yes?' said an elderly clerk, presently appearing from an inner room.

'We are given to understand that the records of Coroner's inquests are kept here,' said Ravenscroft.

'Maybe,' came back the unhelpful reply.

'We are interested in an inquest that was held in Worcester, in the year 1851,' said Ravenscroft.

'Are you?' sniffed the clerk, looking away.

'Could you see whether you still have the records for that year?'

'Can't do that.'

'Why not?' asked Ravenscroft becoming annoyed.

'Records are secret,' mumbled the clerk, giving another, longer, sniff.

'Why?'

'Rules is rules.'

'Yes, but why?' persisted Ravenscroft.

'Confidentiality! That's why,' retorted the clerk.

'Now look here, I am Inspector Ravenscroft of the Worcester Constabulary—'

'Don't care who you are. Records are secret. Not to be disclosed to anyone.'

'—and we are investigating the deaths of two, possibly three people,' continued Ravenscroft showing the man his credentials.

'Still can't help. Anyway if you say who you are, why do you want to look at Coroner's records that are nearly forty years old?' replied the clerk, reasserting his authority, and sniffing again as he did so.

'Are you going to let me see the reports for 1851, or not?' asked Ravenscroft, angry at the clerk's intransigence.

'No!'

'It may prove the worse for you,' said Ravenscroft firmly.

'Doubt that,' sniffed the clerk, making ready to go back into his inner sanctum.

'I want to have a word with your superior,' said Ravenscroft, trying one last throw.

The clerk looked up and gave Ravenscroft a surely look. 'There's no superior. I'm in charge. Rules says you cannot look at the records, so you can't look at them, and that's all there is to it.'

'If you don't let me examine the papers, I will return with a search warrant within the hour, and you will find yourself in a cell in Worcester Gaol facing a charge of police obstruction! I trust I make myself clear? I want to see the coroner's reports for 1851. I will not ask again,' said Ravenscroft, in a determined voice and facing the clerk head on.

'Wait here,' said the clerk disappearing into the back room.

'What a miserable, surly fellow,' said Crabb, as Ravenscroft sought to regain his composure. 'Whole place could do with brightening up.'

After a few minutes the clerk returned with a large ledger which he threw down on the desk.

'Thank you,' said Ravenscroft, opening the volume.

'I'll have to remain while you read it,' said the clerk, taking up a defensive position in the corner of the room.

Ravenscroft ignored him, and turned over the pages of the book as Crabb looked on. 'Ah, here we are: Inquest into the death of Martin Tinniswood, age thirteen, held on the 12 March, 1851. All Press asked to leave and not to report any details of the case.'

Ravenscroft read the rest of the coroner's inquest in silence, running his finger along the lines of ink on the page as he did so. 'Thank you my man,' he said eventually closing the volume. 'Good day.'

'What did the report say?' asked Crabb eagerly, as the pair made their way back along Foregate Street.

'It appears that young Martin Tinniswood committed suicide because of the "distressed nature of his mind" to quote the Coroner's words,' said Ravenscroft deep in thought.

'Then it would seem that his death has no bearing at all on our present investigation?' said Crabb, feeling rather disappointed at the outcome of all their research.

'Far from it. Far from it! I now know what had worried Evelyn for all those years and why he had felt compelled to lead the life of a recluse.'

'You've lost me, sir.'

'The choirboy hanged himself from one of the beams in the library – and it was Nicholas Evelyn who discovered the body!'

CHAPTER ELEVEN

'So it would seem that Nicholas Evelyn had something to do with that choirboy who hanged himself in the library, all those years ago,' said Crabb.

It was the following morning and the two detectives were on their way to see Dr Silas Renfrew.

'I think it was more than that. The event had a profound effect on the rest of Evelyn's life. He became a recluse, immersing himself in his books, spending his evenings alone in that awful room, making no friends and avoiding all company. Somehow he must have felt himself responsible for the boy's death. He withdrew into himself. Then one day someone came along and threatened to disclose Evelyn's involvement in the boy's death unless he stole the *Whisperie* – and when he had carried out the task he was brutally killed and thrown into the river,' said Ravenscroft.

'Then Miss Weston found out who had killed Evelyn, and before she could tell, our murderer hired Billy to kill her as well,' suggested Crabb.

'It would appear to be that way.'

'But how would our murderer have discovered Evelyn's involvement in the boy's suicide? After all there were no newspaper reports and there are no records in King's School concerning the death.'

'Which leads us to the conclusion that either our murderer was there at the time – in 1851 – or that he later became involved with the boy's family and learned of the death that way,' said Ravenscroft.

'If he was around in 1851 that would rule out most of our suspects. Renfrew would have been too young and was living in America, and both Sir Arthur Griffiths and Cranston were either small children at the time or had not even been born.'

'This case certainly throws up more possibilities the further we go back in time. Talking of Renfrew, here we are. Let us hope he has returned.'

The two men alighted from the cab and gave instructions that their driver was to wait for them.

'No sign of the gardener today,' said Crabb, lifting the large knocker and bringing it down on the wooden door. Almost before he had laid the knocker to rest, the door was abruptly opened by Georgio, the manservant.

'Good morning,' said Ravenscroft, 'is your master at home?'

The Italian looked them up and down suspiciously, then remarked, 'You a wait here,' before opening the door wider, and admitting the two men into the hall.

'Blimey!' said Crabb observing the statue of the naked David at the bottom of the stairs, as the manservant disappeared into one of the back rooms.

'Our doctor is a man of liberal tastes,' smiled Ravenscroft.

'Positively obscene I call it!'

The doors to the library opened and Renfrew strode out. 'Good morning, Inspector. I see we meet again,' said the American, offering his hand. As Ravenscroft shook it, he experienced the same iron grip as before. 'Do please come into the library. Can I offer you a drink perhaps?'

'No, thank you, sir. We won't detain you long,' replied Ravenscroft following his host into the room.

'Dear me, Inspector, that all sounds very formal. Thank you, Georgio, you may leave us.'

The manservant gave a slight bow and stared at Crabb again, before leaving the room.

'Now Inspector, have you called upon me to tell me that you have found the *Whisperie*?' asked Renfrew, in his slow American drawl.

'Alas, no, Dr Renfrew,' replied Ravenscroft, as Crabb busied himself by casting glances round the room.

'Then it must be concerning the *Antiphoner*.'

'You are correct, sir.'

'I knew that it would only be a matter of time before you returned, wanting to know more about my purchase of the work,' said the American with confidence.

'It might interest you to know, Dr Renfrew, that I have reason to believe that the *Antiphoner* was stolen some years ago from the library of Worcester Cathedral,' said Ravenscroft looking into the American's eyes to see if his sudden declaration had any noticeable effect on his host.

'I see. Do you have any evidence to support this view?' asked Renfrew unperturbed.

'We examined the catalogue of the collection. The page which contained details of the *Antiphoner* had clearly been removed.'

'Then this is of serious concern,' replied Renfrew looking away.

'You mentioned that you purchased the work from a New York auction house approximately five years ago, I think you said.'

'That is correct, Inspector.'

'Do you have any documentation to prove that you did indeed purchase it?' asked Ravenscroft.

'Do you think that I took it from the cathedral library, or that I paid Evelyn to acquire it for me?'

'I did not suggest that, sir.'

'But you consider it a distinct possibility.'

'I have to keep an open mind,' said Ravenscroft, forcing a smile.

'I think I have proof of purchase. If you will allow me time to search through my papers, Inspector?'

'Of course.'

'I know the purchase cost me a great deal of money. I had to sell a number of my American stocks to fund it,' said Renfrew, opening the top drawer of his desk and taking out a folder of papers.

'Perhaps you would allow me to show my constable the work in question?'

'Please, feel free, Inspector.'

Ravenscroft and Crabb walked over to the glass cabinet which contained the *Antiphoner*.

'Late fourteenth century, I think you said, sir?' said Ravenscroft.

'Yes,' said Renfrew, going through his papers.

'Don't think I've ever seen a work as old as that before.'

'Handwritten by the monks here at Worcester,' added Ravenscroft.

'Ah, here we are. I think you will find that this is in order,' said Renfrew rising from his seat and handing over a sheet of paper.

'Thank you. I see what you mean about a great deal of money.'

'And worth every cent, I can assure you.'

'This paper certainly indicates that you purchased the work in good faith from the auction house. Would you happen to know who the previous owner was?' asked Ravenscroft.

'I'm afraid I can't help you there. Most of these things are said to come from the "estate of an English gentleman", which generally means that either some lord or other has died and his heirs are cashing in on his estate, or that some poor aristocrat has had to sell the family heirlooms to pay off his gambling debts.'

'May I retain this receipt for a while?'

'Certainly.'

'You realize, sir, that if we find that the *Antiphoner* was taken from the cathedral, then the work will almost certainly have to be returned to the cathedral authorities,' said Ravenscroft, neatly folding the paper and placing it in one of his coat pockets.

'That I would be very loath to do – but then, as you say, Inspector, you have to prove that it was taken in the first place,' replied Renfrew defiantly.

'Oh, I think we might be able to do that, sir. In the meantime, I would ask you not to sell or dispose of it.'

'I would be unlikely to do that. The *Antiphoner* is the pride of my collection. I would be unwilling to part with it.'

'Thank you for your time.'

Renfrew rang a bell. 'Please feel free to call upon me at anytime you so wish.'

The manservant entered the room almost immediately.

'Georgio, would you please show these two gentlemen out.'

Ravenscroft and Crabb followed him into the hall.

'Until next time, Inspector,' shouted out Renfrew from the study.

The two men walked back to their waiting cab.

'He seems very sure of himself, and he didn't like it when he thought you might be taking the *Antiphoner* from him,' said Crabb.

'Our Dr Renfrew has an answer for everything. I have the distinct impression that he either stole the book from the cathedral library, or purchased it from someone else who took it. In which case, this paper is almost certainly a forgery. Did you notice how quickly he found the receipt amongst his papers? It was almost as though he knew we would be arriving and had his story and this paper to hand,' said Ravenscroft, patting the horse before climbing into the cab.

'I can't say I liked him much. He was too full of his own importance if you ask me. Don't trust these Americans,' said Crabb.

'Where to now, governor?' asked their driver cracking his whip.

'Back to Worcester if you please.'

'Didn't like the look of that Italian fellow either. Looked a bit suspicious to me,' added Crabb.

'I agree. Not the kind of man you would want to cross swords with in a dark alley late at night.'

Ten minutes later, the two men alighted from the cab and made their way over to Glovers Lodging-house, where Crabb banged his fist on the door.

'Lord above if it ain't the peelers again,' muttered Mrs Glover, reluctantly opening the door.

'I'm sorry to disturb you, Mrs Glover. We wondered whether Mr Cranston has returned from London?' asked Ravenscroft.

'He came in about ten minutes ago.'

'Then may we come in and have a word with him, if you please?'

The old woman said nothing, allowing them to enter and make their way up the stairs.

Ravenscroft knocked on the door to Cranston's rooms.

'Coming, Mrs Glover,' shouted the voice from within. There followed a long silence, during which Ravenscroft shuffled his feet, as Crabb looked down over the banisters.

Presently they heard the sound of a key being turned in the lock. 'Oh, it's you again, Inspector,' said Cranston, opening the door with a look of annoyance.

'Good morning, Mr Cranston. May we come in? We won't take up too much of your time,' said Ravenscroft, trying to sound as polite as he could.

'If you must,' sighed Cranston turning away.

'Thank you, sir, I see that you have just returned from London. I trust you managed to conclude your business to your own satisfaction?'

'I'm sure that my business concerns are of little interest to you,' replied Cranston, affecting an air of indifference.

'Oh, that is where you are incorrect, sir. Your business affairs interest us a great deal. When we spoke the other day, you stated – unless I am mistaken – that before you came to Worcester you were employed by the

Wedgewood Company at Stoke on Trent,' said Ravenscroft, casting his eyes round the contents of the room.

'That is so, Inspector, but I fail to see the significance of all this,' replied Cranston irritably.

'We have reason to believe that you lied to us, Mr Cranston.'

'Now look here—'

'It might interest you to know that they have not heard of you at Wedgewood. There is no trace of you having been employed by them.'

'Then they must be mistaken. I was employed there for six years,' replied Cranston adamantly.

'That is not what they say.'

'As I have just said, Inspector, they must be mistaken. Wedgewood are a large concern. There are a number of departments. I'm sure if you ask again, they will find details of my employment. Now, if you will excuse me, there is a great deal of paperwork that I must complete before the end of the morning.'

'Do you mind if we take a look around your rooms, sir?' asked Ravenscroft.

'I certainly do mind,' replied Cranston angrily.

'It won't take a minute.'

'The devil it will!'

'I could return with a written authorization from my superiors, Mr Cranston,' said Ravenscroft, trying to remain as calm as he could.

'Then I suggest you do so,' snapped Cranston.

'I'm sure that if you have nothing to hide, you cannot possibly object.'

'But I do object, most strongly – and no, I have nothing to hide. I regard all this as police harassment, and will be lodging a complaint with your superiors,' said Cranston firmly, looking Ravenscroft in the eye.

'That is your decision.'

'I don't like your tone, Inspector. I said all I had to say on your last visit here. I am not involved in the murders of either Mr Evelyn or Miss Weston. In fact I was not in Worcester on either of the two nights in question, facts that can be easily checked by reference to my employers, if you consider it worth the effort to do so,' replied Cranston sarcastically.

'You seem remarkably well informed about the events we are investigating for someone who is seldom in Worcester,' said Ravenscroft.

'I read the papers. I like to be kept informed. Now I think it is time you left. I shall be seeking legal representation in this matter and, as I said, I will be lodging a complaint. You have not heard the last of this, Ravenscroft.'

'That sounds remarkably like a threat to me, Mr Cranston,' said Ravenscroft firmly.

'That is your interpretation. Now I suggest you leave, before you say something you may later regret,' said Cranston opening the door.

'Mr Cranston, I am not satisfied with your answers, and further investigation concerning the nature of your activities before your arrival in Worcester, will be conducted. I wish you a good day.'

The policemen quickly made their way down the stairs as the door to Cranston's room banged shut behind them.

'Nasty, unpleasant fellow!' remarked Crabb.

'My sentiments exactly. I tell you, Crabb, I was an inch away from instructing you to put the cuffs on him. Our Mr Cranston has something to hide. I am sure he is involved in these two murders.'

'Shall we come back with a warrant to search his rooms?'

'I doubt we would find anything. It would not surprise me, however, if we discover that Cranston is not his real name.'

'You mean he could have been in prison before he came to Worcester?' asked Crabb.

'Most likely, I would say,' said Ravenscroft reaching the lower floor, where an anxious Mrs Glover was waiting.

'Have you finished then?' asked the old woman.

'For the present, thank you, Mrs Glover,' smiled Ravenscroft.

'I wants to let them rooms. We can't be having two rooms empty where there is no one to pay the rent. Old Glover would turn in his grave if he thought there was no money coming in.'

'I quite understand, Mrs Glover. I don't think we will need access again to either Mr Evelyn or Miss Weston's rooms, so, yes, do go ahead and secure new tenants if you so wish.'

'Then you best have this then,' said the landlady, leading the way into Ruth Weston's old rooms. Ravenscroft followed on behind, wondering what it was that she wanted to give him. 'You best have that. I've no use for it,' she said, handing him the hand-embroidered tablecloth. 'Lad might want it, when he's older.'

'Thank you, Mrs Glover. I'm sure he will,' said Ravenscroft, folding up the cloth. 'Thank you once again for all your assistance.'

The old woman showed them out, and the two men walked away from the lodging-house.

'I think our Mrs Glover will be pleased to see the back of us.'

'Do you want me to take the cloth and give it to the lad?' asked Crabb.

'If you would be so kind; this was the tablecloth that Ruth Weston embroidered with the names 'Arthur and Ruth' – the names which I presume refer to herself and her son. Of course!' said Ravenscroft, stopping suddenly.

'What's the matter, sir?' asked Crabb.

' "One day my son will live in that house", that's what she said to me.'

'Sorry, sir, you've lost me.' said Crabb bewildered.

'The day I met Ruth Weston she said to me that one day her son would live in "that house". We were facing Sir Arthur Griffiths' house at the time. One day her son would live in the house. Come, Crabb, back to the Court offices before they close for the day. There are some more records we need to examine urgently!'

'Yes?' said the clerk appearing from the inner office. 'Oh, it's you again.'

'We require some more information,' said Ravenscroft.

'We're closing in five minutes,' sniffed the clerk.

'Then there is just time for you to bring me the Birth Registers, for the years 1881 and 1882, if you please.'

'Might take me longer than five minutes,' grumbled the clerk.

'We are content to wait. I'm sure it will not take you long to find them,' insisted Ravenscroft.

'Better if you came back tomorrow.'

'I don't want to come back tomorrow.'

'Suit yourselves then.'

'Now look here, we are on urgent police business which can't wait until tomorrow,' said Ravenscroft, remembering his previous encounter with the clerk and becoming annoyed.

'Better tomorrow,' repeated the clerk, giving another long sniff.

'See here, if you do not bring me the registers within the next five minutes, you will find yourself facing a charge of hindering the police in the pursuance of their duty. I need not remind you of the seriousness of this offence. You would almost certainly lose your employment as a result

of facing such a charge. I trust I make myself clear?' said Ravenscroft leaning over the counter in a slightly menacing way.

The clerk said nothing as he shuffled away.

'Why do we need to look at the registers, sir?' asked Crabb.

'I hope we can find details relating to the birth of Ruth Weston's child.'

The clerk returned bearing two ledgers which he banged down on the
table. 'Closing in two minutes!'

'You take 1881, I'll take 1882. Look for an entry for Weston,' instructed
Ravenscroft, ignoring the clerk.

The two men busied themselves in turning over the pages as the clerk
stood in the corner of the room shuffling his feet, and giving the occasional sniff.

'Here we are!' exclaimed Crabb, after a few minutes.

'Well done,' said Ravenscroft, leaning over his shoulder. 'Christian
names – Arthur, Granville, Sackville, Boscawen, Griffiths. Name of father
left blank. Name of mother – Ruth Weston. Informant – Ruth Weston.'

'I've seen those Christian names before,' said Crabb.

'So have I. If I recall correctly, you discovered from your research in the
library that Arthur, Granville, Sackville, and Boscawen were all Christian
names of Sir Arthur Griffiths. Ruth gave her son not only all those names
but also Griffiths as well. It was as though she was telling anyone who
came after her, that Sir Arthur Griffiths was the boy's father, although she
felt compelled not to name him as such on the birth certificate,' whispered
Ravenscroft, so that the clerk would not hear.

'And that is why Sir Arthur did not dismiss her,' said Crabb.

'Exactly! He may have had some feelings for the mother and child, but
could not admit publicly that he was the father. That is why Ruth took
the boy on to the green every day, before she went to work, and why she
said to me that one day her son would live in that house. She hoped that
eventually Sir Arthur would acknowledge his son, and that the boy
would assume his rightful place. The Arthur and Ruth embroidered on
the cloth does not stand for Ruth and her son, they represent Ruth and
Sir Arthur!'

The clerk let out a loud sneeze.

'I'm sorry we have detained you,' said Ravenscroft, closing the ledger.

'Got what you came for?' muttered the clerk.

'Yes, thank you, my man. You can lock up now.'

'Trust you won't be needing anything else?' said the clerk picking up the ledgers.

'At this moment, I do not believe so – but you can never tell,' said Ravenscroft, smiling.

The clerk scowled as he locked the door behind them.

'Well, this puts a new face on the case,' said Crabb, as they walked along Foregate Street.

'Maybe. If Sir Arthur is the boy's father – and the evidence would tend to suggest that is the case – then we need to confront him with our findings. Do you know, Crabb, I am beginning to find that this case is becoming more and more like an onion every day,' said Ravenscroft.

'An onion?'

'As we uncover another layer of the truth, so we near the centre of the onion where the solution promises to be found. The only problem is – our onion is quite a large one, and has many skins.'

Ten minutes later the two men found themselves standing outside the home of Sir Arthur Griffiths.

'I don't think he will be too pleased to see us when he hears what we have to say,' said Crabb.

The maid opened the door.

'Is Sir Arthur in residence today?' asked Ravenscroft.

'Yes, sir.'

'It is very important that we have words with him.'

'If you would both care to wait in the hall, sir. The master has someone with him at the moment, but I will inform him of your arrival.' Ravenscroft and Crabb stepped inside, as the maid knocked on the door of the drawing-room, and disappeared from view.

'I must admit that I am not looking forward to this interview,' said Ravenscroft, walking up and down the hallway.

'My dear Ravenscroft, good to see you again. I hear you have apprehended the felon who killed poor Miss Weston,' said Sir Arthur opening the door suddenly and striding out into the hall. 'Well done. I always knew you were the man for the job.'

'Unfortunately the man was killed before he could tell us anything,' replied Ravenscroft.

'Does that matter?' asked Sir Arthur. 'After all you must have been sure of your evidence.'

'Indeed, Sir Arthur. However, the case has not been completely solved. There have been some recent developments that I need to discuss with you.'

'I see. Well, you'd best come into the drawing-room,' replied the politician leading the way.

'Thank you, sir.'

'May I introduce you to Mrs Marchmont?' said Sir Arthur.

Ravenscroft paused momentarily: the lady sitting on one of the drawing-room chairs was the last person he had expected to encounter that day.

'This is Inspector Ravenscroft, my dear. He has been investigating the death of my servant, Ruth Weston.'

'Mrs Marchmont,' said Ravenscroft, recovering his composure and giving a slight bow in the lady's direction.

'Inspector Ravenscroft,' said the lady, whom Ravenscroft had known as Mrs Kelly.

'You two look as though you have met somewhere before,' said Sir Arthur.

'No. I don't believe Inspector Ravenscroft and I have ever spoken together,' smiled Mrs Marchmont.

'Well, Ravenscroft, what's all this about? You said there had been some developments in the case?' asked Sir Arthur.

'My news is of a rather delicate, personal nature,' said Ravenscroft, giving a sideways glance at Mrs Marchmont.

'I see. I wonder, my dear, if you would excuse us for a few minutes?' said Sir Arthur.

'Of course, Sir Arthur. It is time I was returning home. If you will excuse me, gentlemen?' said Mrs Marchmont smiling.

'Then let me see you out, my dear lady,' offered Sir Arthur.

'Good day to you, Inspector.'

'Good day to you, Mrs Marchmont,' said Ravenscroft stepping to one side of the room, 'Perhaps we shall meet again sometime in the future.'

'I have no doubt of it, Inspector,' replied Mrs Marchmont, with a certainty that Ravenscroft found unnerving, and she left the room accompanied by Sir Arthur.

The door closed behind them. 'That's twice we have seen your lady in black here,' whispered Crabb.

'More than a coincidence?' remarked Ravenscroft, straining to hear what was being said beyond the closed door.

'They seem to be on good terms with one another,' suggested Crabb.

The door opened and Sir Arthur strode in once more. 'Now then, Ravenscroft, take a seat. What can I do for you?'

'I don't quite know how to put this to you,' said Ravenscroft, accepting the offer. 'What I have to say may not be of a welcome nature.'

'Out with it, man. No need to beat about the bush. I always believe in a direct approach,' said Sir Arthur.

'During our investigations into the brutal murder of your maid, Ruth Weston, I had cause to inspect the official registers for the birth of her son, Arthur,' began Ravenscroft.

'What on earth for? What has the birth of Ruth Weston's son to do with her death?' asked Sir Arthur, sitting uneasily in his chair.

'Bear with me, sir. I found that the child had been christened Arthur, Granville, Sackville, Boscawen, Griffiths Weston. You will note, sir, that the first four Christian names are the same as your own, and that the last Christian name – Griffiths – is your own surname. The father is not named however, on the birth entry,' said Ravenscroft in as formal and calm manner as he could.

'I see.' Sir Arthur rose from his seat and walked over to the window, where he remained silent for some moments. Ravenscroft looked across at Crabb and wondered whether he had been too blunt in his approach. 'You have done well, Inspector. So you have discovered my little secret. Yes, I was the father of Ruth Weston's child. My wife had been dead for some years when Miss Weston entered my household – and yes, I must admit that I abused my position as her employer and benefactor – and in a moment of weakness took advantage of her. I am not particularly proud of my actions, and I do not expect you to understand the loneliness I was feeling at the time, although I might add that my attentions were recipro-cated by the other party. You must appreciate, however, that I could not acknowledge the child as my own. That would have led to my ruin and would have served little purpose. All I could do was to see that Ruth and her son were found lodgings in the town, and that she continued in my employ, so that I might be able to see that no harm should befall either of them. I suppose you would seek to condemn my actions.'

'It is not my role to either approve or disapprove of your actions, Sir Arthur.'

'Look, does all this need to come out? As you say, you have caught Ruth's murderer, so what possible good can come of making public the parentage of the boy?' said Sir Arthur resuming his seat.

'Although Billy, the bargeman, killed her, we believe that he was paid to do so by another party whose identity is at present unknown to us. We believe that she had probably discovered the identity of the man who had killed Nicholas Evelyn the librarian, and consequently she suffered the same fate that had befallen him. Whoever took the *Whisperie* and killed Evelyn, also paid Billy to kill Ruth Weston.'

'And do you have any notion as to who this person is?'

'At the moment we are following several lines of inquiry, and have a number of possible suspects under consideration,' replied the inspector, trying to sound as confident as he could.

'Then there is no reason why the parentage of Ruth Weston's son should be made public, as it clearly has no bearing on the case,' suggested Sir Arthur nervously.

'It would seem that way, Sir Arthur.'

'Then can I have your assurance that what I have told you today will not enter into the public domain?' asked the politician.

'I cannot give you a complete assurance on that score,' said Ravenscroft, 'but you have my word, Sir Arthur, that the true parentage of Ruth Weston's child will not be made public, unless I find that it has a direct bearing on this case. That is all I can say at present.'

'Then, that is all I can ask for. I thank you, Inspector,' said Sir Arthur, rising from his seat and offering his hand.

'Rest assured, we will do all in our power to find the murderer of Nicholas Evelyn and Ruth Weston, and bring him to justice,' said Ravenscroft, shaking the outstretched hand.

'I wish you well, Inspector, in your investigations. If you require any assistance, at any time, then please call on me.'

They began to walk out of the room, but were unexpectedly called back by their host. 'Tell me one more thing.'

'Sir Arthur?'

'The boy – where is the boy now?'

'The child, Arthur, is being cared for by the wife of my colleague here, Constable Crabb, but such an arrangement, of course, can only be of a temporary nature,' replied Ravenscroft.

'And eventually?'

'We would need to place him with the appropriate authorities.'

'By which you mean the workhouse?'

'Until he should come of age to secure an apprenticeship of some kind, or unless—'

'Thank you, Inspector,' said Sir Arthur quickly, interrupting and turning away.

Ravenscroft closed the door behind him, and he and Crabb stepped out on to the green and into the early autumn sunshine.

CHAPTER TWELVE

'Sit down, Ravenscroft.'

'Thank you, sir.'

'Not a very pleasant thing to receive,' said Superintendent Henderson, brandishing a sheet of paper.

'No, sir,' replied Ravenscroft, guessing what was about to happen next.

'Apparently you have had dealings with some fellow called Cranston.'

'I have had cause to interview him on two occasions, in connection with our investigations, yes, sir.'

'He says you were rude and objectionable. Wanted to search his rooms, and when he refused, he says that you were heavy handed and threatened him with all manner of things,' said Henderson, glowering.

'That is an incorrect accusation. I certainly wanted to search his rooms, and he did object, but at no time did I threaten him. Nor was I rude or objectionable,' replied Ravenscroft, beginning to feel uncomfortable.

'Well, that's not what he says here. Apparently he's got some smart London brief called Sefton Rawlinson to represent him. Says he knows you.'

'I have encountered the said legal gentleman in the courts of the Old Bailey,' Ravenscroft said, fearing the worst.

'This fellow Rawlinson says you are victimizing Cranston, and that if you have any further contact with his client, he will take legal action against both the force and yourself. I view this as a grave matter, Ravenscroft, a very grave matter indeed.'

'Yes, sir.'

'Damn it man, can't you see that anything which brings the force into disrepute, is not to be tolerated?' barked Henderson.

'I understand.'

'Just who is this Cranston fellow anyway?'

'He is a commercial traveller with the Worcester Porcelain Company. He lives at the same premises as the victims, Nicholas Evelyn and Ruth Weston. That is why I decided to interview him. He proved the most objectionable of fellows and raised my suspicions. In particular, I discovered that although he claimed to have worked for the Wedgewood Company for a number of years – before arriving in Worcester – this proved on further investigation, not to be the case,' said Ravenscroft attempting to placate his superior.

'So you asked to search his rooms?'

'Yes.'

'Whatever for?'

'I thought there might be some evidence there that would link him to the two murders. There was also the possibility that we might have found the *Whisperie*.'

'But you had no reason to undertake such a search, other than the fact that he lied about his past employment?' said Henderson, his face growing redder by the second.

'I considered that there was just cause to undertake such a search.'

'Good grief, you can't go around threatening people—'

'I did not threaten him.'

'That's not what it says here,' replied Henderson, waving the letter again.

'Begging your pardon, sir, but I still believe that Cranston is one of our chief suspects. He has clearly lied about his past, which suggests to me that he probably has a criminal record—'

'But you don't know that?'

'No, sir, but—'

'This just won't do, Ravenscroft. We can't go around getting heavy handed with people and demanding to search their premises, just on the grounds that we dislike them, and suspect them of having a criminal record. That might be how you do things in London; we do things rather differently here in Worcester. If I let my officers behave in the way you have, the reputation of both the force, and myself would reach an all time low.'

'Yes, sir,' replied Ravenscroft, staring at the floor with downcast eyes.

'I'm taking you off the case, Ravenscroft, as from now. You'd best go back to London and leave the rest of the investigation to us. Your assistant, Cribb, can take over,' said Henderson firmly.

'Crabb, sir,' corrected Ravenscroft.

'Cribb, Crabb, whatever. He can carry on for a couple of days. I suppose I shall now have to write to this Rawlinson fellow, offering some sort of apology to his client. I tell you, Ravenscroft, this is just about the last thing I want on my plate.'

'With due respect, sir, I believe that another two or three days will enable me to solve this case,' said Ravenscroft hopefully.

'You've nothing to go on, man. You've been here now over two weeks, and all you have managed to do is track down that ruffian Billy. Accept the fact, that he probably killed Evelyn as well. Let's close the file and have done with it.'

'I don't believe that to be the case, sir – and we have not yet recovered the *Whisperie*,' protested Ravenscroft.

'It's probably at the bottom of the Severn.'

'I believe it may be in the possession of Dr Silas Renfrew.'

'What evidence do you have to support this view?' snapped Henderson glaring at him.

'I believe that the *Antiphoner*, which is currently in his possession—'

'What the devil is an *Antiphoner*?'

'It's an early medieval manuscript, which I believe was once in the possession of the cathedral authorities. Renfrew maintains that he purchased the work in New York some years ago.'

'And I suppose you don't believe him.'

'I have my suspicions, that he may be telling us an untruth.'

'So you think this Renfrew has got the *Whisperie* as well?'

'That remains a strong possibility,' replied Ravenscroft, beginning to see a faint glimmer of hope that he had engaged his superior's interest at last.

'But you don't have any evidence?'

'Not at present.'

'And I suppose you want to search his premises in an attempt to find it?' said Henderson sarcastically.

'It might resolve the matter and draw the case to a satisfactory conclusion.'

'Good grief. If I allowed you to ride roughshod all through Renfrew's home, there would be a public outcry. Renfrew is a respected figure in this town. Met him myself a couple of times and found him a pleasant enough fellow – not bad at all for an American.'

'If I could just have a few more days, sir,' pleaded Ravenscroft. 'With due respect it would not look good if the case was not bought to a satisfactory conclusion. It would reflect badly on the force – and on yourself as well, if the *Whisperie* was never recovered.'

'Hmm, I suppose you have a point,' grumbled Henderson.

'The force would be derided for its failure to solve the case. I know the Dean and Chapter would be particularly annoyed if the work was never recovered,' said Ravenscroft, sensing that a reprieve might just be in sight.

'Yes, yes,' replied Henderson irritably 'All right, all right. I'll give you just two more days to tidy up this affair, but after that I'm drawing a line under the case.'

'Thank you, sir,' said Ravenscroft, rising from his chair eagerly, anxious to leave the room as quickly as possible before his superior changed his mind.

'On one condition, Ravenscroft, one condition: you are to keep away from this Cranston fellow, and there is to be no search made of Dr Renfrew's house. Do I make myself clear?' snapped Henderson.

'Absolutely, sir, I quite understand. Will that be all?'

The superintendent dismissed Ravenscroft with a flick of his hand, and looked back at his paperwork.

Ravenscroft stepped out into the street and gave a sigh of relief. He had managed to deflect Henderson's wrath and had gained another two days to continue with his inquiries – but the realization that he was now virtually forbidden to have any further contact with his two principal suspects now appeared as a severe blow to his hopes.

'This is becoming something of a habit, Inspector,' said Dr Edwards rising from his seat, as Ravenscroft and Crabb entered the room.

'Our visit should prove but a short one, Dr Edwards. We would like some information regarding one of your past pupils,' said Ravenscroft.

'You mean the boy whom you thought committed suicide?'

'Yes. Our investigations have shown that the information provided by the Tovey sisters was in fact true. One of your pupils did indeed kill himself, all those years ago,' said Ravenscroft.

'I see.'

Ravenscroft thought the headmaster sounded almost disappointed by his news. 'The boy's name was Martin Tinniswood. I would be obliged, sir, if you could consult your records to see what information they could provide us with,' he requested.

Edwards rose from his seat and opened the door of a large cabinet in the corner of the room. 'We keep an alphabetical list of all present and past pupils on cards. T – here we are – Tinniswood, Martin,' he said, removing a card from the index.

'May I see, please, sir?'

Edwards handed the card over to Ravenscroft, who read the entry aloud—

Tinniswood, Martin. Born, 1838, Radnor Lodge, Hay-on-Wye, son of Mr and Mrs Tinniswood. Admitted to the school in 1849. Member of the choir in 1850.

'There is nothing else on the card' said Ravenscroft, handing the card back to the Master.

'I suppose the school did not wish to record the unfortunate circumstances of the boy's demise,' suggested Edwards returning the card to its place in the cabinet.

'Thank you,' said Ravenscroft, disappointed and about to take his leave.

'There was apparently a brother,' said Edwards, removing another card from the index and handing it to Ravenscroft.

Tinniswood, Malcolm. Born, 1853, Radnor Lodge, Hay-on-Wye, youngest son of Mr and Mrs Tinniswood. Admitted to the school in 1864. Member of the choir in 1865. Chess, Athletics Clubs. Left 1866.

'He was not here for very long,' said Ravenscroft.

'Just two years, sir,' added Crabb.

'That was surely unusual, for a boy to leave after just two years,' said Ravenscroft handing the card back.

'It would seem so Inspector. Most of our pupils remain with us for at least five or six years.'

'Can you think of any reason why the boy might have left?'

'Perhaps his parents were unable to pay the fees, or there could have been a family bereavement,' suggested Edwards. 'Or there is always the possibility, I suppose, that he could have been expelled for some violation of the rules.'

'Would that not have been recorded on the card?' asked Crabb.

'Not if the school wanted to keep that quiet as well,' suggested Ravenscroft, answering the question.

'This is all in the past, Inspector. It might be prudent to leave it there. It can do neither the school, or your investigation, any good to pursue the matter,' said Edwards closing the door to the cabinet.

'Just one last question: where is Hay-on-Wye?'

'It's a small town in Herefordshire, on the Welsh borders,' replied Edwards.

'Thank you, Dr Edwards. You have been most helpful,' said Ravenscroft as he and Crabb left the room.

'Well, that was most interesting,' said Ravenscroft, as the two men walked away from the school. 'So Tinniswood had a younger brother who was born two years after his death, and who also became a pupil at the school. Don't you find it rather strange, that the parents of the dead boy would want to send another son to the same school where their first son had clearly been unhappy?'

'Perhaps they had every confidence in the school, despite the death of their eldest son. After all we don't know what caused the elder Tinniswood to take his own life,' suggested Crabb.

'I wonder why the younger brother left the school so suddenly? The boy, Malcolm, was born in 1853. That would make him 35 now, if he was still alive.'

'Cranston and Renfrew's age, I would say.'

'It seems to me that we could have been looking at this case from the wrong direction. Up to now we have assumed that Evelyn was killed for the *Whisperie* alone. We now know that he could have been involved in some way with Martin Tinniswood's suicide all those years ago. Perhaps Malcolm found out the true cause of his brother's death when he was a pupil here. That knowledge, in some way, leads to his expulsion from the school, but years later he returns and claims his revenge on Evelyn?' said Ravenscroft thinking aloud.

'It all sounds a bit too involved to me,' said Crabb, a puzzled expression on his face.

'Yes, perhaps you're right. Sometimes I feel we are clutching at straws. Probably the death of Martin Tinniswood has nothing whatever to do with this business after all, and we are being distracted from our main line of enquiry.'

'Good morning, Inspector!' shouted a voice from across the green.

'Mr Taylor. Might we have a quick word with you?' shouted back Ravenscroft, quickening his pace in the choirmaster's direction.

'Always at your service, Inspector, but I must warn you that thirty rebellious choirboys are threatening to burn down the cathedral, unless I can bring my restraining influence to bear within the next five minutes,' said the young choirmaster smiling.

'We won't detain you long,' replied Ravenscroft. 'Does the name Tinniswood mean anything to you?'

'Tinniswood? Tinniswood? Can't say it does, Inspector. Sounds like the name of one of those three-legged horses at the Worcester Races,' said the young man running his hand through his untidy hair.

'He was a member of the choir. He committed suicide in 1851.'

'Good Lord, was his singing that bad?'

'This is a serious line of inquiry, Mr Taylor,' said Ravenscroft sternly.

'Yes, I'm sorry, 1851 was long before my time, Inspector. At that date I was but a mere thought in my mother's eye.'

'How long have you been choirmaster here?' asked Ravenscroft quickly changing the subject.

'I came last year. There wasn't a vacancy going at the time at St Paul's, so London's loss was Worcester's gain – or is it the other way round?'

'Have you ever had any association with the town of Hay-on-Wye?'

'Hay-on-Wye? The Lord has saved me from that dreaded experience! Some dreary backwater on the edge of Wales, I believe. Sounds the kind of place you send your maiden aunt to, in the hope that she may never return!'

'Thank you, Mr Taylor. We won't detain you any longer.'

'Then I bid you farewell. Tallis and Tompkins await the ruination of their works, yet again, by the angelic voices of the cathedral song birds.

Will nothing survive the murderous onslaught?' said the choirmaster, shaking his head and quickly heading off in the direction of the cathedral.

'You think he might be our Malcolm Tinniswood? He did treat the whole matter somewhat lightly,' said Crabb.

'Mr Taylor sees himself as nature's jester. But to answer your question, he would certainly be the right age, and it would have been easy for him to have changed his name from Malcolm Tinniswood to Matthew Taylor. In this world, Crabb, you can never be sure of anything,' replied Ravenscroft. 'But I know one thing.'

'What's that?'

'It's time we sought some refreshment. Let's go to the Diglis. It's not far from here and a breath of air by the river would be most welcome.'

A few minutes later Ravenscroft and Crabb entered the Diglis where they were welcomed by the landlord like old friends.

'Good to see you again, gentlemen.'

'And to you, landlord,' said Ravenscroft.

'Same as last time, is it?'

'If you will.'

'Shame about old Billy; I would never have thought he would have been the murdering type,' said the landlord wiping the bar with a cloth.

'People will sometimes do anything for money,' replied Ravenscroft, as their host disappeared round the back of the bar.

The two men seated themselves by the window, which afforded them a view over the river.

'Henderson has given us just two more days to solve the case. Time is running out for us, Crabb. I'm sure that the death of that choirboy has something to do with this case.'

'It was a very long time ago.'

'Yes, but if Nicholas Evelyn was responsible in some way for the boy's death, and the younger Tinniswood later found out the truth when he was a pupil here, then he could have returned many years later and black-mailed Evelyn with that knowledge, forcing him to steal the *Whisperie* for him – and possibly the *Antiphoner* as well.'

'Thank you,' interjected Crabb, as the landlord placed two tankards of ale before them.

'Tinniswood. Who is the younger Tinniswood? Who is our murderer?' asked Ravenscroft.

'There is the choirmaster, Matthew Taylor. Sir Arthur would be too old. My money would be on Cranston,' said Crabb, taking a drink of his ale.

'I'm inclined to agree with you. Cranston is certainly an unpleasant enough fellow. We must not forget Renfrew however.'

'But he is an American, sir.'

'The Tinniswood family might have moved to America when young Malcolm was just thirteen, which would account for him leaving the school so early. When he grew up he could easily have changed his name to Renfrew before he returned to England. He also has the desire to possess early valuable manuscripts.'

'There is also Edwards.'

'No. He is far too old. Had he been our murderer he would never have shown us the other card which contained details of Malcolm Tinniswood.'

'What do we do next then?' asked Crabb.

'I think we should pay a visit to Hay-on-Wye tomorrow, and see what we can find out about the Tinniswood family. I am still convinced that this present mystery has its origins back in 1851, when that poor choirboy took his own life. How far is Hay from here?'

'It must be about sixty or seventy miles. It's the other side of Hereford. I'll consult the railway timetables, and find out when the trains are running.'

'Could be a long day, Crabb. We will need refreshments.'

'That will be all right, sir. I've got my Jennie. She'll see me right,' said Crabb.

Ravenscroft suddenly banged his tankard down on the table.

'Whatever is the matter?'

'What was that you just said?'

'I said, I've got my Jennie. She'll see me right,' repeated Crabb, mystified.

'Of course! That's it. How stupid I have been not to have seen the connection before. We've been following the wrong path all this time. Drink up. It's time we made an arrest. I think I now know who paid Billy to kill Ruth Weston!'

'Do sit down, Inspector,' said Sir Arthur.

'Thank you, sir. Good afternoon to you as well Miss Griffiths,' said Ravenscroft accepting the seat. The young lady nodded briefly in his direction.

'You have some news regarding the case?' asked the Member for Worcester.

'Yes, sir. I hope to be making an arrest shortly,' replied Ravenscroft with confidence.

'That is good news. It will give me great pleasure to see the villain who paid old Billy to kill Miss Weston behind bars,' smiled Sir Arthur. 'Did you hear that, my dear? Ravenscroft says he is about to make an arrest. We will have justice at last.'

'Yes, Father,' replied his daughter, staring out of the window.

'Before I begin, sir, can I assume that your daughter is fully acquainted with the facts that you disclosed to me the other day?'

'My father has never kept any secrets from me,' said Miss Griffiths nervously turning her fingers in her lap.

'Come to the point, Ravenscroft. What have you unearthed?' asked Sir Arthur anxiously.

'Since we discovered the body of Miss Weston I had always assumed that her death had been linked with that of the librarian, Nicholas Evelyn, particularly as they both lived at Glovers Lodging-house. It seemed highly probable that Ruth had discovered the murderer of her fellow lodger, and that the murderer paid Billy to kill her before she could go to the authorities with that knowledge. But then I asked myself, what if that assumption was totally wrong? What if the two murders were not linked at all and there were really two killers, one who killed Evelyn and stole the *Whisperie*, and one who killed, or rather paid, old Billy to murder Ruth Weston?'

Ravenscroft paused for the effect of his words on his listeners.

'Go on. All this is very fascinating,' said Sir Arthur.

'Then I began to wonder, if Ruth Weston was not murdered because of her possible connection with the Evelyn murder, why was she killed? She had no wealth or fortune. She lived quite modestly with her son, bringing him every morning before she started work to play on the green outside your house, believing that one day you, Sir Arthur, would accept the child as your own.'

'My father could never do that. His reputation would be ruined,' said Miss Griffiths firmly.

'You are correct, Miss Griffiths, and that is the whole point. Then I realized that the only reason why Ruth Weston was killed, was because of the knowledge she held – knowledge not about the Evelyn murder, but the secret about the birth of her own son. Once I accepted that, everything seemed to fall into place. Our murderer took advantage of the investigation into the murder of Evelyn, to hire Billy to kill Ruth Weston, thereby creating the impression that the killer was the same person who had committed the first murder.'

'I see. Then you believe that I killed Ruth because I wanted her to be kept silent, in order to protect my reputation and standing in society?' said Sir Arthur.

'The day after Billy killed Ruth, and after he had placed the body in a sack on his boat ready for him to dispose of later, he decided to drink away some of his payment in the Old Diglis. That is where my constable and I encountered him. He was rather the worse for drink at the time, and my constable here had to eject him from the inn. Before he left, though, I remember him saying – "I'll be all right. I've got my lady. She'll see me all right", meaning that he had been paid by "a lady" to carry out the murder. Miss Griffiths, why did you have Ruth Weston killed?'

'Look here, Ravenscroft, you can't go around making accusations against my daughter! This is ridiculous. Why on earth would my daughter want to have her maid killed? The idea is foolish in the extreme,' exclaimed Sir Arthur staring at Ravenscroft in an aggressive manner.

'Your daughter is not a well woman, as you have stated, Sir Arthur. I believe she wanted Ruth removed because she was afraid that one day Ruth would reveal the truth concerning the true parentage of her child. Is that not correct, Miss Griffiths?' asked Ravenscroft, turning towards the lady in question.

'Really, Inspector, this whole thing is a work of fantasy on your part. I must ask you to leave my house at once. I find your manner insulting and I will certainly have words with my lawyers,' said Sir Arthur rising angrily from his chair.

'Miss Griffiths,' protested Ravenscroft, 'It will do no good to conceal the truth.'

'Mr Ravenscroft is correct, father. I paid Billy to kill Ruth!'

'Be quiet Anne. Don't say another word until I have arranged for our lawyer to be present,' urged Sir Arthur, walking over towards her.

'There is no point, Father. I had Ruth killed. Mr Ravenscroft is quite right when he says that I could see that the police were looking for the murderer of the librarian, and I thought if Ruth was killed as well, they would think that the same person had committed both crimes,' she said, rising from her seat.

'But, Anne, why?' Sir Arthur stared at his daughter, distraught, before burying his face in his hands.

'Do you need to ask why, Father? I did it to protect you. I knew that one day that woman would want everything, and that you would be ruined as a consequence. I could not let that happen. After all we had worked for over the years. Inspector, I am indeed a sick woman. The doctors have given me but three months to live. I wanted to do this for my father before I died, so that he would be secure,' said Anne, tears beginning to fall down her cheeks. 'Don't think too harshly of me, Father, I have always loved you, and will do anything for you, you know that.'

'But not this, Anne! Surely not this?' said her father reaching out for her and encompassing her fragile body in his arms.

The two policemen remained silent, looking uncomfortably at one another, listening to the sobs of the young woman. Presently Sir Arthur turned to face them.

'Look, you can see the state of my daughter. She has but a short time to live. Is there some way in which all this can be covered up? I will do anything you ask – money, advancement, a title – anything you want, if only my daughter can be protected?'

'Sir Arthur, you know better than that. A crime has been committed and I must act accordingly. I'm afraid I must take your daughter into custody. She will appear before the magistrates tomorrow morning on a charge of incitement to murder,' said Ravenscroft, hating every word that he was saying, and wishing he was anywhere other than the drawing-room of the Member of Parliament for Worcester.

'For God's sake, have you no feelings? At least show some compassion, man. Have mercy,' implored Sir Arthur.

'No mercy was shown to Ruth Weston. She was an innocent young woman, the mother of your child, who was lured to the banks of the river where she was strangled to death by a cord being placed round her throat and being pulled tight until there was no life left within her. Where was the compassion then?' said the inspector, trying not to let his feelings get the better of him.

'Mr Ravenscroft is right, Father. It is a terrible thing I have done, and the memory of my actions will prey upon my soul until my dying day. I am prepared to accept the consequences. I am ready to go with you Inspector,' replied Anne Griffiths, drying her eyes on her handkerchief.

'Anne, you don't have to do this. I'll secure the services of the best lawyer in London, Mr Sefton Rawlinson. I'll telegraph him in the morning. He'll know what to say in your defence. We will say it was your illness that drove you to commit this desperate act. That you were not thinking at the time. Trust me, Anne. Is there no way, Inspector, you can help my daughter? You must be able to do something for her? God, man, we'll do anything, but not this.'

'I'm sorry, sir, but I have to uphold the law. It is out of my hands. If you would be so good as to accompany us, Miss Griffiths, when you are ready.'

Later that night, Ravenscroft made his way back to the Cardinal's Hat. It had given him little satisfaction to have arrested Anne Griffiths, but at least he had discovered who, and why, Ruth Weston had been killed, and that file could now be closed. He had eventually secured justice for the poor unfortunate woman whom he had engaged in conversation shortly after his arrival in Worcester, and he now knew that the two killings were not related to one another. There still remained, however, the murder of Nicholas Evelyn to be solved; the *Whisperie* had not yet been recovered and returned to its rightful place – and he was more than aware that time was running out for the truth to be finally unravelled.

CHAPTER THIRTEEN

'Nasty business, sir.'

Ravenscroft looked up from his breakfast. The landlord of the Cardinal's Hat was pointing to one of the pages in the local newspaper.

'There's never any good news in the newspapers these days,' said Ravenscroft, placing a piece of sausage on the end of his fork.

'Two of them killed on one night in London. First one apparently had her throat cut,' continued the landlord dramatizing the scene. 'Killer was likely to have done more to her, but was disturbed and ran off before he was caught. Then the fellow goes on to kill another woman an hour later; can you believe it? Cuts her throat and does horrible things with her insides, displaying them all out on the pavement for everyone to gawp at.'

Ravenscroft returned his fork and sausage to his plate.

'Mind you, I suppose those women got what was coming to them, if they will insist on carrying on like that. Still no one deserves to be cut up like that, and their insides taken out for all and sundry to view. Cut out her kidney as well, by all accounts, then, when he had satisfied himself there he had a go at her face. Cut her ear right off, he did. No need for that, was there? Breakfast not to your liking this morning, Mr Ravenscroft?'

'I'm not particularly hungry, thank you,' replied Ravenscroft, pushing his plate away from him.

'The terrible things they get up to in London. Who'd live there?' said the landlord picking up the plate.

'Indeed. Who would? Is that the hour? Time I was on my way to catch my train. I might be back rather late tonight.'

'Right you are, sir. Perhaps you would care for some reading matter on your journey? Read all the ghastly details like,' said the landlord, smiling and holding out the newspaper for him to take.

'I don't think so, thank you all the same,' said Ravenscroft, quickly making his way towards the door.

'Don't forget the beam, sir! Oh – too late!'

Ravenscroft escaped from the inn, and rubbed his head as he made his way down Friar Street and along Foregate Street, in the direction of the railway station.

After purchasing his ticket, he made his way up the steps and on to the platform. He checked his pocket watch with the large station clock and, realizing that his train would not be due for another ten minutes, pushed open the door to the waiting-room. A number of people were sitting on the benches, some engaged in conversation, others reading, one or two staring vacantly before them. An old bearded man, wearing a large hat and a ragged overcoat, was sleeping in the corner. One lady, dressed in black, looked up from her reading and glanced at him as he made his way across the room.

'Good morning, Mrs Marchmont – or should I say, Mrs Kelly?' said Ravenscroft raising his hat.

'Inspector Ravenscroft. I thought it would not be long before we encountered one another again,' she replied in a quiet assured voice.

'May I join you?' he asked, noticing that she seemed paler and more worn, than when he had seen her last.

She nodded her approval, and Ravenscroft sat down on the bench beside her. 'Are you waiting for the Hereford train?' asked Ravenscroft, not quite sure what he should say in the circumstances.

'London,' she replied. 'And yourself?'

'I go in the other direction to Hereford and then on to Hay.'

'Your investigations take you far afield,' she said, in the same plain, matter-of-fact voice that he remembered from the previous year.

'In this case, yes.'

'I hear that you have arrested Miss Griffiths for being involved in her maid's murder.'

'News travels very fast in Worcester,' answered Ravenscroft, beginning to feel uneasy in her presence.

'In a small town such as Worcester, you cannot keep secrets for long. But presumably your investigations still continue, Mr Ravenscroft?'

'Yes. The killer of Mr Evelyn is still at large, and the *Whisperie* has not yet been recovered.'

'Ah, the *Whisperie*.' She smiled briefly for the first time during their conversation.

'You are familiar with the work?'

'I have never seen it myself, but I am aware of its value to the cathedral.'

'You seem well acquainted with Sir Arthur.'

'I have met him on a number of occasions. He was very helpful to me in the administration of my late husband's estate,' she replied quietly.

'I see.'

'And you are wondering, Mr Ravenscroft, if I am not mistaken, as to why I am known as Mrs Marchmont, when my real name is apparently Mrs Kelly.'

'I must admit that the thought had crossed my mind.'

'Always the detective! Marchmont was my maiden name. After his death, and the disgrace he had brought upon us by his behaviour, I thought it prudent to revert back to my former family name. So you see, there is nothing at all sinister in my motives. I am sorry to have to disappoint you on this occasion.'

'I had thought that there was a logical explanation,' said Ravenscroft looking away. 'Do you live in London now?'

'No. I purchased a small property just outside Worcester, in the village of Hallow, after I left Malvern. Why do you ask?'

'Last year, I thought I saw you in London – and you said you were waiting for the London train today.'

'You must have been mistaken. I have not been to the capital for some years now. Today I am awaiting the arrival of the London train. I am meeting an old friend who is to stay with me.'

Ravenscroft felt that she was not telling the truth, but knew that it would be futile to continue with that line of questioning. 'And how is your situation now, since we last spoke?' he enquired, without thinking what he was asking.

'Are you asking, Mr Ravenscroft, if I still feel bitterness over the cause of the death of my husband and son? Of course: that pain can never go away. Why should it?' she replied, a look of resignation forming in her eyes.

'Then I am sorry,' was all that he could say.

'You might be interested to learn that Sir Arthur has asked me to marry him,' she said suddenly.

'I had no idea—' said Ravenscroft, but she cut him short.

'I think, Inspector, you are trying to be over polite. You have seen me there twice, at Sir Arthur's house, and no doubt observed how the gentleman addressed me.'

'And have you accepted him?'

'Now you are being impolite.'

'Forgive me, my dear lady,' said Ravenscroft, uncomfortable and wishing that his train would arrive.

'Sir Arthur is a good man. He is also very lonely since the death of his first wife. He thinks I could bring him happiness. In that, he is mistaken. To answer your question, Inspector – no, I will not be accepting his proposal. My destiny lies elsewhere. I am not well; the illness that struck down my husband and my son, has I fear, also begun to cast its shadow over me. No, please do not say that you are sorry for my condition. I would find such sympathy patronizing.'

'I was merely going to say that it is a shame that you are unable to bring some comfort to Sir Arthur. Now that his daughter has been taken into custody, he will have need of friends, as indeed will you.'

Mrs Kelly reached into the pocket on her dress, and in so doing a small packet dropped on to the floor of the waiting-room, startling its owner as it did so.

'Allow me,' said Ravenscroft, leaning down and reaching out for the packet. As he grasped it, however, its contents – three brass rings – rolled away from his feet. He rose from his seat and, recovering the rings, wrapped them in the paper, and handed them back to their owner. The old man in the corner of the waiting-room coughed and pulled his hat further down over his face.

'Thank you, Mr Ravenscroft,' she said, replacing it in her pocket, 'I should take greater care.'

Ravenscroft smiled – and wondered why she should be carrying three such items on her person.

'And how are you?' she asked quickly, breaking into his thoughts. 'Do you still live in London?'

'Unfortunately so,' he replied, resuming his seat.

'I think you would rather be here in Worcester – or Ledbury.'

'I would indeed. Worcester is a pleasant enough city,' he replied, wondering why his companion should have mentioned the latter place.

'Then perhaps you should consider the change. I am sure you would be more content. Sometimes we need to put our fears behind us. Only by confronting our failures can we eventually hope to achieve our heart's desire.'

Ravenscroft smiled. The station master, outside on the platform, began to announce the arrival of the Hereford train. 'I must go,' he said, rising from his seat. 'Until we meet again, Mrs Kelly, or should I say, Mrs Marchmont.'

'I do not think that will be possible. Our paths go in different directions,' she said, in a formal reassuring tone, which Ravenscroft found slightly unnerving.

As the train arrived on the station platform, Ravenscroft hesitated, not knowing whether he should stay and prolong his conversation, or embark on his journey to Hereford and Hay.

'You will miss your train, Mr Ravenscroft, and that will never do. There is someone, I am sure, who will be pleased to see you. Do not leave it until it is too late.'

Ravenscroft nodded briefly and making his way out of the waiting-room, boarded the departing train, deep in thought.

'Good morning,' said Crabb, boarding the train at Great Malvern station.

'And to you, Crabb. We have chosen a fine day for our excursion, although I believe the forecast is not so good for the west of Hereford. There could be some rain later, but we must take it as it comes.'

'I have sent a telegram to the local station in Hay, and someone should be meeting us off the train. We have to change at Hereford and on to the Brecknock Railway,' said Crabb. 'You look deep in thought this morning, sir, if you don't mind my saying.'

'I've just encountered an old acquaintance,' replied Ravenscroft looking out of the window at the hills. 'Crabb, I've decided to get off at Ledbury for a while; there is someone I need to see. You go on ahead, and I'll join you in Hay off the later train.'

'Very well, sir. I'm sure Miss Armitage will be pleased to see you again,' replied Crabb smiling.

'Of that I cannot be sure, but I am resolved to be bold.'

'That's always the best way. Why, if I had not been so bold with my Jennie, someone else would have snapped her up and no mistake!'

'When you get to Hay see if you can find Radnor Lodge. See if the Tinniswood family is still there – or if not, find out as much as you can about them.'

'Leave it to me, sir.'

A few minutes later, the train drew into the station at Ledbury and Ravenscroft alighted from the carriage. Ignoring the waiting horse-drawn cabs outside the station, he set off at a brisk pace down the road that led into the centre of the town. Reaching the busy market place, he paused for a moment at the entrance to Church Lane, not knowing whether he should continue or retreat and retrace his steps back to the station. Perhaps he had been foolish to have broken his journey on what seemed little more than a sudden impulse. After all, he had been rejected once – why should he expect that he would succeed this time?

'It's Mr Ravenscroft, is it not?' said a voice at his elbow.

'Er, yes,' he replied.

'You probably don't remember me, sir. I'm Miss Armitage's maid,' replied the young woman.

'Yes, of course. Please forgive me. It has been some time,' he apologized, looking anxiously all around in case the maid had been accompanied by her mistress.

'That's all right, sir,' she smiled.

'And how is your mistress?'

'Miss Armitage is well, sir.'

'And her son, is he well?'

'Very well, sir. He can be quite a handful at times' she laughed.

'I expect so.'

'Will you be calling on Miss Armitage?'

'I'm not sure. Perhaps another day,' he replied, despising his lack of endeavour.

'I'm sure she would be very pleased to see you. She often speaks very highly about you, sir.'

'Does she?'

'I'm just returning from market, if you would care to accompany me?' said the girl looking up into his eyes.

He hesitated, aware that he could still make his excuses and return to the station. Instead he nodded and followed the young woman up the narrow cobbled street.

There was the snug little cottage, just as he remembered it, with its baskets of hanging flowers outside, and its prospect of an inviting interior within.

'If you would care to wait here, sir, I'll just tell Miss Armitage that you have arrived.'

Ravenscroft forced a smile as the maid entered the cottage. He reached up to admire the flowers and looked up at the bedroom windows, half expecting to see a familiar face gazing down upon him from one of the leaded paned windows. He began to walk up and down outside the building for what seemed like an eternity, looking down the street one minute, staring at the closed door the next, removing his spectacles for the third time so that he might polish the lens. He wondered how shocked she would be to hear that he had returned, and what her reaction would be to seeing him once more. He could feel a cold sweat forming on his brow, and his stomach felt hollow and unsettled. Thoughts of abandoning such a foolish adventure flooded into his mind. He turned and resolved to leave quickly before the door reopened. There was still time to abandon his quest.

'Miss says you are very welcome, sir,' said the maid suddenly opening the door.

'Thank you,' he replied, quickly walking up the path, then pausing momentarily before stepping into the hallway.

'Mr Ravenscroft, how pleasant to see you again.'

She was just as he remembered her – the same striking appearance, auburn hair and welcoming smile that had remained in his thoughts since the first day he had seen her. 'Miss Armitage,' he said kissing her outstretched hand.

'Do, please, come into the sitting-room.'

He followed her and accepted the seat that was offered.

'Would you like some tea?'

'That would be very pleasant,' he replied, looking around him, reassured that the room still retained its light, airy, homely appearance.

Lucy gave instructions to the maid, who smiled, and left the room. 'And what brings you to Ledbury today, Mr Ravenscroft? Are you here on police business? Will you be staying long?' she asked, the questions issued in a formal but nervous manner.

'I was invited to come to Worcester by the dean of the cathedral, to help solve a murder and recover one of their priceless books,' he replied, the words displaying his uncertainty.

'Your reputation is obviously well established,' she said smiling.

'I have been in Worcester for nearly three weeks now,' he said quickly and, as she turned away, he realized that she would have been perhaps upset by the fact that he had not visited her during that time.

'And have you caught your murderer?' she asked.

'Not yet. The case has been of a protracted nature, but I am hopeful that we may be able to bring things to a satisfactory conclusion. I am on my way to visit Hay-on-Wye to investigate a possible line of inquiry.'

'So you thought you would break your journey in Ledbury.'

He thought he detected a note of sadness in her voice, realized that he had hurt her, cursed his clumsiness and wished he was elsewhere. 'I...er,' he started to say, but was disturbed by the maid entering the room holding a tray.

'Thank you, Sally. You may go now. How do you like your tea, Mr Ravenscroft?'

'Just a little sugar, thank you.'

'Of course, I should have remembered. How foolish of me to forget.'

'It has been a long time.'

He sat in silence as she poured out the tea and handed him the cup.

'And how have you been Miss Armitage – sorry, Lucy.'

'I have been well. Thank you.'

'And your son, Richard, is he in good spirits?'

'He is very well, thank you. He has grown such a lot since you last saw him. You would hardly recognize him now,' she answered, smiling briefly as she did so.

'That is good – and your brother, is he still at the almshouses in Colwall?'

'Yes.'

'I trust he is happy in his work.'

'I believe so. He still calls on me, once a week.'

'That is good. I know that you and your brother are very close. And how are you finding things in Ledbury?' he asked, sipping his tea.

'I like Ledbury very much. The people have been very kind to us here, and the town has a warmth and charm that is very pleasing.'

'I am glad of that.'

Ravenscroft, realizing that his left hand was beginning to shake, took another sip of his tea, and looked out of the window, not knowing what he should say next. He had not expected such aloofness, such formality, but now considered he had been foolish to expect otherwise.

'Do you still dislike London?' she asked, suddenly breaking the silence.

'I would prefer to reside in Worcester – or perhaps even Ledbury,' he replied.

'But your work is in the capital?'

'Alas, yes.'

'Perhaps you could secure another appointment.'

'Miss Armitage, Lucy, I realize that my last visit caused you some distress and placed you in a predicament. For that, I wish to apologize,' he said, the words coming quickly and unsure.

'You have nothing to apologize for, Mr Ravenscroft. It is I who must apologize to you. I was perhaps too cruel in the way in which I treated you.'

'Never! You could never be cruel to me. It was my impulsive nature that came to the fore. I was entirely to blame.'

'You sound as though you regretted your decision?' she said, turning away, leaving Ravenscroft unsure as to what he should say next. Instead he took another drink of his tea, and listened to the slow tick of the clock in the corner of the room.

'And what will you do, once your case is concluded?' she asked, 'Will you return to London? There have been some terrible murders there recently, I understand.'

'I believe so, although I must admit that I have not had time to read the London papers, so am not fully acquainted with all the details,' he replied, replacing his cup on the tray.

'Your colleagues will be missing you there.'

'I would doubt that.'

'You would like some more tea?'

'No, thank you,' he replied, glancing at the clock face, 'I must go,' he said rising from his seat, accepting that his mission was impossible, and anxious to leave as quickly as possible.

'Yes, your train. You must not miss your train to Hereford,' she said, a look of anxiety clouding her face.

'Perhaps I might call on you again, Miss Armitage,' he said, seeing the sadness in her eyes, and knowing that he might never see her again.

'You would always be welcome here, Mr Ravenscroft – Samuel.'

'Lucy, I—' he began, anxious to declare his true feelings, but afraid that his determination might yet cause more unhappiness.

'You should catch your train, Samuel,' she replied, sensing his unease, and touching his arm gently with her hand.

'Yes. You are right,' he said, kissing her hand. 'Good day to you, Lucy.'

As he stepped out into the street, and made his way slowly back to the station, he was overcome with feelings of failure and emptiness. He had wanted to say so much, to have told her how his life had been lonely and without purpose since their last meeting, but her detachment and formality had been like a barrier, which he had felt unable to climb. As he sat on the platform, waiting for the next train to arrive, he began to curse his lack of resolve – and realized that he had faced the most important challenge in his life, and had again been found wanting.

'Good morning,' said Crabb, as Ravenscroft stepped down from the train. 'Welcome to Hay. I trust your enterprise at Ledbury went well?'

'Have you located Radnor Lodge?' asked Ravenscroft, ignoring the question, and looking up at the black sky which seemed to match his mood.

'About a five-minute walk from here, sir, but I don't think we are in luck. The place looks deserted; all boarded up,' replied Crabb.

'Nevertheless, lead on,' said Ravenscroft.

The two men left the station and made their way down a dusty road, on the edge of the town.

'I don't like the look of that sky, sir. The heavens look as though they are about to open. Ah, here we are.'

Ravenscroft found himself outside a large house. 'I see what you mean,' he said, observing that all the doors and windows of the property had been covered over with wooden boards, that several tiles were missing from the roof and that the gardens were full of nettles and long grass.

'Looks as though no one has lived here for years.'

'I wonder why they went away? Have you enquired at the nearby houses?' asked Ravenscroft.

'One or two of the neighbours can recall a family living here called Tinniswood, but they can't remember much about them.'

'It seems as though our journey may prove pointless. Let's make our way into the town and find some refreshment before this sky opens up on us,' replied a gloomy Ravenscroft.

Making their way into the centre of Hay, they were met with a rumble of approaching thunder as the rain started to fall. Quickly passing the old clock tower in the market square, Ravenscroft and Crabb ran up the steep slope and turned the corner before making their way into one of the nearby inns.

'Just made it in time,' remarked Crabb, as the rain cascaded down on the pavement.

'Two tankards of your best ale,' said Ravenscroft, addressing the landlord.

'As you wish, sir, won't keep you long.'

'That fire looks inviting,' said Ravenscroft, rubbing his hands and moving closer to the hearth. A group of three men busily engaged in smoking and drinking, looked up briefly from their game of dominoes.

'There you are, gentlemen,' said the landlord, placing two tankards on the table, where they had seated themselves. 'You are not from these parts then?'

'No, we've journeyed from Worcester. Tell me, do you have anything to eat?' asked Ravenscroft.

'I could rustle up some bread and cheese, and some of the wife's home-made pickle, if you like.'

'That sounds most acceptable.'

'What you doing in Hay then?' asked one of the domino players, looking up from the game. 'We don't get many visitors round these parts.'

'We're here on business,' replied Ravenscroft.

'Ain't no business to be done in Hay,' remarked the second player, letting out a thin wisp of smoke from the corner of his mouth.

'Picked a good day for it,' laughed the third, his voice almost eclipsed by the sound of the rain beating on the windows of the inn. 'This casselty weather dunna suit most owd folks.'

'So it would seem,' replied Ravenscroft.

'Be beazy by afternoon though,' said the first man.

'We are trying to trace the Tinniswood family. Do you know of them?' asked Ravenscroft raising his voice.

'Maybe,' said the first player, taking a long draw on his clay pipe.

'They used to live at Radnor Lodge,' said Crabb.

'Radnor Lodge, you say?'

'The house which is all boarded up, on the edge of town, with the overgrown garden,' said Ravenscroft.

'Oh there, Radnor Lodge,' nodded the second smoker.

'Yes, the Tinniswood family,' added Ravenscroft hopefully.

'You remember them Tinniswoods, Glyn?' asked the first speaker.

'Lived at Radnor Lodge. They kept themselves much to themselves, them being English like. Just arrived one day,' offered the third man.

'How long were they here for?' asked Ravenscroft.

'Oh, about twenty year or so, then they left one day, and ain't come back since.'

'Can you tell me anything about them?'

'There were MrTinniswood and his wife. They had two sons, I believe. One of 'em died when he was young,' continued the man.

'That would be the family,' said Ravenscroft, realizing that he might be getting somewhere at last.

'Buried in churchyard, along with them others, he is.'

'What others?' asked Crabb.

'Other Tinniswoods,' replied the man irritably, before resuming his game.

'I see. Thank you, gentlemen,' said Ravenscroft, turning back to Crabb. 'It looks as though we don't have much to go on. Our only chance is to pay a visit to the local church and see what we can discover there, once this wretched storm has passed over, but in the meantime let us first partake of some of this promising cheese and pickle which I see our host is bringing over to our table.'

Thirty minutes later, as the storm moved away from the town to be replaced by a light drizzle, the two made their way along the road towards the Church of St Mary. 'Let's get out of this rain and take a look inside first,' said Ravenscroft pushing open the door to the church. 'You take that side of the building, I'll look this side.'

'What am I looking for?'

'A plaque, stone, effigy – anything which has the name Tinniswood on it.'

The two men walked around the church in silence, straining to read any form of lettering they could find in the darkened interior.

'Nothing! No record of anyone called Tinniswood.'

'They probably just weren't important enough, sir,' sympathized Crabb.

They turned, as the door to the church opened suddenly. 'Good morning, gentlemen. I see you have come to admire our lovely church, although this terrible weather does not show it in its full glory,' said the new arrival, removing his hat and shaking the wet from its surface.

'We are here to look for information. Perhaps you can assist us, Vicar,' said Ravenscroft.

'I will do my best, although I've only been parish priest here for the last fifteen years,' he replied.

'We are trying to find anything related to a family called Tinniswood. They probably left the parish over twenty years ago. Used to reside at Radnor Lodge.'

'Ah yes, Radnor Lodge. Rather a fine building in its day; a shame that it has stood empty for so long. You would have thought that the owners would have returned by now,' said the cleric, shaking his head.

'Indeed.'

'Tinniswood. Let me see. The name strikes a chord somewhere in my memory. Ah, yes. I have it. I've seen their gravestones in the churchyard.'

'Can you tell us where they are?' asked Ravenscroft, eagerly.

'Are you related to them?' enquired the vicar.

'No, we are police officers investigating the death of a man in Worcester. We believe that a member of the Tinniswood family might be involved in some way.'

'I see. Well, gentlemen, if you take the path that leads down from the church until you reach nearly the bottom of the hill then turn to your left, on the edge of the churchyard, you should find what you are looking for.'

'Thank you, sir,' said Ravenscroft shaking the clergyman's hand.

'If you will excuse me, gentlemen, I will remain in the dry. I have to prepare my sermon for the Sunday service.'

'Of course.'

They left the church and made their way down a steep slope that led away from the building. 'Rather overgrown in some places. I think we have gone far enough. Make your way along there, and see if you can find any Tinniswood stones,' instructed Ravenscroft. 'I'll take this path.'

The two men began their search, bending down to examine each stone as they made their way through the wet undergrowth.

'Over here, sir. I think I have found one,' shouted Crabb excitedly.

'Well done. Let's clear away some of these thorns and grass,' said Ravenscroft, joining him.

'There, sir, the name Tinniswood.'

Ravenscroft dried his spectacles before reading the words on the slab. 'In memory of Martin Tinniswood, Eldest son of Robert and Martha Tinniswood. Born 1838. Passed Away 1851. Always Remembered.'

'Rather sad.'

'Yes, they evidently brought the poor boy back to Hay and buried him here. Now he lies, all alone in this churchyard, forgotten and with no one to tend his grave. There must be others,' said Ravenscroft moving on to the next stone in the row, and pulling out the grass obstructing the inscription.

'Any luck?'

'Yes, I can just make it out. Tinniswood. Oh, no!'

'Whatever is the matter, sir?'

'Take a look,' said Ravenscroft standing up.

Crabb read the words on the stone – 'In loving memory of Malcolm Tinniswood, youngest son of Robert and Martha Tinniswood. Born 1853. Unexpectedly Taken from Us After a Short Illness. 1866.'

'So that is why Malcolm never returned to King's at Worcester. He must have fallen ill and died. Perhaps there was a cholera outbreak in the town or some other pestilence that caused his death in the school holidays?'

'I pity the parents, to have lost one son must have been hard enough, to have lost another must have been terrible,' said Crabb, shaking his head.

'I wonder why there was such a long gap between the birth of the first son in 1838 and the second in 1853?' said Ravenscroft, mopping the rain from his face with his handkerchief.

'Could be that they decided to have a second child after their first had died?' suggested Crabb.

'You could be right. There might have been a middle child.'

'If there was, sir, there's no record of him at King's.'

'Either way, it does not seem to matter. It looks as though our journey here has been futile. With Malcolm dead, that puts an end to our theory that a younger brother came back to Worcester many years later to gain his revenge on Evelyn. I'm afraid we have been following the wrong trail all along. Evelyn's death clearly has no connection with the Tinniswoods. We have been wasting our time. Will this case ever have an end, Crabb? We are back at the start yet again,' said Ravenscroft dejectedly.

'It seems so.'

'Come, let's get out of this rain and catch the next train back to Worcester. There is nothing more we can do. Time I returned to London,' said Ravenscroft, walking away from the stones.

'Just a minute, sir, there's another stone here.' Crabb was kneeling before the next grave in the row. 'Yes, I can just make out the name Tinniswood.'

Ravenscroft joined his constable, and the two men eagerly pulled the grass and weeds away from the stone, so that they could read the words.

'Martha Tinniswood. This must be the mother's grave. Born 1818, eldest daughter of— Good God, Crabb! See the name engraved there!'

'This puts a whole new light on the case,' replied Crabb.

The two men looked at one another, each not quite believing what they had just uncovered.

'So our journey has not been in vain after all!' cried Ravenscroft. 'I think we now know who killed Evelyn. Time we returned to Worcester and laid a trap for our murderer!'

INTERLUDE

LONDON

Dusk was falling, and the old lamplighter was about to commence his duties outside the old, decayed church, as she made her way up the path to the main entrance and gently pushed open the door.

The church was dimly lit – a few candles burned on the offertory table – and seemed unoccupied, and for a moment she hesitated thinking that perhaps she had arrived at the wrong place, or had ventured out upon the wrong day, but the note had given clear instructions and she realized that she had no alternative but to carry them out if she wanted to bring her plan to its climactic conclusion.

She made her way across to the confessional box, and entered the confined space. The compartment smelt of damp and decay, and she sat there for a few moments adjusting her eyes to the near darkness, her breathing coming in short gasps betraying her anxiety.

Eventually she spoke, not knowing whether he was there or not. 'Bless me Father, for I have sinned.'

'We will both suffer in Hell for our deeds,' replied a voice that she recognized, from behind the partition.

'You have carried out your work?' she asked, ignoring his remark. 'Two in one night, as you said.'

'Stride was difficult. I had so little time before I could bring matters to a satisfactory conclusion. You received the ear-ring I sent you?'

The same calculating, methodical voice, that she remembered from their previous encounters.

'Yes, but the kidney—' she began.

'Eddowes. You said you would leave the choice to me!' snapped the voice suddenly.

'Yes, but not that!' she protested.

'If you do not have the stomach to continue, I am satisfied that our agreement should be at an end,' he said, a note of determination in his voice.

'No, I am sorry. I realize that I should not question your methods,' she replied seeking to calm his anger.

'You have the money?' he asked abruptly.

'Yes. One hundred and fifty sovereigns as we agreed.'

'Good. When you depart, leave the purse containing the money on your seat. I will collect it after you have gone,' said the voice resuming its earlier, formal composure.

'As you wish.'

'You spoke of a final victim?'

'Yes. She is the one I hate the most.' She paused for a moment. 'The one who brought the most harm to my family. I have left her to the last.'

'I understand. What is her name?'

'Her name is Mary Jane Kelly, although she sometimes likes to call herself Marie Jeanette Kelly, giving herself French airs and graces. She lives at 13 Miller's Court, Dorset Street. A small, filthy hovel of a place. She lives with a man called Barnett. That might prove difficult. You will have to wait until he is out of the way.'

'Why?' asked Monk.

'Because I would have you kill her in her room, after I have spoken to her.'

'That is impossible. I work alone – or not at all,' he said, a note of finality in his voice.

'I will pay you well,' she pleaded, afraid that her final desire might not be fulfilled, that her last victim would go unpunished.

'It is too dangerous. Why would you need to speak to her?'

'I would have her atone for the evil she has wrought on my family, before her death. It is important to me. I have so little time left. Afterwards our work will be finished. We will have no further need of one another.'

'I will not permit you to accompany me. The police are closing in. I cannot afford a mistake. You have already been too careless.'

'How?' she asked. 'No one has ever followed me to our meetings, I can assure you. I have always taken precautions.'

'You allowed yourself to speak to that man Ravenscroft – when you dropped Chapman's rings,' he sneered.

'How do you know that?' she asked, a cold shiver running down her spine. Was he aware of her every move? Had he been following her?

'I was there in the waiting-room. You did not notice me. That is why I am never discovered. People never realize that I am there.'

'They fell from my pocket—' she began.

'—And he picked them up and returned them to you. The foolish man! He will never know that London's most notorious criminal was sitting within feet of him, and that he had touched one of the victim's rings! What a lost opportunity. He will never again be so close,' he said, in a mocking voice.

'I told him nothing,' she protested.

'I know.'

'I will give you two hundred sovereigns for this last killing. I will give them to you when you have taken me to her room.'

He did not reply, and she grew anxious, fearing that her insistence on this had alienated him.

'If I agree to your terms, you must do exactly as I tell you. There can be no deviation.'

'Of course, I understand that.'

'We must do nothing for the next few weeks. The police will be redoubling their efforts, ever seeking to entrap me, thinking that I am some imbecile whose lust must be satisfied at all costs, and that I will strike again soon. In that they will be disappointed. Let them think that I have gone away, that all has returned to what it was before. Then, when they are least expecting it, we will act. I will send you a letter. There will be a time and a place. That is all. You will meet me there. My face will be covered, but you will know when I am there. You will follow me to her room. After you have confronted her, you will give me the money and leave. I will kill her after you have gone. We will never see each other again. You understand all this?'

'I do,' she said, relieved that he had agreed to this one last proposition.

'Then go. There is nothing else left to say.'

She rose, and after depositing the purse of coins on the seat, left the confessional and walked quickly out of the church.

Crossing over the road, she paused for a moment and, after looking around her and seeing that she was unobserved, she stepped back into the darkness of one of the doorways and watched and waited for the door of the church to open again. Realizing that her hands were shaking in the cold autumn air, she drew her coat closer to her.

The minutes seemed to her to inch forward, as the early evening fog began to drift across the square. Surely he would be leaving soon, she told herself? There would be little point in his remaining inside the building, but perhaps there had been another exit.

The church clock struck eight, as the door of the church slowly opened. She drew back even further into the darkened doorway, lest she should be seen. An old man, with a long white beard, dressed shabbily in a black coat, head bent, features hidden under a large hat, shuffled his slow way down the path that led from the church entrance to the road.

Surely this old, insignificant man, bore no resemblance to the man she knew as Monk? She had imagined someone younger, more agile, more – but then she remembered his words: 'You did not notice me. That is why I am never discovered. People never realize that I am there.'

Reaching the edge of the church precincts, the old man looked around him briefly, before shuffling his way down the road. Then he turned the corner and disappeared from view.

She waited for some minutes, alone in the dark and cold, fearing that he would return and see her leaving if she left her hiding place too soon.

The church clock struck the quarter hour. Stepping out into the street, she walked quickly away from the square, not wanting to look behind her, trusting that the thickening fog would conceal her very existence.

She knew now that her work would be completed. Soon all would be set in motion; the final act would be played out. She would meet the woman whom she hated above all others; the woman who had caused the death of her husband and son. It was ironic that they should both share the same surname – Kelly – one the destroyer of families, the other the victim of another's lust. Only with the woman's death could she hope to feel cleansed and released – and could perhaps be purified before her final reconciliation.

CHAPTER FOURTEEN

WORCESTER

It was late afternoon, on the following day, when Ravenscroft made his slow way up the winding steps of the tower of Worcester Cathedral. Although he had made the journey before, on the day when he had spoken with Brother Jonus, he still found the climb arduous, and paused frequently to ease the congestion in his lungs. He knew that he would soon be drawing the case to a conclusion, and the anxiety that even now he might not succeed in bringing Evelyn's murderer to justice, or retrieve the *Whisperie*, weighed heavily upon his mind. A few weeks ago he had welcomed the opportunity of leaving the heat and noise of the capital behind him, to involve himself in a case which he could call his own, free from the interference of his superiors at the Yard. He had found the comparative calm, and ancient history of the city and its cathedral, strangely reassuring and rewarding in its own right, and there had always been the thought that the person for whom he most cared in all the world was but a short distance away over the other side of the hills. But now that hope had been dashed, and it was as though the narrow streets of the city and the ancient stones of the cathedral were seeking to overwhelm him with their mockery and stature. All he desired now was to bring the case to an end so that he could return once more to his home and place of work, where he knew that the encompassing arms of the metropolis would subjugate his thoughts and feelings, and where new challenges might yet await him.

He breathed a sigh of relief as he reached the topmost step, and gently pushed open the door, half expecting to see someone standing on the platform but relieved that he had arrived first. Fastening the top button of his coat against the wind, he walked to the edge of the parapet and traced the course of the ever important river, as it threaded its way through the city on one side and the meadows on the other; the same river which had born witness to the great battle of centuries before, and which had recently seen the deaths of Nicholas Evelyn, Ruth Weston and Billy, the bargeman. Then Ravenscroft's thoughts returned to the young choirboy, who, all those years ago had lived in the precincts of the cathedral and who had sung within its confines, until one day he had sought release from his anxiety and shame in the only way that had been left to him, in the taking of his own life.

Then he remembered again the choirmaster, Matthew Taylor raising his arms before him, urging his charges to greater levels of excellence, the American Renfrew turning over the pages of one of his ancient books, and Cranston, ever on the defensive and anxious to guard his secrets. Other figures began to crowd in upon his mind – Touchmore enjoying his newly acquired status as the dean of the cathedral; Edwards shouting disapproval at his pupils; Sir Arthur, seeking to retain his status and importance in the light of his daughter's actions; the Tovey sisters talking amongst themselves – ever the eyes and ears of the building; Brother Jonus, a calm presence offering words of comfort and advice to those that would listen, and finally Mrs Kelly, the woman in black who had long occupied his thoughts and deliberations. Ravenscroft knew that when the last scene of this drama was played out, the truth would be revealed, and the killer would be within his grasp. Only then would he be free to leave.

The sound of approaching footsteps, nearing the end of the climb, reminded him of the purpose in hand.

'Good God, Ravenscroft. What the blazes did you pick this place for?'

'I thought we needed to be somewhere quiet, where our killer would think it safe to converse with us,' said Ravenscroft, addressing his superior.

'Damn it, you could have chosen somewhere less strenuous,' said Henderson, mopping his brow and attempting to recover his breathing. 'I am getting on in years, you know.'

'Sorry, sir, but I knew you would be anxious to confront our murderer and would enjoy the satisfaction of arresting him yourself.'

'So who is he?' asked Henderson.

'That we shall both learn shortly. This morning I sent letters to all our chief suspects, the contents of which would no doubt prove of little interest to the majority of them. One person, however, would see the importance of my words, and would desire to meet me here in an attempt to prevent his unmasking,' said Ravenscroft with confidence.

'All sounds rather too far-fetched for me. Are you sure you know what you're doing, Ravenscroft?' said Henderson, mopping his brow once more, before returning his handkerchief to his pocket.

'Absolutely. In a few minutes, our killer will be making his way up those steps. He will think that I will be alone. What he has not counted on is that you will be here as well.'

'Suppose you know what you're doing,' replied Henderson grudgingly.

'Look down there, sir, on the green. Matthew Taylor, about to make his way into the cathedral,' said Ravenscroft, pointing out the figure of the young choirmaster.

'He's your chief suspect then?' enquired Henderson. 'You think he could be on his way up here?'

'We will see. Our killer may already be within the confines of the cathedral, awaiting his opportunity to make his way up here unnoticed.'

'So, what have you unearthed about the case that makes you so confident?' asked Henderson, gruffly.

'When I first started my investigations, I believed that the case was all about the theft of the *Whisperie*, that someone had compelled Evelyn to steal the work, and that once he had done so, the murderer had no further need of him and killed him, so that the true circumstances of the theft would remain a secret. But then I learnt about the suicide of the young choirboy, Martin Tinniswood, all those years ago.1851 to be precise. At first it seemed as though the two events could not be in any way connected, but the more I found out about the boy, the more I came to the conclusion that the reason for the events of this year had its origins back in that earlier event,' said the inspector, walking up and down, and warming to his subject.

'Sounds interesting, I suppose. Go on,' interjected Henderson.

'So I asked myself, why would a thirteen-year-old choirboy seek to take his own life? Perhaps he had been bullied at school, or was concerned about events at home, or was just desperately unhappy. But then when I read the report of the inquest, I discovered that the boy had been found hanging in the library, and I began to wonder why the boy had chosen that place above all others within the cathedral. Then it occurred to me that the boy had deliberately chosen the library because he wanted to show people that it was the place that had been witness to the scene of his own degradation – for, you see, Nicholas Evelyn had been the cause of the boy's death. He had taken advantage of a young innocent boy, had violated his person to such an extent that the boy was so full of shame and remorse that he felt eventually compelled to take his own life, seeing his own death as the only way to escape from his torment. Nicholas Evelyn was therefore the main criminal in all of this.'

'All this sounds rather too fanciful for me Ravenscroft. Can't see the relevance of this to your case,' muttered Henderson.

'Bear with me, sir, and I will explain. After the boy's suicide, Evelyn was full of remorse and withdrew into his own private world where he spurned company and sought solace in the ancient books and manuscripts of the cathedral library, but every day as he entered his place of work he will have remembered it as the place of violation and death. Then, thirteen years after the death of Martin Tinniswood, a younger brother, Malcolm, came to the school, became a choirboy and the whole ghastly business started again.'

'Good God!' exclaimed Henderson.

'Yes, young Malcolm must have become Evelyn's next victim. He probably learnt of the real cause of his brother's death, or if he did not, must have at least deduced that Evelyn had played a major part in his brother's demise. But then, when Malcolm returned home in the holidays there was a cholera outbreak in the town where he lived. He contracted the disease, fell ill and suddenly died. His gravestone says "Unexpectedly taken from us". Evelyn must have breathed a sigh of relief when he learnt of the boy's death, for he realized that his secret was safe, and his life continued as it had before, full of loneliness and shame. And I suppose that would have been the end of things, and eventually Evelyn would have died taking his secret with him to the grave. But then I asked myself, what if young Malcolm Tinniswood had told of his suspicions regarding Evelyn to someone before his death, perhaps a schoolfriend, or a master, and that this confidant had kept the secret for over twenty years until he saw the opportunity to confront Evelyn and to use him to acquire precious manuscripts from the cathedral collection.'

'Go on,' urged Henderson.

'Our murderer was very clever. He never confronted Evelyn direct. He used the hidden cavity in the old ruined house down by the river to leave notes for Evelyn, so that he would not reveal his true identity. After he had threatened the librarian that he would reveal the secret of Evelyn's past, he demanded the theft of the *Antiphoner* in exchange for his silence. After he had acquired this work, he was not satisfied and instructed Evelyn to steal the *Whisperie*, in exchange for his release. Evelyn felt compelled to comply with this request and returned to the cathedral late one night when he thought no one would see him, but where in fact he was observed by both the Tovey sisters and Brother Jonus. After taking the *Whisperie* and creating the impression that someone had broken in and stolen the work, he left the manuscript in the usual hiding place, and was coming back towards the cathedral when our murderer killed him and pushed his body into the river.'

'This is all very well, Ravenscroft, but there is one flaw in all of this,' interrupted Henderson.

'And what is that, sir?'

'Surely it would have been easier for your murderer to have just taken the *Antiphoner* and the *Whisperie*, without all this supposed recourse to blackmail?'

'You would have thought so, but the library was kept locked with the dean and Evelyn having the only keys. I have no doubt that our thief could have overcome this obstacle, but there was always the risk that he would be caught in the act. By blackmailing Evelyn and using him to take the manuscripts, he would avoid the chance of being caught himself.'

'Very clever!'

'As you say, sir, very clever – or that is what we were supposed to think, that the main motive was the theft and acquisition of the manuscripts. But I believe our murderer desired one thing more than all this. He wanted to see Evelyn dead, for you see his main purpose was not the theft of the *Antiphoner* and the *Whisperie* – although he could see that he could sell the works and make a tidy sum – no, his main desire was for revenge,' he said, turning away and looking out over the town.

'If your theory is correct, is it not time that your murderer made his appearance?' said Henderson, taking out his pocket watch and examining the hands. 'It looks to me as though he is not going to show up. Got cold feet and backed off, I'll be bound. All this has been a complete waste of time, if you ask me.'

'Far from it. You see, I did not expect anyone else to join us. There were no letters written to our chief suspects. I informed only one person that I would be up here tonight – and that was you! The person who killed Nicholas Evelyn was none other than yourself,' said Ravenscroft, turning round and looking his superior straight in the eye.

'For God's sake, man! You're rambling! Now I know this has all been far too much for you,' protested Henderson.

'Yesterday I went to Hay-on-Wye, where the Tinniswoods lived. I learnt that they had left the town over twenty years ago, or rather one of them did, the other three remain buried in the churchyard – the two boys, Martin and Malcolm, and their mother Martha. There was no trace of the father, Robert Tinniswood. That is because he shut up the house after the death of his wife, and left the town, adopting his wife's maiden name and entering the army where he rose to the rank of major, later retiring, before being elevated to the position of Superintendent here in Worcester. For you see the name on his wife's gravestone was Henderson!'

'Very clever,' said Henderson, staring into the distance.

'Something always worried me about this case. I was invited to investigate the crime by the Dean and Chapter of the cathedral, because of the lack of progress that had been made by your force in finding either Evelyn or the missing manuscript. Of course, you had no desire to solve the crime; you hoped that in time it would all go away. It must have been very irritating for you when I turned up. When Evelyn's body was recovered down at Upton, you had not even searched the corpse to see what possessions he had on him, because you did not want the keys to the library to be found on his person. You always maintained that someone else had broken into the library, and when we later established that it had been Evelyn all along who had stolen the manuscript, you suggested that the work probably lay at the bottom of the Severn. You were annoyed when I took men away to search the grounds near the river and revealed the hiding place, and hindered our further requests for manpower claiming that your men were needed for the policing of the Worcester Races. You were no doubt relieved when Billy, the bargeman, was killed, and were more than anxious to pin the blame for both murders on him, being reluctant for me to continue with my investigations. You could see that I was not getting anywhere, and knew that eventually my lack of success would give you the excuse you needed to demand my recall to London. That is why you gave me just two days to conclude my investigations – and, of course, you did not want to organize a search of Renfrew's house where you knew we might find the *Whisperie* and discover that he had purchased the work from yourself.'

'I see you have worked it all out, Ravenscroft. It was that damned headstone that gave it away! You were right. Shortly before my son Malcolm died of that dreadful fever, he spoke of his suspicions regarding Evelyn. A few weeks after his death, my wife also died. I had no desire to remain in Hay, and, as you said, joined the army using my wife's maiden name, Henderson. My service took me out to Africa, and then India for a number of years, but all the time I was out there I could not forget my wife and my two children, and swore that one day I would make Evelyn pay for the way he had abused my boys! Then last year, I was appointed as the superintendent of the force here in Worcester. I found that Evelyn was still alive, and wanted to kill him for what he had done all those years ago – but first I used him to acquire the two manuscripts, which I then sold on to Renfrew. The man was an evil predator who took innocent young boys and corrupted them. He deserved to die.'

'I understand that. Nevertheless, a crime has been committed and you know that I must arrest you for the murder of Nicholas Evelyn,' said Ravenscroft firmly.

'Damn it, Ravenscroft, can't you see the justice in all this? The man finally paid for his crimes. What good would it do to arrest me? Any father would have done the same,' pleaded Henderson.

'I'm sorry,' replied Ravenscroft looking down.

'Then you leave me with no alternative.'

Ravenscroft looked up to see that Henderson had removed a pistol from his coat pocket.

'I don't want to do this, Ravenscroft. You are a decent enough man, but I'm not prepared to face the gallows. It's your word against mine, but I can't take the risk in letting you go. I'll say I came up here and found you dead. Shot by our murderer before I arrived. People will accept my word. I am, after all, the superintendent of the local force. I'll arrest Cranston, plant the gun in his rooms, and charge him with your murder.'

'Very neat; you seem to have thought of everything.'

'I really am sorry. There's no other way out,' said Henderson pointing the gun at his junior officer.

'And I'm sorry to have to disappoint you, sir, but before you press that trigger, you might consider that I would not have been so foolish as to come up here alone.'

'Don't be stupid, man! There's no one else here but us. That's just foolish bravado!'

'That's where you are wrong. You see, after you climbed the stairs, I gave instructions that you were to be followed. Our conversation and your confession have been witnessed by Constable Crabb, Brother Jonus and two officers who have been situated all this time at the top of the steps.'

'Stuff and nonsense! You're bluffing!' protested Henderson, going red in the face and waving his pistol around.

'I assure you that I am not. Show yourselves, gentlemen!'

Crabb, Brother Jonus and a number of police officers emerged from the stairwell and stepped out on to the top of the tower.

'Damn you, Ravenscroft!' shouted Henderson.

'So you see, there is no point in continuing. Give me your revolver, if you please.'

Henderson glanced at the others, and then stared at Ravenscroft a look of hatred on his face.

'My son, do as the inspector says. Atone for your sins,' pleaded Brother Jonus taking a step forwards.

'Stay back!' yelled Henderson.

'You can't shoot us all,' added Crabb.

'Damn you all!' shouted Henderson, flinging the gun over the parapet. 'Damn you!'

'Take him, men,' instructed the inspector.

Two uniformed officers stepped forwards and placed a set of handcuffs around Henderson's wrists.

'Constable Crabb, perhaps you would be good enough to see that you and the other officers escort the superintendent back to the station.' said Ravenscroft.

'Right you are, sir. Come along, Mr Henderson,' said Crabb laying a hand on the arrested man's arm and leading him down the steps.

'So, my son, you have caught your murderer at last,' said Brother Jonus.

'Indeed. It was Henderson who took the monk's habit that night and used it to conceal himself, as he made his way down to the river, where he killed Evelyn.'

'Terrible. Quite terrible!'

'I must say I have a degree of sympathy for him. He had lost both his sons and his wife. I suppose, though, that the real criminal in all this was Evelyn himself,' said Ravenscroft.

'Yes, the poor man. I should have been able to help him.'

'You could do little for him, Brother Jonus. He lived with his guilt for nearly forty years. The last thing he wanted in this life was to confess his sins to anyone,' suggested Ravenscroft.

'It is to be hoped, Inspector, that in his moment of death, he might have finally asked for forgiveness and have been granted salvation by our Lord.'

'Who knows, Brother? I know one thing, however.'

'And what is that, my son?'

'I will be mighty relieved to get off this roof. Heights and I do not go well together.'

'Then it is to be hoped that your eventual passage to Heaven will be made as easy as possible,' smiled Brother Jonus, as the two men began their descent.

'Before that occurs, Brother, there remains much work to be done. I must now recover the *Whisperie*, before Renfrew learns of Henderson's arrest and flies the coop!'

Darkness was beginning to fall, as Ravenscroft, Crabb and a group of uniformed officers found themselves standing outside the house of Dr Silas Renfrew.

'At least the house does not appear to have been locked up, so we can hope that the owner is still in residence,' said Ravenscroft, lifting up the knocker and bringing it down heavily on the wooden door.

'Let's hope that he still has the manuscripts, sir,' said Crabb.

The door opened to reveal the manservant Georgio.

'We wish to see your master,' said Ravenscroft.

'My master, he is a'busy. Cannot see you,' said the Italian, glaring at the policemen, before attempting to close the door in Ravenscroft's face.

'I'm sorry that will not do,' said Ravenscroft pushing past the servant, closely followed by Crabb and his colleagues.

'What is a'this?' protested the Italian.

'You three men take the upstairs. You other two take the kitchens. You know what you are looking for. On no account let anyone leave the house,' instructed Ravenscroft.

'You cannot, a'do this,' replied Georgio, grabbing Crabb by the shoulders.

'That's all right, Georgio. Let him go. The police are only doing their duty', interrupted an American voice.

'Doctor Renfrew,' said Ravenscroft.

'So, Inspector, we meet again. I see your curiosity has got the better of you. May I ask on what grounds you have sought to violate my house?'

'We have reason to believe that you are in possession of stolen property,' answered Ravenscroft, making his way across the hallway towards the library.

'Ah, you mean the *Antiphoner* and the *Whisperie*. I have already proved to you, Inspector, that I purchased the former work legally in New York some years ago, before I came to this country. As to the *Whisperie*, you will not find it here because I have never been in possession of it in the first place,' said Renfrew, in his familiar, confident, slow American drawl.

'We have arrested Henderson who has told us everything. How he sold you both manuscripts,' said Ravenscroft, quickly looking round the study, reassured that the *Antiphoner* still lay within its case.

'My God, Inspector, you must be desperate if you have arrested your own superior officer,' laughed Renfrew.

'Then you deny the accusation, Dr Renfrew?' asked Ravenscroft.

'Of course I do. The whole idea that Superintendent Henderson sold me two stolen manuscripts is the height of absurdity – or perhaps this is all an example of your strange English humour?'

'We have contacted the auction house in New York, and await their reply. I am confident that their response will indicate that they did not sell the *Antiphoner* to you. I believe you obtained a copy of their headed notepaper and wrote out the receipt yourself. I'm sure that a close analysis of the handwriting on the receipt and a copy of your own hand will prove that they are one and the same.'

'I see, Inspector,' replied Renfrew, looking somewhat crestfallen.

'It would save us all a lot of time and bother, sir, if you confessed to the purchase of the *Antiphoner* knowing it to be stolen,' said Ravenscroft, confronting the American face to face, knowing that at last he had disturbed the other's usual calm exterior.

'Very well, Inspector,' sighed Renfrew. 'I confess that Superintendent Henderson did approach me a few months ago with the *Antiphoner*. He said that the work had been stolen from the cathedral, but had been personally recovered by himself, and that he was making investigations as to who the culprit was. In the meantime, he did not wish to return the manuscript to the cathedral authorities, and asked me to house it here in my own collection for safe-keeping, whilst he was continuing with his investigations, pending its eventual return to the library. Of course, had I known that Henderson had stolen the work himself in the first place, then I would have contacted the appropriate authorities straight away, but then I had no cause to suspect him,' said Renfrew recovering his composure.

'That is all rather too plausible, sir,' said Ravenscroft sarcastically.

'It is what I shall say in my defence, Inspector, should you foolishly still feel compelled to press charges and bring the case to court. I warn you that I have a very good lawyer in London.'

'Is that a threat, sir?' Ravenscroft said, getting warm under his collar.

'Oh, certainly not, Inspector; I am merely informing you of my intentions,' replied Renfrew, giving a brief smile.

'I will ask you and your servant to accompany my officers to the station, where a statement will be taken from you later,' said Ravenscroft, turning away.

'Of course, Inspector, I will be more than pleased to assist you in your inquiries.'

'In the meantime, we will take possession of the *Antiphoner*, and return it to its rightful place.'

'If you insist.'

'Where is the *Whisperie*, Dr Renfrew?'

'I have never received the *Whisperie*, from anyone.'

'Henderson told us that he sold you the work.'

'Then he is mistaken.'

'I have to tell you that we will make a thorough search of these premises until we recover it,' said Ravenscroft, pacing up and down.

'You will be most welcome, Inspector, but I fear you will be wasting your time: I do not have the *Whisperie* in my possession,' said Renfrew, a note of defiance creeping into his voice.

Ravenscroft stared at his adversary. He knew he was lying, and he was determined to find the work. 'Escort Dr Renfrew and his manservant to the station, and take their statements,' he said, addressing two of his uniformed officers.

Renfrew smiled and turned to leave the room.

'We will find the *Whisperie*,' announced Ravenscroft, trying to sound as confident as he could.

'I sense that your search will prove fruitless, Inspector,' said Renfrew, a superior tone to his voice. 'I look forward to receiving a full apology.'

'Close the door, Crabb,' instructed Ravenscroft after they had gone.

'He's a slippery cove, if ever I saw one,' said Crabb.

'The man is insufferable. It was more than I could do to restrain myself from laying my hand on that supercilious face. The worst thing is that he's probably right. He will no doubt hire the cleverest brief in London and get off on all charges unless we can find the *Whisperie* first.'

'The men are searching the rest of the house. It will only be a matter of time before they turn up the work,' said Crabb optimistically.

'I'm not so sure. If you wanted to hide the *Whisperie*, where would you hide it?'

'Under my bed, in a chest-of-drawers, in that desk over there,' Crabb suggested pointing at the item of furniture. 'Or perhaps the house has a secret room or cavity somewhere.'

'All obvious places, I fear, which we will check, nevertheless. No, if I wanted to hide a particular coloured stone I would place it in the middle of a group of similar coloured stones where it would not stand out. I feel that the *Whisperie* is probably somewhere in this room, lying on the shelves between similar volumes or within one of these cases with other manuscripts.'

'You could well be right, sir.'

'Then we'd best set to work. You take those shelves over there; I'll do this bookcase. Take down every book and see that there are no loose manuscripts inside.'

Dawn was breaking as Crabb pulled back the curtain of the library. Ravenscroft, slumped in one of the armchairs, raised his hand to shelter his eyes from the light.

'Nothing, absolutely nothing. We've searched through every book and manuscript. Nothing!'

'The men made a search of the rest of the house, and checked both the cellars and the outbuildings. I sent them home three hours ago, sir,' replied a weary Crabb.

'Where the devil is it, Tom? It has to be here, but the deuce knows where,' sighed Ravenscroft, 'We've even checked the walls and furniture for hidden cavities.'

'Perhaps Renfrew has moved the manuscript elsewhere. Placed it in a bank vault somewhere in London, or even posted it off to America,' suggested Crabb.

'Somehow I don't think so. Renfrew is not the kind of man who would lock things away. He would want to gaze upon his recent acquisition every day, revel in its detail and history, run his fingers over the ornate lettering and decipher its meaning. No, he would want it close at hand – the question is where?'

'Perhaps we should go home, and get some rest. Come back later in the day?'

'We would then have to let Renfrew go, much against my better judgement and humour, and once he returns here he could quickly leave Worcester taking the *Whisperie* with him, before we were able to return.'

'We could always place some men on guard to see that he did not do that, sir.'

'Then we would have his brief breathing down our necks, saying we were hounding his client. No, Renfrew would lie low, until all this had died down, then he would take his opportunity to slip quietly out of the country, no doubt taking it with him. The manuscript would then be lost forever to the cathedral,' replied Ravenscroft dejectedly.

'We can search again, sir.'

'You're right, Tom, we have obviously missed something. It's probably right here under our very noses, and we have been too blind to see it. Renfrew is a proud, self opinionated man, and I am determined to see that his fall from grace is a mighty one, and—' Ravenscroft stopped suddenly.

'What is it?'

'That's it! Renfrew has left us a clue. He is such a vain man and confident of his own success, yet unable to resist the temptation of teasing us. His arrogance, however, may well have got the better of him this time,' said Ravenscroft walking over to one of the cases. 'See here, Crabb, the first folio of the works of William Shakespeare. Open at King Henry VIII. Those lines are spoken by Cardinal Wolsey after his fall from grace—

> *And then he falls, as I do. I have ventured,*
> *Like little wanton boys that swim on bladders,*
> *This many summers in a sea of glory,*
> *But far beyond my depth: my high-blown pride*
> *At length broke under me, and now has left me,*
> *Weary and old with service, to the mercy*
> *Of a rude stream that must for ever hide me.*

'Bit beyond me, sir,' said Crabb puzzled.

'Open the case, Tom. Don't you see? The words say that his pride has left him, leaving him to the mercy of a stream that will forever hide him,' said Ravenscroft excitedly.

'I still don't see. There's no stream here to hide the *Whisperie*,' said Crabb, opening the case.

'No, but there is a book. What Wolsey, or rather Renfrew, is telling us is that the *Whisperie* is hidden within this work. When I first saw this volume, I accepted it at face value, the First Folio of the Works of William Shakespeare published in the early part of the seventeenth century,' said Ravenscroft reaching into the case, 'But I think we may find that the work is not all that it purports to be. Look, the first few pages appear to belong to the First Folio – but see how they lift up, to reveal a secret cavity of some sort underneath.'

'You think Renfrew has hidden the *Whisperie* within it?' asked Crabb.

'We shall see. Let's find how to open the lid of the compartment.'

Ravenscroft ran his fingernail along the edge of the lid, and opened the top of the cavity.

'Good Lord, sir! You're right!'

Ravenscroft carefully lifted the manuscript from its hiding place and laid it upon the table. 'Renfrew hid it in the last place where anyone would think of looking for it, in a secret compartment concealed within another work. And this, Tom, if I am not mistaken, is the *Whisperie*!'

The two men stood in silence, looking down at the ancient work, admiring the ornate cartouche on its outer page.

Ravenscroft smiled, and breathed a sigh of relief. His quest was at an end – the *Whisperie* had been recovered!

CHAPTER FIFTEEN

'Well, Inspector, words fail me.'

The three men were standing in the library of Worcester Cathedral, some days after the arrest of Henderson and the recovery of the lost manuscripts.

Ravenscroft smiled, knowing that Touchmore would continue.

'To see the *Antiphoner* and the *Whisperie* returned to their rightful places here in the library, is joy indeed. I must admit there were times when I thought we would never see them again. Lost on the bottom of the River Severn, or spirited away to some foreign country, but no, here they are, safe and sound, for future generations to gaze down upon and rejoice. Our prayers have been answered!'

'I am pleased that we were able to recover them,' replied Ravenscroft gazing down at the works displayed in the glass cabinet.

'Rest assured, Inspector, that we shall take far greater care of them than we have done in the past.'

'I am pleased to hear that, Dean.'

'A new librarian has already been appointed. But I hear that you are leaving us today?'

'Yes, my work is completed. I have given evidence at the trials of Henderson and Miss Griffiths. Both have, of course, been found guilty of their crimes.'

'What a terrible business this has all been. What will happen to both of them Inspector?'

'Hang, sir,' interjected Crabb.

'Oh dear me,' said Touchmore, shaking his head,

'In Henderson's case, he will be brought to the gallows next week. Miss

Griffiths has been granted clemency in view of her failing health. She will remain in prison. I fear she is not long for this world,' replied Ravenscroft.

'The poor woman. I will pray for her. Such a shame. And what of Dr Renfrew?' asked the Dean.

'It is my one regret that in this case that I was not able to bring that man to book. Almost certainly he paid Henderson a great deal of money to acquire the two works for his collection. However he also acquired the services of a top London barrister, who claimed that his client had purchased the manuscripts in good faith, and that he was merely acting as their custodian, with the full intention of eventually returning them to the cathedral. Unfortunately, the jury believed him rather than me in this matter, and so he has walked free. The man is as slippery as an eel. There is nothing more I can do to bring him to justice,' replied Ravenscroft, with more than a hint of regret in his voice.

'Well, at least we have recovered the manuscripts,' said Touchmore, smiling.

'Indeed we have, sir.'

'Apparently Renfrew has vacated the house. One of our men saw him and his manservant leaving the day after the trial,' said Crabb.

'Gone to London, no doubt. Perhaps he will eventually return to America,' suggested Ravenscroft.

'If he returns to Worcester, he will certainly be denied access to the library,' said Touchmore.

'I doubt he will do that,' said Ravenscroft. 'He may have escaped justice, but his reputation will have been harmed. Well, sir, it is time I bade you good day.'

'I cannot thank you enough, Inspector Ravenscroft. You cannot hope to imagine the gratitude that the Dean and Chapter feel towards you. The Bishop also sends his kind regards and words of thanks,' said Touchmore shaking Ravenscroft's hand with vigour.

'I thank you, sir. Perhaps our paths might cross again one day.'

'I do hope so. There will always be a warm welcome for you here at the cathedral.'

As the two policemen made their way down the stairs and into the nave of the cathedral, they could hear the sound of boys' voices. They paused to listen to the choir, and to look upwards towards the stained-glass windows.

Matthew Taylor was conducting the boys with his usual casual flourish, and waved in their direction. Ravenscroft signalled back and smiled, before making his way out.

'Mr Ravenscroft, I would be glad of the opportunity of a few words with you, before your departure,' said Sir Arthur Griffiths who had clearly been waiting for them to leave the building.

'Certainly, sir. May I say how sorry I am for your daughter's imprisonment,' offered Ravenscroft.

'Thank you. We are trying to persuade the authorities to allow her to spend her final days at home.'

'I am sure they will give your request a sympathetic consideration.'

'You may be interested to learn that I have decided to relinquish my seat in the House of Commons. It is not prudent that I should continue with my parliamentary career given the present circumstances.'

'That is a pity. I am sure you will be a loss to both the country and your party. What will you do now?'

'I have a large number of business interests within the county which will occupy my time. I do not intend to be idle. I realize that I have been a very foolish man. If I had accepted the boy as my own all those years ago, none of this would ever have happened, and my daughter would not now be languishing in a prison cell. I seek now to make recompense, and to regain that which I had thought lost. I may have lost a daughter: it is not my intention to lose a son. I understand the boy is being cared for by you and your wife, Constable Crabb?'

'He is indeed, Sir Arthur,' replied the constable.

'If you would return him to my house, you will have my assurance that the boy will be well cared for and acknowledged as my true son and heir. He will want for nothing.'

'I will bring him over this evening, sir.'

'Thank you, Constable Crabb. If I can in anyway recompense you for all your trouble, I would be happy to do so.'

'It is no trouble, Sir Arthur. My wife Jennie, has taken quite a liking to the lad, and will be sorry to see him go.'

'Then you must tell your wife that I am eternally in her debt, and should she care to visit us at any time to see the boy, she would be more than welcome.'

'Thank you, Sir Arthur.'

'Now, I wish you good day, gentlemen. It is my regret that we could not have met under different circumstances,' said the Member for Worcester extending his hand.

'I wish you well, sir,' replied Ravenscroft, shaking the politician's hand.

The two detectives watched as Sir Arthur strode towards his house.

'So Ruth Weston's words have come true at last,' said Ravenscroft.

'And what were those, sir?'

'On that morning when I met her here with her son, she said that one day her son would live in a fine house. It is a pity that she was not here to see it,' said Ravenscroft sadly.

'At least the boy will grow up a gentleman,' said Crabb.

'Yes, that is indeed so.'

'I think that someone else is trying to attract your attention, sir,' said Crabb.

'Good morning to you, Inspector,' said the eldest Miss Tovey walking towards the two men, a greeting that was echoed by her two younger sisters.

'Good morning to you ladies. I trust I find you well?' replied Ravenscroft.

'Very well Inspector, thank you. But we hear you may be leaving us?' said Mary Ann, looking wistfully into Ravenscroft's eyes.

'We are going to miss you so much,' said Alice Maria sadly.

'That is very kind of you to say, but my work is completed here, and my superiors will be expecting my return to London at any moment.'

'It is so good to hear that the books have been returned—' began the eldest sister.

'—to their rightful place in the library—' continued the middle sister.

'—where they can be enjoyed by everyone who desires to see them,' completed Alice Maria.

'Indeed so, ladies,' said Ravenscroft, smiling.

'It is such a pity that you have decided not to stay with us,' said Mary Ann.

Crabb coughed and gave Ravenscroft a puzzled look.

'You are too kind, ladies. It is true that I have been offered a position with the local force here in Worcester, but I suppose I can be of greater service in London. There is nothing now to keep me here,' said Ravenscroft, wondering how the sisters had gained knowledge of the offer that had been made to him only hours previously.

'What a shame!'

'We are so sorry.'

'But we quite understand your decision.'

'Thank you, ladies. Of course, I have not finally—' began Ravenscroft.

'We understand that a new librarian has been appointed.'

'We shall have to have him to tea one afternoon, sisters.'

'I am sure he would appreciate that,' said Ravenscroft.

'We thought you would like a little something to take back to London,' said the eldest sister handing over a brown paper parcel.

'My sister's cakes are the envy of the town,' said Emily proudly.

'Hush, Sister!' said the youngest sister turning bright red.

'You are most kind. I am sure your cake will be delicious, and when I am eating it in my rooms in London I shall remember all the kindness I have received here.'

'Time we went to the station, sir,' interrupted Crabb.

'We must not detain you, Inspector.'

'You must not miss your train.'

'That would never do.'

'Thank you again, ladies,' said Ravenscroft raising his hat, before they walked away.

'I was not aware, that you have been offered a place with the force here in Worcester,' said Crabb, as they made their way back towards the Cardinal's Hat. 'I hope you will accept such a position. May I say it has been a great honour to have served alongside you, sir.'

'Stop it, Crabb! I have not yet refused the offer. I need to return to London and have time to consider the matter.'

'I understand. I suppose if a certain young lady—'

'Enough, Crabb!' said Ravenscroft firmly. 'If you want to make yourself useful, you can carry my bag from the Cardinal's to the station.'

'A pleasure, sir,' he grinned.

After collecting his bag and paying the landlord his account, Ravenscroft made his way to the station with his colleague. They climbed up the steps to the station platform.

'You know, Tom, it was a good thing that we went to Hay, otherwise we would never have discovered Henderson's true identity. Until then, I was so sure that Cranston was our murderer, but I now realize that my intense dislike of the man clouded my judgement,' said Ravenscroft.

'Good job we didn't arrest him then,' replied Crabb, 'otherwise we would have had that smart London lawyer after us.'

'That idea does not bear thinking about. But enough of Cranston and the *Whisperie*. Tom, give my best regards to your wife and son.'

'I certainly will, sir. Things are going to be a little flat around here, now that you are returning to London,' said Crabb sadly.

'Good morning, Inspector,' interrupted a familiar voice.

'Brother Jonus. How pleased I am to see you again,' said Ravenscroft shaking the monk's hand, 'I was hoping to see you at the cathedral before my departure, but I see you are also travelling to London.'

'The cathedral has a number of business interests in London, which necessitate my presence there from time to time,' replied Jonus.

'Then perhaps we might share a compartment together,' suggested Ravenscroft.

'That would be an honour, Inspector.'

The group were suddenly disturbed by the arrival of a uniformed officer, who emerged running from the stairway and on to the platform. 'Inspector Ravenscroft, sir. I'm glad I've caught you.'

'Whatever is the matter?' enquired Crabb.

'I'm so sorry, sir. This arrived for you yesterday. I meant to give it to you then, but placed it on the station desk and forgot all about it. I hope it is not anything important?' said the breathless constable, handing Ravenscroft a letter.

'Thank you, Constable.'

'A young girl delivered it. Said her mistress had sent her all the way over from Ledbury, saying it was most urgent and that you were to read it straight away. Sorry for the delay, sir.'

'That's quite all right, Constable, better late than never, as they say,' said Ravenscroft recognizing the handwriting. 'Gentlemen, if you will excuse me for a moment.'

'Of course, my son.'

Ravenscroft withdrew a little way down the platform, leaving Jonus and Crabb talking to the constable. He stared down at the envelope, his heart beating, a sudden hope taking possession of his mind, his hand shaking and unsure whether he dare read its contents now, or later.

The sound of the approaching train, brought him back to the reality of his present situation. He tore open the envelope and read its contents.

My Dearest Samuel,

I do hope that this letter is able to reach you before your departure to London. I had hoped that you would have found it in your heart to have visited me again, here in Ledbury, now that you have brought your investigations to a satisfactory conclusion, but I realize that after my coldness towards you during our last meeting, you would be too hurt and would want to put me out of your mind as quickly as possible.

When you arrived – so unexpectedly – I was unsure how you would be with me, after my foolishness of last year. I hope you will forgive my aloof manner towards you. It was never my intention to be so distant and seemingly uncaring. The truth is, since your generous offer of marriage last year, there has hardly been a day gone by when my thoughts have not turned in your direction wondering what you would have been doing at that moment, and whether you would still be thinking of me, and cursing my own foolishness.

There I go again – repeating the word 'foolishness'. You must excuse such repetition, but it is an apt word to describe my behaviour towards you. I hope you will excuse these strange ramblings from one who cares for you. In time you will forget all about me – and it is all that I can expect.

However, should you find it in your heart to forgive the pain I have caused you in the past, and desire to see me again – and wish to repeat your more than generous offer that you made last year – you would receive a more than favourable response.

If I have said too much, then please excuse me, but the contents of this letter are what I feel, and are written from the heart.

Your ever loving

Lucy

'I think your train has arrived, sir,' interrupted Crabb.

'Yes. Yes, of course,' replied Ravenscroft folding over the letter and replacing it within its envelope. 'Brother Jonus, you will have to excuse me. I find that I am unable to travel with you today.'

'I understand my son. Follow your heart,' said the churchman shaking Ravenscroft's hand vigorously, before boarding the train, 'I'm sure our paths will cross again sometime in the future.'

'Yes, indeed,' said Ravenscroft, closing the carriage door.

'Good news, sir?' enquired a smiling Crabb.

'It is very good news indeed, Tom! When is the next train to Ledbury?'

'In about five minutes, I believe.'

'It looks as though I might be staying after all.'

'Capital news, sir. Capital news indeed!'

'Oh, and Tom, how would you like to be best man at a wedding?'

'Delighted, I'm sure. Delighted!'

CHAPTER SIXTEEN

WHITECHAPEL, LONDON

She could hear the distant sound of a church clock striking the night hour of two as she arrived outside the drinking house in Commercial Street. Despite the lateness of the hour, the voices of people singing and shouting drifted out into the cold night air. One or two ladies of the night waited for clients further down the road, and an old blind beggar lay slumped in an adjoining doorway, his empty cap before him on the cobbled stones.

She had drawn the veil over her face, not wishing her features to be seen by anyone, as she had made her way to this final encounter. The instructions had been short and to the point, giving her the time and place, and warning her to ensure that she had not been followed on her journey.

As she moved away from the lamp, seeking the shadows, coughing as she did so, she wondered whether he was there already, watching her every move, awaiting his opportunity, his moment, when he would make himself known to her, and lead her to Kelly's rooms. She looked down at her shaking hands, anxious that the final act should begin, and straining to see whether he was there in the swirling damp fog.

The doors of the inn suddenly flew open.

'Get out, you drunken sod!' came an angry voice from within.

The ejected drinker, a rough-looking unshaven man, wearing mud-splattered trousers and a torn coat, picked himself up from the floor, uttering loud curses as he did so, and waving his fist in the direction of the drinking house.

She withdrew further into the shadows as the man, noticing her presence, staggered towards her, waving his arms in the air. 'Hello, my little fine doxy,' he said, in a slurred voice. 'Like to come back to my place, and I'll give you a good time?'

She recoiled. Surely this drunken man could not be Monk?

'Come on, my little Polly. Don't be shy. We all know what you are here for,' said the man lunging towards her and attempting to seize her by the shoulders.

'Go away!' she protested, seeking to distance herself from this new intrusion.

'Are you all right, miss?'

The voice was that of the beggar.

'What's it to you?' growled the man turning his attention towards the speaker.

'Are you all right, miss? Has he hurt you?' called out the beggar again.

Trembling, and coughing, she retreated into a nearby doorway, as she heard the sound of a creaking cart approaching somewhere in the distance.

'Shut up, you old piece of horse meat!' shouted the drunken man, lashing out with his foot at the blind beggar.

'Please don't hurt me!' cried out the other, covering his face with his hands.

She turned in the direction of the cart, as it made its noisy way towards the buildings, an old bearded man pushing the vehicle before him.

'I told you to shut your mouth!' The drunken man landed his boot in the chest of the old beggar, making him cry out in pain. Instinctively she began to move forward, seeking to help the unfortunate victim.

'Follow me!' instructed the man with the cart, in a voice barely audible as he passed by.

'Now shut your mouth, you old tramp!' shouted the drunken man, lashing out once more at the beggar, but missing his aim and collapsing on the cobbles.

She stood still and watched the old man and the cart turn the corner.

So he had kept his word.

He had come for her.

Quickly she walked away from the inn, leaving the drunkard and the blind beggar still in dispute. Turning the corner, she was relieved to see the cart and its owner making their slow way down one of the narrow alleyways.

She knew now, that he would take her to where their final victim would be waiting – to where she would be able to confront the woman who had been the main cause of the downfall of her family, and to where she would at last be avenged.

The cart and the old man continued on their way. She wondered why he did not turn round to see whether she had followed his instructions, but then she realized that such a man as Monk would have been aware of her every movement.

Suddenly Monk stopped. He abandoned the cart at the side of the alleyway, glanced briefly in her direction, before quickening his pace and turning the corner, disappearing from view.

She hurried after him, fearful that the night fog would encompass the figure before she regained sight of him.

As she turned the corner, she felt herself being grabbed and thrust violently up against the brickwork.

'You made sure that no one followed you?' he whispered.

'Yes. Yes, I am alone,' she replied, trying to recover her breathing as she attempted to free herself from his grasp.

'We must be quiet. She is asleep in her room,' he whispered again as he relaxed his grip upon her, his face hidden by the darkness.

She nodded, her face wet with perspiration as she attempted to stifle her coughing with her trembling hands.

'You are sure?' he asked.

'Yes,' she replied, the words being uttered in no more than a faint whisper, and in a voice that seemed not like her own.

'Then come!'

Taking her hand, he pulled her into a small courtyard and on towards the window of a room, where she saw the faint flicker of a candle from within.

At last, the final page could be written.

She would be fulfilled.

He pushed open the door and almost dragged her into the small room.

'There is no one here!' she protested, but before she could continue, she felt herself being thrown on to the bed that lay in the centre of the room.

'You waited for me to come out of the church!' he sneered, his breath coming in short gasps as he looked down at her.

She tried to climb off the bed, but before she could do so, she felt his strong hands forcing her back on to the sheet, as his body came down on top of her.

'I told you, I work alone. You should have left me alone, but your curiosity got the better of you. You had to see who I was!' he snarled again, tearing at her clothes.

She tried to cry out, but instead felt his hand clasping her throat, forcing her head back on to the bed.

She knew then, that he had betrayed her and that she was to be his final victim.

'It is no use! All you can do is die!' he hissed.

As she struggled to break free, she could feel his grip tightening around her throat. She looked up at his face and saw the hatred and frenzy there.

She had failed her husband and son!

As the blackness came over her, the last thing she saw was the blade, as it prepared to make its downward thrust.

EPILOGUE

DINARD, NORTHERN FRANCE, NOVEMBER 1888

On 12 November, a well-dressed, middle-aged gentleman could be found sipping coffee on the terrace of the Gandolphi Hotel in the fashionable French resort of Dinard. The late autumn sunshine felt warm against the side of his face, as he looked out across the bay to where he could just see the outline of the ancient walls of the imposing fortress of St Malo in the distance. Closer to the shore, the ferry boat was making its slow progress across the waters. On the beach, below the terrace, a small group of children played happily on the sands under the watchful eye of their guardian. A number of sea birds circled overhead in the blue sky. On either side of him, fine stately villas adorned the edges of the cliffs.

Somewhere in the distance a church clock struck the hour of eleven. To this man, the peaceful, tranquil setting seemed a million miles away from the narrow, congested streets of Whitechapel and the ancient stones of Worcester that he had known. As he lay back in his chair, he closed his eyes, knowing that he had at last achieved the inner peace which he had so long desired.

'*Monsieur* would like the newspaper?' inquired a French voice breaking the tranquillity of the scene.

'*Merci*, Philippe,' replied the man taking the paper.

The waiter smiled, collected his empty coffee cup and walked back into the interior of the hotel.

The man, after cleaning the lens in his spectacles, opened the newspaper and turned over the pages, casually glancing at the various news stories, not welcoming the intrusion of the real world into his thoughts.

221

After a brief examination of the cricket scores, he opened the newspaper at the centre page, where a particular item caught his attention.

TERRIBLE MURDER IN WHITECHAPEL
Further Horrific Outrage

Reports are being circulated in the London newspapers regarding the discovery of a woman's body in the Whitechapel district of the city, early on the morning of 9 November last. We have reason to believe that the unfortunate woman was another victim of the infamous killer who has stalked this area of London over the previous three months. What is particularly disturbing upon this occasion, however, is that the victim was savagely killed in her own rooms. We understand that the victim's name was one Marie Jeanette Kelly who lodged at 13 Miller's Court off Dorset Street, although it may not be possible to effect a positive identification of the deceased, as the body was brutally mutilated by her attacker in his frenzied assault. The death of this latest woman has caused widespread outrage within the capital, and we have also learnt that Sir Charles Warren, the Metropolitan Police Commissioner has resigned over the failure of the police force to apprehend the murderer of these poor—

'Anything interesting in the newspaper today?' asked a voice at the reader's elbow.

'It seems that another poor woman has met with an untimely death in London,' said the man rising from his seat.

'I am sure that had you been there, you would have apprehended the villain by now,' smiled the lady.

'You overestimate my abilities, my dear,' replied Ravenscroft, discarding the paper on the table. 'Anyway, I would much prefer to be here in your company, than tracking down some depraved maniac in the grimy streets of Whitechapel. I only wish we did not have to return to England today.'

'I have been so happy here, Samuel,' she replied, taking his arm, 'and would be content to remain here for the rest of our lives, but I'm sure little Richard will be missing us, and—'

'*Pardon*, Monsieur Ravenscroft, Madame Ravenscroft. Your carriage is ready to take you to your boat at St Malo,' interrupted the waiter.

'Thank you, Philippe,' replied Ravenscroft.

'Your bags have been sent on ahead, *monsieur*'

'Thank you.'

'I trust *madame* and *monsieur* have found everything to their satisfaction at the Hotel Gandolphi, and that we may have the satisfaction of seeing you again some other day?'

'Indeed,' said Ravenscroft, tipping the waiter, before taking Lucy's arm and leading the way towards the front entrance of the hotel, to where a horse-drawn carriage awaited them.

Ravenscroft opened the door of the carriage, as another vehicle suddenly swept into the entrance way. 'After you, my dear,' he said, helping his wife up the steps of their carriage, whilst the driver steadied the horse.

The manager of the Gandolphi walked down the entrance steps and opened the door of the other conveyance. 'Welcome to the Hotel Gandolphi, *monsieur, madame.*'

Ravenscroft looked across and saw an elderly gentleman with a long white beard alighting from the vehicle. Wearing a black cloak over a shabby black suit, and a large hat, the new arrival stared round at his new surroundings. His companion, a young woman of striking appearance, laughed and smiled as she placed her arm within his and looked up into his face.

For a brief moment, Ravenscroft thought the old man looked across in his direction, before shuffling up the steps of the Gandolphi.

'Come, Samuel, or our boat will sail without us,' called Lucy from within the carriage.

'I'm sorry, my dear. It's just, I thought I recognized someone, but I must have been mistaken.'

Ravenscroft climbed into the carriage, and their conveyance set off at a brisk pace in the direction of St Malo.

Inside the Gandolphi, the manager was examining the papers of the strange couple who stood before him. 'These all seem in order. You are Mademoiselle Mary Jane Kelly?'

'Marie Jeanette,' corrected the young woman, laughing and squeezing her elder companion's arm.

'Pardon, mademoiselle. Marie Jeanette Kelly, of course. Here are your papers as well, *monsieur*.'

'Thank you,' replied the old man.

'We hope you will enjoy your stay in Dinard, Monsieur Cranston.'

'I'm sure I will. Thank you. You are most kind. I'm sure I will enjoy my stay here a great deal,' replied the old man smiling. . . .